D112084 3

NO ONE TO TRUST

JULIE MOFFETT

———

carina
press

carina press®

Recycling programs
for this product may
not exist in your area.

ISBN-13: 978-1-335-43042-7

No One To Trust

First published in 2011. This edition published in 2021 with revised text.

Copyright © 2011 by Julie Moffett

Copyright © 2021 by Julie Moffett, revised text edition.

This edition published by arrangement with Harlequin Books S.A.

For questions and comments about the quality of this book, please contact us at CustomerService@Harlequin.com.

Carina Press
22 Adelaide St. West, 40th Floor
Toronto, Ontario M5H 4E3, Canada
www.CarinaPress.com

Printed in U.S.A.

This book is dedicated to my family because they've always stood beside me no matter what and encouraged me to follow my dreams.
Thank you for being my pillars of strength.
I love you guys so much! oxoxox

NO ONE TO TRUST

Chapter One

When I was seven my older brother Rock gave me a camera for Christmas. The science of photography fascinated me—the angles, depth and lighting. But I was more interested in how the camera worked than in what I was pointing it at. Fast-forward a few years and here I am, a twenty-five-year-old, single, white, geek girl who can't take a decent picture of anything.

I'm also a semi-reformed computer hacker, a numbers whiz and a girl with a photographic memory. The whole photographic memory thing is totally overrated, though. Every human has the physiological capability. Most people just don't have the film.

Lucky for me, I've got the film, but I'm also stuck with a geeky reputation. Counter to the stereotypical image, I don't wear thick glasses held together by duct tape and I no longer own a pair of high-water pants. On the other hand, I'm no Miss America—just your basic tall, skinny girl with no curves and long brown hair. I double-majored in mathematics and computer science and have zero social skills. These days I'm employed by X-Corp Global Intelligence and Security, as Director of Information Security or InfoSec for short. It sounds impressive and maybe it is, but I'm so fresh in the job, I can't be sure yet.

This morning the top company brass, including me, had an important client meeting. It was our *first* client meeting, which made it all the more significant, not to mention nerve-racking. At a few minutes before ten, I grabbed a cup of coffee and my laptop, heading into the conference room. One of the cofounders of X-Corp, Ben Steinhouser, was already sitting at the table looking over some papers, his bifocals practically hanging off the edge of his pudgy nose. He used to work at the National Security Agency, or the NSA, just like I did and is a living legend among hackers, programmers and cryptanalysts. He is brilliant, difficult and unconventional, but by his sheer genius, he commands everyone's respect. He intimidates me, even if I try to pretend he doesn't. When I first met him, I reverently called him "Mr. Steinhouser." He glared at me and told me if I called him that again, he'd fire me. I'm still not sure if he was kidding.

"Hey, Ben." I tried not to wince as I called him by his first name. It's not easy to pretend to be comfortable when you're nervous.

Ben glanced up at me and my knees knocked together. "You're punctual. That's an admirable quality in an employee. Did you have a chance to look over the materials on Flow Technologies?"

Apparently not the type for small talk. Me neither, although a simple "good morning" would have been nice.

I nodded. Why did I need to be here? My job as Info-Sec Director required mostly identifying and assessing threats, vulnerabilities and attacks on our clients' networks and then implementing plans to either mitigate or eliminate these threats. Client acquisition was not in my job description and frankly, I liked it that way. Not much of a people person.

"Do we know why they are seeking our services?"

"Not yet. But I presume we shall shortly find out." He jerked his head toward the door as Finn Shaughnessy led a group of three men into the room.

Finn is the other cofounder of X-Corp. Sexy, Irish and an all-around decent guy, he lured me from the NSA with the promise of manager responsibility, more freedom in my work than the government could offer and a higher paycheck. My history with Finn is complex and includes handcuffs, a bed and no sex.

Ben and I stood while Finn seated the group. Before we'd taken our seats, Finn's gorgeous secretary, Glinda McBain, brought the guests coffee and danishes and then vanished. We all stared at each other until Finn began the introductions.

He looked at our visitors. "I'd like to introduce you to our staff. This is the cofounder of X-Corp, Ben Steinhouser. And this is our Director of Information Security, Lexi Carmichael. Lexi, Ben, meet Niles Foreman, Randall Tryosi and Lawrence Delaney of Flow Technologies."

I smiled and tried to look like I belonged. Why were they staring at me and ignoring Ben?

We all shook hands politely and then sat down. I opened my laptop as Finn leaned back in his chair and steepled his fingers.

"So, how can X-Corp help Flow Technologies?"

Niles Foreman, the leader of the trio, leaned forward on the table, his eyes narrowing. He was a very thin man with silver hair and a hard, angular face, dressed in an impeccable three-piece navy suit and gold tie.

"I must be assured that anything spoken about here today will be kept in the strictest confidence." For some strange reason, he looked pointedly at me. I wasn't sure whether it indicated a lack of conviction in me because I was young, female or both. His focused gaze made me so nervous I had to discreetly wipe my hands three times on my slacks to keep my fingers from slipping off the keys.

Perhaps Finn noticed. He tapped his pen on the table, drawing attention back to himself. "Confidentiality is a given. Now, how can we help you?"

Niles flicked an imaginary piece of lint off his lapel. "I suppose it would be prudent to give you a little background on Flow Technologies. Two young men, Darren Greening and Michael Hart, founded the company just over two years ago. They had some revolutionary ideas about how to use nanotechnology to produce an alternate energy source. We liked what we saw and came aboard with significant capital to see these ideas actualized."

Niles paused and took a sip of his coffee. The danishes sat in the middle of the table untouched, although I was having a serious fantasy about leaping across the table and snagging the cherry one.

"It became fairly clear from the beginning that most of the original ideas were coming from Darren, whereas Michael was better at the practicality and production of the science. Since at this point we were dealing only in ideas, it became obvious that in order to protect our investment we needed to take out an insurance policy on the most valuable asset the company had—Darren Greening."

I blinked in surprise. I'd never heard of such a thing, but looking at it from a coldly, calculating business view, it made sense.

If Finn was surprised by the revelation, he didn't show it. Then again, he was a lawyer by training.

"But you didn't take out an insurance policy on Michael Hart?" he asked.

Niles shook his head. "No. It wasn't necessary. To be brutally honest, Michael was replaceable in the bigger scheme of things. Darren was not."

"Unfortunately, while it was a sound business decision, it wasn't a popular move," Randall Tryosi stepped in. "The two men came to us. They thought we were trying to drive a wedge between them. They were quite unhappy with our decision and didn't want to have anything to do with an insurance policy of any kind. Regardless, we overruled them."

Niles crossed his hands on the table. "To say they had even an inkling of how to run a business is an overstatement. But the call was ours and we insisted. The company bought an insurance policy for Darren."

Finn wrote something down on his pad of paper. "And the insurance policy was worth how much?"

"Twenty-five million dollars."

That was one heck of an insurance policy. I studied the three men from Flow, not sure where they were going with all this. How did it tie in to computer security?

Finn was apparently wondering the same thing. "So, what happened?"

"The two men finally resumed their work. Their initial experiments were wildly successful, and frankly, the potential we could see for their work was breathtaking."

Ben Steinhouser finally spoke up. "Exactly what kind of experiments are we talking about here?"

"Energy replacement," Niles answered. "Frankly, the prospects of energy-related nanotechnology are stagger-

ing. The science could make solar energy widely available to the masses, replace gasoline in cars with liquid
methanol and make oil virtually obsolete."

I hadn't realized energy-related nanotechnology was
that far along, but then if it wasn't computers, it wasn't
on my radar.

"And this applies to your problems with Darren
how?" Finn asked.

"Do you know that the U.S. government buys forty
percent of the world's oil?" Niles's voice rose slightly.
"One-third of America's deficit is due to our dependency
on foreign oil. Oil is also the underlying reason we med-
dle in the affairs of the people of the Middle East, why
people hate us, join terrorist groups, attack us and force
us to spend billions encouraging peace and democracy
in the region. This is not to mention the money we spend
combating pollution and environmental disasters. Oil is
the root of a national, financial drain on this country,
and if we don't do something to change it, oil will eventually be the nation's downfall."

It was a pretty dramatic statement, but I couldn't
think of a single reason to disagree with him. That kind
of scared me. Especially because some days, just the
fact that Dunkin' Donuts was out of blueberry muffins
was my biggest worry. Now I realized, in the big scope
of things, a national disaster could be just around the
corner.

"Obviously, something happened," Finn said.

Niles nodded. "Less than six months after we came
aboard, Michael Hart was killed in an unfortunate car
accident. It was a horrid blow to all of us, especially Darren. He was inconsolable. But the work had to go on. To
protect the company, we bought out Michael's share and

brought in a new man to replace him. Darren was devastated and completely unable to concentrate. We had some bitter arguments and it was quite a difficult time." He sighed. "I should mention that Darren is young, and as many geniuses are, emotionally unstable."

"Did he eventually recover?" Ben asked.

"A few months later," Lawrence Delaney, the third of the men, chimed in. "Thanks to Michael's father. He convinced Darren that Michael would want him to continue his work. So, to our great relief, he finally did."

"But to our dismay, things got worse, not better, for the company," Niles said. "Somehow word leaked out about Darren's progress on the energy nanotechnology and we began to fear for his life."

"Fear for his life?" Finn's normally impassive face showed a hint of surprise. "Why would you fear for his life?"

Niles laughed. "Do you have any idea how many people would like to see Darren's energy nanotechnology buried? Oil-rich countries for starters. What do you think would happen to the sheiks if the U.S. no longer needs their products? What would happen to the oil executives who would lose their incomes, positions and privileges if such a science is perfected? This is not to mention car manufacturers, gas-station owners and so on. You understand where I am going with this. Darren's ideas threaten extremely powerful groups around the world."

"Are you suggesting that Michael Hart's death was not an accident?" Ben asked.

Niles shrugged. "We don't know for sure. But we decided that just in case, we needed to take extra precautions with Darren."

I frowned into my coffee cup. Frankly, it seemed like these investors were way more worried about protecting their money than the life or mental health of a kid. I guess that's standard operating procedure in the cutthroat business world of today, but it somehow made me feel unclean.

"So, what kind of extra precautions did you take with Darren?" I asked.

"Bodyguards, extra security at his apartment," Randall answered. "But it was of no use."

Finn raised an eyebrow. "Why not?"

"Because he vanished a week ago."

For a moment, no one spoke. Finn regained his composure first. "Do you think he was kidnapped?"

"To this point, we have received no ransom note."

"Did you go to the police?"

Niles shook his head. "No, and for many reasons. We don't want to put the company at risk. We have no desire to go public and spook any potential investors. Also, we aren't certain Darren disappeared under suspicious circumstances."

"Why do you say that?"

"Because he left us a note of sorts." Niles pulled a piece of paper out of his briefcase and put it on the table.

For a moment, Ben, Finn and I just looked at each other, wondering if this conversation could get any odder. Then we stared at the paper.

"Are you sure it's from Darren?" Finn inquired.

Niles nodded. "It's in his handwriting. Of course, we have no idea if he wrote this under duress."

"So, what does it say?" Ben sounded rather annoyed. I guess he wondered if we were all going to sit and stare at the note all day. He doesn't suffer fools easily and this trio from Flow Technologies seemed to be taking an awfully long time to get to the bottom line.

Niles slid the paper toward Finn. "We wondered if you might help with that."

Finn took one look at the paper and frowned, pushing it toward Ben. Ben studied it for a full minute or so and then slid it down to me.

"What do you think, Lexi?"

Puzzled, I took the paper and saw why Finn had given it to Ben, and why Ben had studied it for so long. It was several lines of handwritten text—all in code. I recognized this one from my Cryptanalysis 101 course at Georgetown.

"It's the Navajo code used by the U.S. in World War II. That's pretty weird." I looked up at Ben who nodded at me in approval.

Finn turned to Niles. "Lexi is an expert cryptanalyst."

I erupted into a coughing fit, both embarrassed and flattered by his assessment of my capabilities. "Um, technically I'm not an expert."

Niles shifted in his seat. "So, can you read it or not?"

"Yes. But not without the reference. If you wait a minute, I'll be right back with it."

I walked back to my office, pulled down one of my reference books on code breaking and carried it back to the conference room.

"It'll take me a few minutes." I jotted some notes on my pad.

Hooray! I wouldn't abjectly humiliate myself in front of X-Corp's first client. This would be an easy code to break, not only because the Navajo code was useless since it had been revealed and anyone could do exactly what I did, go get the reference book and crack it in minutes. But also because it was glaringly apparent an amateur had written it. At the very least a professional would have tried to make the code somewhat difficult by doing what the Navajos had done—add extra letters to the Navajo words to act as substitutes for each of the six commonest letters in the English language—*e, t, a, o, i* and *r*. But whoever had written this code hadn't even bothered with the substitutes.

After a minute of working, I realized that no one was talking. They were all staring at me. I jotted down a few more letters and then suddenly I got a sick knot in my stomach. With a sinking feeling of dread, I looked up at Niles Foreman and met his eyes across the table. In an instant, I could see he already had this code broken and knew exactly what it said.

I knew what it said, too, even though I had only translated part. With a miserable feeling in the pit of my stomach, I finished and slid it across the table to Ben.

Ben looked down at the translation and I saw his eyes go wide as he looked back at me. Clearly impatient, Finn reached across the table and snatched the translation from Ben without even asking.

Silence hung in the room until Finn looked up and glared at our clients. "Is this some kind of joke?"

Niles shook his head. "I assure you, it is not."

Frozen to my chair, I watched as Niles snatched the translation from Finn and slid it back to me. "So, young lady, what do you make of all this?"

Once again, I looked down at the paper, hoping that by some miracle the translation had changed during its trip around the table.

But it hadn't. There, written in my neat handwriting, were two lines: *SOS. Need Lexi Carmichael's help. GU*

Chapter Two

Everyone's eyes were glued to me. Great. I tried to untangle my tongue to talk. "I don't know Darren Greening. I have no idea why he would write this."

"You went to Georgetown University." Niles sounded as if he thought I was somehow responsible for Darren's disappearance. "So did he. I presume that's why he wrote GU at the end of the note."

I lifted my hands in the universal gesture of "who knows?" "Well, thousands of other students have also attended Georgetown University, including Mr. Shaughnessy here. But I assure you, Darren Greening was not in my social circle." I didn't even *have* a social circle except for Basia, but no need to point that out right now.

"Then why did he write this?" Randall asked. "Why did he name you in particular?"

I leaned forward on the table. "Do you know how many Lexi Carmichaels there are in the world? Maybe another one went to Georgetown University."

Niles laughed. "I find that highly unlikely."

Statistically I knew he was right. Jeez, why couldn't my mom have named me Jane Smith?

"That still doesn't mean it's me."

"Perhaps not, but don't you think it's rather coincidental that the message was written in code and you just happen to know cryptanalysis?" Lawrence tried to stare me down.

He had a point, but their problem still wasn't my fault. "Well, how do we know for certain that GU even stands for Georgetown University?" I countered.

"Perhaps because he went there." Randall looked as if he was losing patience.

Ben looked across the table at me thoughtfully. "You have another theory, Lexi?"

I didn't, but I didn't want to admit it. "Well, there is always…say, Griffith University," I said, groping for another, or *any* other, possible explanation.

Finn jotted it down. "Where is it located?"

"Australia."

Finn stopped writing and rolled his eyes at me. Okay, it was a long shot, but it was all I could come up with on short notice.

"All right, so that wasn't my best theory. But honestly, GU could mean anything. It could be a company, a location, a scientific notation."

"Did anyone check with Darren's parents?" Finn's question gave me a slight reprieve from the accusing looks of the Flow trio. "Perhaps the name Lexi Carmichael is familiar to them."

"Darren's parents are both dead and he's an only child."

"Well, maybe he has a childhood friend or a long-lost relative by that name." I was really reaching now, but being named in that note seriously freaked me out.

Niles turned his steely gaze on me. "Whereas speculation is sometimes helpful, Miss Carmichael, I think that in this particular case it would be more prudent to search your memory in the event you might have run across Darren Greening at some point in your life and had some kind of a meaningful encounter."

I sighed. It was becoming quite clear why I'd been invited to this meeting. Good old Niles had probably specifically requested I attend once he'd figured out this is where I worked. I wondered how much they already knew about me, and then decided I didn't want to know.

"Do you have a picture of Darren?"

Niles reached into his briefcase and slid a photograph of Darren across the table to me. "It was taken two months ago at the lab."

Darren was supposedly twenty-five years old but he didn't look a day over eighteen to me. He was tall, gangly and his white lab coat hung on his thin frame like a sack. Light brown hair badly in need of a cut curled over his ears and fell across his forehead as if he were using it to hide from the camera. Thick-framed glasses dominated his entire bony face. I didn't have to be a psychologist to see that this was a guy who was painfully shy and didn't like having his picture taken. I felt an instant, kindred connection—one geek to another. But other than that, the face didn't ring a bell. Nothing. No niggling familiarity and no recognition. *Nada.* I couldn't ever remember seeing or meeting him.

I pushed the photo back toward Niles. "I'm sorry. I don't think I've ever met him before."

Niles's lips thinned in anger. "Regardless, we apparently have little choice. We'd still like to put X-Corp on the case. Find this young man and recover our investment."

Finn cleared his throat. "As much as it pains me to say this, I'm afraid X-Corp doesn't really deal in missing persons. We're a technology-based computer and intelligence security firm, protecting virtual information and assets. You'd be better off getting help from a private detective agency."

Niles leaned across the table. "Darren's mind *is* our company's most valuable asset. Consider him as you would a piece of commercial information that needs to be kept safe from our competitors. To put it bluntly, we need you to recover and secure our company's greatest intelligence secret. But most importantly, for some unfathomable reason, Darren is frightened and has clearly instructed us to put Miss Carmichael on the case. For all we know, she may be the only person able to aid us in our recovery of him. Can you help us or not?"

Finn stood up. "Will you permit me a few minutes to discuss this with my colleagues?"

When Niles nodded, Ben and I filed out with Finn to the corridor. After Finn shut the door, they stared at me for a long time.

"What?" I lifted my hands. "I told the truth. I don't know this guy."

"I believe you," Finn said. "I'm just not certain we should take the case. What do you two think?"

Ben shrugged. "In my opinion, it doesn't sound that ominous. Probably the kid is just paranoid after his friend died and he ran away to hide from the vulture investors and get his thoughts together."

"Then what's with the wacko note in Navajo code with my name on it?"

"Maybe he admired you from a distance when he was at Georgetown," Ben offered.

Finn frowned. "Or perhaps this is just a stunt from

a socially warped guy who is too afraid to call you up and ask you out."

He didn't look happy about that at all, and part of me hoped he was just a tad bit jealous.

"Um, I don't think so. I don't really see myself as so intimidating that a guy wouldn't call me."

There was a moment of thoughtful silence but unfortunately, no one seemed inclined to argue with me.

"Well, there has to be some connection to you," Ben insisted.

"None that leaps to mind. Really."

"Do you think we should take the case?" Finn paced a few steps. "It is a little out of our realm."

Ben rubbed his chin. "Well, most detective work is done on the computer anyway these days. I figure it won't take us long to find the kid. And if that's all they want from us, it should be a piece of cake."

Finn turned to me. "Lexi?"

"I'm on board if you really want to do this. I'll try to figure out where our paths might have crossed, *if* the person named in that note is really intended to be me."

"I suppose it's settled then. Lexi, I'll need you to check your old yearbooks and talk to friends to see if you can find anything else that may link you to Darren Greening."

"Leave the technology side to me," Ben said. "I'll ask around and find out how well-known this kid is among the energy-related nanotechnology set. I can also do a standard run on this kid's credit and bank account, see if anything unusual comes up."

"I'll go have a talk with Michael Hart's father and see if I can get a copy of the accident report. Maybe we'll find something useful there." Finn put a hand on the doorknob. "Now I'll return to our friends from Flow Technologies and hammer out the business details. You two can get to work."

I started to leave and then stopped. "Ask if you can keep the photo of Darren. Maybe if I discreetly show it around, it'll jog someone's memory."

Finn nodded and disappeared back into the conference room. Ben headed for his office without another word to me, so I trudged back to mine feeling guilty for something I didn't even do.

This whole mess was so indicative of my luck. The last thing in the world I wanted to do was to make Finn and Ben sorry they had brought me on board. Why couldn't our first case be something simple like a company wanting us to test their computer security? Why did it have to be a note from a troubled guy who, for some unfathomable reason, pointed a finger at me?

My Georgetown University yearbooks were at home, but I did a quick search on the GU Alumni Association website. Darren had signed up, but the information was minimal. He'd graduated the same year as I did and had double-majored in physics and biochemistry—two subjects I liked but didn't particularly excel at. Other than that, there was no other obvious, glaring connection. So, what was the supposed correlation between the two of us?

I refilled my mug with coffee from the kitchen and then returned to my office to search Google for Darren's name. I perused the most popular hits—a few papers he had apparently published online as an undergraduate. I quickly skimmed through the titles: "Nanotechnology as Key to Energy Solutions," "Developing Energy Sources Responsibly Using Nanotechnology" and "The

Downsides of Nanotechnology," before printing all three of them to read. I had just stapled the first article together when Finn came in and dropped Darren's photo on my desk.

"It's a done deal."

"Congratulations." I tried to smile. One of us should at least pretend to be cheerful. I had once fantasized about the two of us drinking champagne to celebrate the company's first new case. Fat chance of that now. Finn looked about as merry as a gargoyle.

"I just hope we can bring a quick closure to this one."

"I'll do my best to find the connection. If Darren wanted to get my attention, he's got it. Now I've just got to follow the clues to him."

Finn smiled at me. "That's what I like best about you, Lexi—dogged determination."

Not exactly what I hoped Finn would like best, but geek girls can't be too picky. "Just call me Rover for short." *Rover? Did I just say that? Why couldn't the floor open up and swallow me whole?*

Note to self: Keep mouth shut.

Finn chuckled. "Hey, I've never noticed your glasses before."

I blushed, taking them off and setting them on my desk. "Computer glasses. Too much time staring at the screen has whacked out my eyes."

"Cute. They suit you."

"They're only for screen," I insisted.

"Nonetheless, right now I have an interesting fantasy going on in my head involving you and those glasses."

"Jeez," I murmured, wishing I could figure out if he were joking or not. I was at a triple disadvantage here because a.) We met under life and death circumstances involving international intrigue, lies and spies; b.) He was my boss; and c.) I sucked at social skills. There had been a couple of kisses, but I didn't have a clue what they meant to him, whether we even had a relationship and what would happen next.

To my disappointment, he didn't comment further on this. "Well, let me know if anything on Darren Greening pops for you," he said instead, heading for the door.

"Sure. Will do."

He left my office and then, to my surprise, popped back in. "Oh, I almost forgot. Are you free tomorrow evening?"

"Free?"

"Yes, as in available to go out with me. On a date."

"A date?" I squeaked.

"As in a social appointment or engagement arranged beforehand with another person."

"I know what a date is." My cheeks heated. "Um, let me check my schedule." I pretended to consult the digital calendar on my phone which I already knew was blank for the next three hundred and sixty-five days. "Hey, good news. It looks like I'm free. Where are we going?"

"I'd like you to accompany me to a fundraiser. It's a gathering to support young Irish artists trying to make it in the U.S."

"It sounds great." I wasn't sure what one did at a fundraiser but at least I would be surrounded by other people who could help me carry a conversation with him and wouldn't be left wondering what I should say on our so-called date.

"Excellent. I'll RSVP for us. Lexi, I'm really looking forward to this."

After he left, I sank back in my chair and fanned myself with a manila folder. Finn had just officially asked me out and I was hyperventilating to prove it.

Taking a deep breath, I set the folder on the desk. As much as I wanted to savor the moment, I couldn't dwell on it now. I had to figure out my connection to Darren Greening and fast.

I opened my browser and began reading more on Flow Technologies. The firm had been started just over two years ago with one and a half million dollars from Darren Greening and Michael Hart. Hart's father, a pharmaceutical mogul from Manassas, Virginia, had contributed most of the start-up capital for the boys. Within nine months they had easily raised over fifteen million dollars in additional financing from three other wealthy, private investors.

A copy of an article from the *Washington Post* on the company quoted one of the venture capitalists as saying *"nanotechnology is a megatrend of the type that biotechnology and wireless have been."*

I was interrupted in my reading by a noise in the doorway to my office. I glanced up to see my best friend Basia Kowalski leaning against the open door, perky and cute. Basia had also been hired by Finn to work for the company. She speaks about a dozen languages and had, before coming aboard X-Corp, been running her own freelance translation business and working part-time for Berlitz—the company that makes those nifty little foreign-language phrase books. Finn made her an offer she couldn't refuse and so here we are working together.

Today Basia was dressed in a crisp peach-colored blouse and black skirt, and her short brown bobbed hair and makeup looked perfect. I looked down at my rumpled slacks and the light blue blouse I had only halfheartedly run an iron over this morning. When I look at people like Basia and Finn, I feel an ugly flare of jealousy that they can look so professional and cheerful when I feel like a gangly version of the green ogre from the movie *Shrek*.

Yet as soon as Basia bounced into my office, I remembered why we're best friends. She's all smiles and sunshine to my gray, non-adventurous existence, outgoing to my introversion, and the only close girlfriend I've ever had. She knows me almost as well as my mother does and has an uncanny ability to make me feel good about myself even if I am feeling like that ogre.

She smiled. "Good morning. How are things?"

"Great, I think."

She stared at me for a moment and then leaned back in the chair, crossing her legs. "So, what's up?"

"What's up with what?"

"That look. You've got that look."

"What look?"

"The look that you know something I don't. I can see it in your eyes. You've got a secret you aren't telling me. I haven't been your best friend for all these years not to recognize it. Come on now, out with it."

Sheesh, I seriously needed to work on a poker face. Leaning forward, I lowered my voice. "Okay. Finn asked me out for tomorrow night."

She squealed in delight. "Freaking awesome."

"That's what I thought."

"You did agree to go, right?"

"No. I told him my social calendar is full."

She gave me a look of such utter horror, I had to laugh.

"Jeez, Basia, of course I said yes." I started to chew

my thumbnail. "Do you think it was a good idea? I don't want people here to think I'm sleeping my way to the top."

She rolled her eyes. "You're already at the top and, although it truly pains me to say it, sex had nothing to do with it."

"My mom doesn't think it's a good idea to date people you work with. Maybe, for once, she's right. What if he takes me out and decides he can't stand me? Then we'd have to work together and it'd be horribly awkward. Besides, isn't there some kind of social stigma attached to people who go out on dates with their bosses?"

"Since when have you cared about a social stigma, or for that matter, even been aware of one? Finn is smart, single, gorgeous and a really nice guy. Any female with a pulse would want to date him. Lucky for you, he's interested. Go out with him, have fun. Lighten up."

"I guess you're right."

"Of course, I'm right. Now where are you going on this first official date?"

"A fundraiser for Irish artists or something like that."

"Ooooh, classy. What are you going to wear?"

My stomach dropped to my toes. "Wear? My red dress, I guess." It was my *only* dress.

She rolled her eyes. "You don't just wear a *dress* to a fundraiser. You wear an evening gown."

Panic grabbed me by the throat. "Gown? I don't have an evening gown."

"You'd better get one by tomorrow night."

I felt sick. "Tomorrow? How am I going to do that?"

"Go shopping?"

I chewed my thumbnail harder. "Forget it. I can't do this. I'll just cancel. Dating is too stressful."

Basia leaned over and slapped my thumb out of my mouth. "It is not too stressful. It just requires shopping. Lucky for you, I'm an expert at shopping."

"You'll help me?"

"Of course."

I blew out a deep breath. "I owe you."

"Yes, you do."

I rubbed my temples. "Jeez, now I'm completely freaked out and I don't have time to panic about this."

"Why not?"

I quickly filled her in on what had happened at the meeting.

Her mouth fell open in shock. "Your name was in the note?"

"Yep. It said '"SOS. Need Lexi Carmichael's help. GU.'"

"What's the GU stand for? Georgetown University?"

"That's the most logical explanation. Apparently, Darren went to GU the same years as we did. I'm hoping you'll remember him." Basia and I had been roommates at Georgetown, and she might recognize him from somewhere. I slid the photo across my desk.

"I don't know. He seems vaguely familiar. But since he's kind of ordinary-looking, that may not mean anything significant."

"Great. That's a lot of help."

She put the photo back on my desk. "No need to get snippy. You apparently didn't recognize him either."

"I know. I'm sorry. It was just kind of a shock, you know, seeing my name in a note from a guy I don't even know. What if he's some kind of wacko stalker or something?"

Basia snorted. "Look at that guy. A stalker? I don't think so. A good wind would blow him over."

"Sometimes the quiet and unassuming ones are the worst psychos of all."

She rolled her eyes. "Oh, please. There must be something else. Let's brainstorm."

"Okay. Where do we start?"

"With the obvious connection. Georgetown University. Can we find out whether he lived on campus or not? Maybe he lived in our dormitory and admired you from a distance."

"No one has ever admired me, from a distance or otherwise."

"You are so wrong. But this is not the time to get into that."

I sighed. "Okay. Finn will probably come back with the dorm information. He's going to try and reach Michael Hart's father. If the two boys were roommates at Georgetown, Finn should be able to find out. But what's my connection to Darren? If he did admire me from a distance, why wait three years after graduation to contact me, and why in such a weird way?"

Basia shrugged. "Who knows what lurks in the eccentric mind? But you have a good point. Maybe he saw you again recently and it reignited the crush. What might you have done lately that put you in contact with him?"

"I don't have a clue. As far as I know he had no contact with the NSA, although I suppose I could use my sources to find out if he ever wanted to apply. But it seems to me that his lifelong dream was founding Flow Technologies with Michael Hart—not joining the NSA."

Basia thought for a moment. "All right, then let's go

back to the Georgetown correlation. It's the only obvious one we have. Might he have been in one of your classes?"

"I don't see why not. We were both science majors and had required courses to fill. But I'm sure I would remember if I had ever worked on any project with him."

"So, what we really need is to get a peek at his school records."

"How? The university won't release them without a subpoena."

She lifted her eyebrow. "You don't need a subpoena."

"Oh, no. I am *not* hacking into his university records. I like this job and I've got to do it by legal means."

"I know. But it would be helpful if we could see them."

"I'll figure out something else."

"Well, whatever you figure out will have to wait until *after* our shopping excursion tonight."

I felt my blood drain from my face. "Shopping excursion?"

"The gown, remember?"

"Um, I thought maybe you'd pick one up for me."

She snorted. "Not a chance. You have to try them on and check the fit. Meet you in the food court at seven," she said and left my office.

"Crap," I muttered as I turned back to the computer. Shopping for an evening gown sounded as appealing as a root canal, but since Basia was the fashion expert, I had to at least be game.

But it didn't mean I had to be happy.

Chapter Three

For the rest of the day I remained holed up in my office, skimming through Darren Greening's online undergraduate papers and racking my brain to see if I could come up with any connection to this guy. It soon became apparent I needed to conduct a more thorough search and I knew just the guys to do it.

I left my office and stopped at the cubicle of the first of my two employees, Kenji Kurisu. Ken is a Japanese-American kid fresh out of Virginia Tech with a degree in computer science and a specialty in intelligence security and protection. He'd been the first person I'd interviewed for X-Corp and I'd liked him right off the bat. Unfortunately, he'd only been in the office for a week and I suspected he was bored. My new assignment probably wouldn't perk him up much, but it was better than nothing.

"Hey, Ken. I've got a little something for you to do, if you're not busy."

He was reading the latest computer news at NetSecurity.org. "Please, boss. Give me anything to do."

I told him to dig around about Darren and Michael. He didn't look thrilled to pieces at the assignment, but with nothing better to do, he started right in on the job. Just to show I wasn't playing favorites, I gave the same assignment to my other employee, Jay Telles. Jay was a quiet, chunky guy with acne and a rap sheet for hacking. Since I'd done my share of hacking before becoming legit, I didn't hold this against him. After our interview, it was clear he knew his stuff and then some. He didn't say much, but not being much of a people person myself, that was a plus in my book.

After giving Jay his assignment, I returned to my office and continued to zoom around the net. I wanted to check out some possible chat rooms where a guy like Darren might hang out. I visited a slew of websites that seemed promising, making a mental note to check some of them out more thoroughly later. By the end of the day I was exhausted and had had two dozen emails from Ken and Jay. I'd go through them when I got home. But first, I wanted to make a quick detour to visit the Zimmerman twins. No one knew technology better than they did and I wanted to bounce some thoughts off their genius brains.

At about five-thirty, I packed things up and headed for the office stairwell. While climbing down the seven flights of stairs toward the garage, I congratulated myself on foregoing the elevator and renewing my commitment to improved stamina and health. I entered the garage and headed toward my car when, out of nowhere, someone grabbed me from behind, clamping a gloved hand over my mouth. He dragged me behind one of the concrete pillars.

I kicked, scratched and fought like a wildcat on drugs, but the guy was like a pillar himself, completely unmovable.

"I'm not going to hurt you." The voice was deep, male. But I didn't stop until he twisted my neck in a very uncomfortable way. "I can snap it with no effort. I'd advise you to hold still so I don't do it by accident."

"Amhogurgsill," I garbled.

"Huh?" he said, but the pressure on my neck eased.

I sucked in a deep breath. "I said I'm holding still. Obviously, I'm in no shape to fight you."

He snorted. "No kidding. That was a pretty pathetic attempt to escape. You need to get more exercise."

Okay. Time to humor the bad guy. "Um, I just took the stairs instead of the elevator."

"Cardio isn't enough. Try strength training. A woman your size should be able to bench press about thirty pounds. It especially works the upper arms and biceps. Great for helping you get out of situations like this."

"Thanks, but I think I get enough exercise just pressing my luck."

That apparently reminded him of why he'd grabbed me because his grip tightened again.

"Okay, no more Mr. Nice Guy. I'm going to ask you a question. If you answer quietly and correctly, you get to live. Understood?"

I nodded as gingerly as I could.

"Where is Darren Greening?"

I gulped. "This is about Darren Greening?"

"Just answer the question."

"I don't know where he is."

"Don't lie to me," he growled.

"I'm not lying. I mean it. I don't even know Darren Greening."

"Tell me or I'll kill you."

Why wasn't anyone else coming into the garage? It was five-fricking-thirty. Didn't anyone keep regular hours these days?

My breath hitched in my throat. "I swear. I don't know my connection to him. I'm certain I've never met him.

We went to Georgetown University at the same time, but that's it. I'm trying to figure it out myself. Honest."

I closed my eyes and waited. To my enormous relief, the grip around my neck disappeared.

"You'd better be telling the truth. If I find out you've been lying to me…" He made a horrid hissing sound like something getting sliced across the neck. I gulped. Loudly.

He pushed me into the pillar and walked away. I stood shaking, turning around just in time to see a very large dark-clad form disappear into the stairwell.

I hugged myself, breathing in and out until I was sure I could walk without collapsing. I wanted to call the police, but I didn't have reception in the garage basement. I thought about going back to the office to tell Finn what happened, but that would require following Neck-Snapping Man into the stairwell. Not a good plan either. I could wait for the elevator, but that meant standing next to the stairwell where Neck-Snapping Man might reappear after changing his mind and coming back to finish me off.

Half stumbling, half running, I retrieved my briefcase and made it to my car. My hands were shaking so bad, I could hardly press the key button to unlock it. Once inside, I locked the doors and put my head on the steering wheel. I willed my breathing to slow and then started the ignition.

After I pulled out of the garage and into rush-hour traffic, I took out my cell phone and called Finn. It went right to voice mail which meant he was probably on the phone. I left him a short message about what had happened. Five minutes later he called me back.

"Lexi, are you all right?" he asked before I could even say hello. "Where are you?"

"I'm fine. Just shaken up a bit. I'm in the car on my way home."

"I've already contacted building security and the police. What is going on?"

"Looks like we aren't the only ones anxious to find Darren Greening." I quickly filled him in on my exchange with the thug.

He swore. "I'd never have taken this case if I'd known it would put you in danger."

My heart warmed at the concern in his voice. "It's okay, Finn. How could you know? I'm fine, really. I think it was just information he was after."

"You didn't get a look at him?"

"No, he came at me from behind. But he had a slight accent."

"Accent?"

"Yes. I couldn't place it, though. Slavic, I think."

A loud noise cut off part of Finn's reply and then I heard, "Lexi, the police are here. They'll want to talk to you."

"Can I talk to them in the morning? I've already told you everything I know."

"Hold on. I'll ask."

He spoke to someone and then came back. "They said it's okay. Building security already made a thorough sweep and the guy is long gone. Since you didn't get a good look at him, I suppose there's not much they can do at this point anyway."

We talked for a few more minutes before I signed off. I had calmed down significantly now that I knew my death wasn't imminent. Still, I drove carefully, heading north toward my apartment in the small but loveable town of Jessup, Maryland.

I had rented the apartment several years ago because it

was close to the NSA and it had a Dunkin' Donuts nearby. I could live without a garden or a garage, but in my book, a Dunkin' Donuts is a critical amenity. Now that I work in Crystal City, Virginia, the commute is terrible. But I don't want to move just yet. Not until I'm certain this whole new job thing will work out. Frankly, after today's events, things weren't looking that promising for me.

I'm an insecure and cautious person by nature. That means I find security living close to my only other friends in the world, my neighbor Jan Walton and the Zimmerman twins—the genius computer security architects of most of the government's important systems.

I remembered I'd been heading to their house after I'd left work, so I made a turn a couple of streets earlier than mine. Xavier and Elvis probably made more money than the entire population of Jessup put together, but still live in the same old house they'd bought when they were starting out as computer nerds at the NSA. Now they are employed by ComQuest in Baltimore and work out of their house. The twins prefer to work in isolation, and the big wigs at ComQuest are so thrilled to have their genius at their disposal that they basically let them do whatever they want, wherever they want to do it.

The twins and I met at the beach when I was on vacation with Basia and still working at the NSA. They had already left the NSA for the private sector, but had taken an instant liking to me, probably because I spoke their nerdy language and was the only person they knew who could beat them at Quake. I also play a decent game of pool—a game they adore—and we're all crazy about anchovies on pizza. Apparently, that's the only criteria they have for friends, since this odd combination was enough to make me a kindred spirit.

I parked the car and walked up to the door. Ringing the bell, I waited until Xavier opened the door. He was tall and slender with dark brown hair, sharp blue eyes and nice, elegant hacker hands.

"Hey, Lexi." I saw his eyes light up. Then he glanced over my shoulder. "Did you come alone?"

Xavier had a serious crush on Basia. He had probably hoped she had come with me. "Sorry," I said. "Just me."

He shrugged. "No problem. Come on in."

I stepped across the threshold, into the foyer and automatically walked to the left where the twins had converted a living and dining room area into what they called their operations center. Although frugal in other areas of their lives, they owned only spectacular, state-of-the-art computer equipment that left me salivating every time I visited.

The décor of the room consisted of a myriad of wires snaking across the floor, wedged beneath tables and hanging from the ceiling. No paintings, no artwork—just high-tech interior design.

More than three dozen computers sat on several long custom-made tables. All the computers had at least two monitors. In one corner stood the twins' Linux cluster of thirty-two computers that they used to break encryption and do serious number crunching. To the right of that cluster was an area with just laptops—some wired, some not—all running different systems in order to test and simulate a variety of software.

The room was arctic cold with a special-ordered air-conditioning unit running twenty-four hours a day. I always froze my buns off when I came to their house until they'd started keeping a blanket handy just for me. I saw it draped over the back of one of the chairs.

The twins had their work spaces in separate corners of the room. Xavier's desk was covered with papers, manuals, cables, various pieces of hardware and tons of small sticky notes stuck to every available surface. Elvis's area stood in sharp contrast to Xavier's mess. Several reference manuals sat neatly stacked on a shelf across the top, along with a pile of files, all labeled. His computer played a screen saver that showed the Star Trek Enterprise in a battle with a Klingon War Ship. But his chair was empty.

That sucked. I adored both the twins, but Elvis and I were more in sync in terms of life, computers and chocolate. We both floundered with social conversation, lived on our computers and had an eternal commitment to créme-filled éclairs and gaming.

How cool was that?

"So, where's Elvis?" I asked.

Xavier jerked his head upstairs. "Taking a shower. Should be down momentarily."

My mood perked as I moved an empty pizza box from one of the swivel chairs and sat down. Several beer bottles littered the area under the chair. Glancing up, I saw the enormous plasma television that hung over the never-used fireplace was turned to the finance channel and muted. Market information scrolled across the bottom of the screen. This was interesting because I hadn't realized the twins were interested in finance. They had an uncanny genius for just about every subject they tackled and if they had finance in their sights, I felt sorry for the global market.

"Looks like you guys had a wild party." I snatched up the blanket and swirled it around my shoulders. A party was bit surprising since the twins were about as adept as I at social events, which put in mathematical terms, equals less than zero. To my knowledge, they'd never been to a party, let alone thrown one.

"No wild party." Xavier grinned at me. "Only a bit of a celebration for the two of us. Elvis finished designing a spectacular security program—probably the first and best of its kind." No bragging here, just stating the truth and nothing but the truth. "Can't say more about it but the suits were delirious with the results and sent us a half dozen pizzas and a case of beer as a reward."

The suits knew their geniuses well. I was sure the twins had been quite pleased with the gesture. "Cool," I said.

"Got some pizza leftovers in the fridge if you're hungry," Elvis said as he came into the room. His dark hair was damp and curling at the nape of his neck. I noticed with some surprise that he had dressed differently from Xavier today in a red-checked flannel shirt and jeans. Usually the twins dress alike, which is a real mystery because they are the most absent-minded people I know, myself included. Maybe as they approached their thirties they were beginning to be more comfortable with having separate identities.

"No thanks, I'll pass on the pizza. But congrats on the new program."

Elvis smiled and I could see he was in a good mood. "It's ace, Lexi. Wish I could show you, but corporate privacy and all that, you know."

"I know. I'll take your word for it."

Elvis sat down in a chair next to me. "So, what's up?"

I sighed. "I've got a problem. Have you guys ever heard of a nanotech researcher named Darren Greening?"

"He sounds familiar." Elvis glanced over at his brother for confirmation.

"I've done some digging of my own, but I wonder if there's something I may have missed."

Xavier nodded. "Give me a minute, will you?"

He sat down at a terminal and started to type as Elvis leaned toward me, speaking softly. "You've caught him on a good day. Did you hear he has a date with Basia tomorrow?"

I just about fell out of my chair. Basia had gone out with Xavier a couple of months ago, but only because she owed me a big-time favor. She hadn't said a word about the date and I'd presumed nothing had come from it. Now she had agreed to go out with him again and hadn't told me. What was up with that?

"Wow, that's…great," I whispered back. "Is he happy?"

Elvis laughed. "Giddy is more like it."

Xavier threw a pencil at us over his shoulder. "I hear you guys talking about me. Knock it off. You're interfering with my concentration."

Elvis rolled his eyes, picking up the pencil. "He's just embarrassed."

"Am not."

"Are too."

I held up my hands. "Jeez. What are you guys, four?"

Elvis grinned. "All right then, tell us what's up with this Darren Greening guy."

I gave him the brief version of the story, speaking just loud enough to clue in Xavier who was listening in. Elvis whistled in concern when I told him about being accosted in the garage. He reached out to take my hands when they started to tremble.

"That is beyond uncool," Elvis said. "Are you sure you're okay?"

"Better now," I assured him. "Just wondering what's the deal with this Darren Greening guy."

"Wait a minute, I think I know where I've heard of him." Elvis suddenly swiveled around in his chair and began typing on the nearest keyboard.

"Way ahead of you, bro." Xavier tapped his monitor. "He's a member of STRUT."

"STRUT?"

"The Society for The Responsible Use of Technology," Elvis explained, pulling up the group's website on his terminal. "Xavier and I are members."

I blinked in surprise. "You are?"

"Yeah, and so are about three thousand other people."

"Why?"

"Why not? We think it's useful to be part of a group interested in keeping technology as ethical as possible," Elvis said.

The twins never cease to amaze me and that's one of the things I like best about them. I glanced at STRUT's web address and memorized it for a closer look later.

"Do you know anything else about Darren other than he's a member of STRUT?"

"Well, a couple of months ago he posted a paper on the site about the dangers of nanotechnology," Xavier said. "It stirred up quite a controversy."

"But he founded a nanotech company," I protested.

"Energy-related nanotechnology," Elvis said.

"Okay. So, what's the big danger?"

Elvis fixed his intense blue gaze on me. "Some people are worried that the nanotechnology Darren is trying to develop as an environmentally safe energy replacement could be used in more sinister ways."

"Sinister? How?"

He leaned forward. "Nanobots, of course. If we aren't careful, using sophisticated nanotechnology, we could one day create intelligent self-replicating molecular machines that would be able to reproduce unchecked and possibly convert most of the biosphere into copies of themselves, if they so desired."

It took a minute for that to sink in. "Okay, that's pretty sinister. So, Darren wants to make sure that whatever he develops in the nanotechnology field will be used strictly for the good of mankind. It sounds reasonable. What's so controversial about that?"

Xavier swiveled slowly back and forth in his chair. "Well, some people read his paper and thought he was advocating a ban on all research and development of nanotechnology to avoid any adverse consequences from the science."

"Like that would ever happen. Since when has an approach of saying no to the progress of science been effective?"

"Never," Elvis said. "You can't tell scientists not to explore nanotechnology when there are so many excellent possibilities and benefits to be gained from the research."

"Not to mention fortunes," Xavier added.

"So, then what *was* Darren saying?" I asked.

"I think he's just trying to raise the bar," Elvis explained. "Like encouraging us to address the ethical use of nanotechnology *before* we start designing things all willy-nilly."

"How can I get a copy of the article?"

Xavier stood and walked over to a printer and pulled off some sheets for me. "Way ahead of you, Lexi."

"Thanks." I stood. "Does STRUT have a chat room?"

"Of course," Xavier said.

"You can hang out there if you join STRUT," Elvis told me. "It's a member-only section."

"How do I join?"

"Just proclaim your ever-dying devotion to using technology responsibly."

I wasn't sure I was well read enough on this topic to join, but it didn't look like I had a lot of choice. Time was of the essence and I'd do what I'd have to do, especially if it helped me figure out why Darren Greening had fingered me in a weird cryptic note.

"Well, I guess that means I'm your newest member." I replaced the blanket on the chair. "Thanks, guys."

Elvis walked me to the door. "I'll ask around about Darren. Maybe he has some connection to you that we're all missing."

"You guys are the best," I said and Elvis smiled.

"I'll walk you to your car."

"I appreciate that," I said, even though I didn't think Neck-Snapping Man would follow me around.

When we got to my car, he reached out and twirled a strand of my hair around his finger. "You be careful, okay?"

Xavier called out from the doorway, "Yeah, and don't forget to tell Basia I'm looking forward to tomorrow night."

"He's counting the nanoseconds."

Again, I felt a flash of annoyance that Basia hadn't told me about the forthcoming date, but I promised to give her Xavier's message when I saw her later tonight.

I turned up the heater in my car to offset the cold November air as I drove home to my cozy little one-bedroom apartment. It's tiny more than cozy, but I had started trying to be more of a glass half-full type of person. I made a conscious decision to look on the bright side of things—like being alive, having a job and living in my own *cozy* apartment.

I tossed my keys on the kitchen counter and went to the living room. I pulled out my Georgetown yearbook and lugged it back to the kitchen. Sitting at the small, round kitchen table, I opened a Diet Coke, and chugged it straight from the can. I flipped pages until I came to Darren Greening's picture and spent some time gazing at it. In this photo, he looked all of twelve years old, skinny with faded acne scars. But his gaze was intense, almost scary. I could see the genius lurking there.

I scanned the rest of the yearbook, but there was nothing else of interest on Darren. No cocky phrases, famous quotes, and as far as I could tell, he hadn't had any other extra-curricular activities at Georgetown. Just your everyday regular, geeky college kid.

I shut the yearbook and stood. I was starving, but figured I'd just pick up something to eat in the food court at the mall. Finishing my Coke, I smashed the can flat because it made me feel powerful, and chucked it into the recycle bin.

In the bedroom, I stripped off my work clothesI pulled on a pair of jeans and an oversized burgundy sweater. Since I was going to be trying on gowns, I pulled my hair back into a long ponytail and pinned it up, adding some lip balm for effect. Like that would really help me appear elegant as I tried on gowns.

A bit depressed, I left my apartment, looked around carefully in the parking lot for strange men, and headed for Columbia Mall, which happens to be my and Basia's favorite spot. It was Basia's favorite hangout because they had a lot of clothes and shoe stores and she was the ultimate shopper. I liked it because they had not one, but two of the nifty stands that sell those fabulous hot cinnamon-sugar pretzels. I got to the mall before Basia for that very reason and was just licking the sugar off my fingers when she plopped down beside me on the bench.

"Do you know how much saturated fat is contained in just one-third of that pretzel?" She looked at it in disgust.

"If only that fat would go straight to my boobs." I sighed.

"I refuse to be jealous because I know you won't be skinny forever. Do yourself a favor and come out of denial now. How many times have I told you that after reaching the big three-oh, your metabolism will slow down and you will get seriously fat if you keep eating like you do. That's *if* you don't have a heart attack first."

"Sticks and stones may break my bones." Then I paused. "Speaking of breaking bones…" I quickly filled her in on what had happened to me in the garage.

"You've got to be kidding. It's not safe anywhere these days. What is going on with Darren Greening?"

"That's the million-dollar question. In return I might ask what is going on with you and Xavier?"

I clearly caught her off guard. Avoiding my pointed stare, she took off her hat and shrugged out of her coat. "How'd you find out?"

"From Xavier, of course. Why all the secrecy?"

"It's no big deal."

"No big deal?" I repeated incredulously. "Are you nuts? This is Xavier we're talking about. You know, the geeky guy you've never looked twice at before."

"Need I remind you, we've already been on one date?"

"Yeah, a date *I* set up. A date you didn't say one word about."

"And from that you presumed what?"

"That you had no interest in him."

"Well, you were wrong. I had fun."

My mouth dropped open. "So, you *like* him?"

"For heaven's sake, Lexi, this is exactly why I didn't tell you. You're too emotionally involved. Xavier is like a brother to you. I'm going on another date with him, period. If it doesn't work out, I don't want any additional grief from you."

"But I thought you were dating Lars," I protested.

Lars Anderson was Basia's one-time karate instructor. A tall, gorgeous Swedish-American with hands licensed as killing machines. He owns a small karate academy in Laurel, Maryland to which I now belong, and where I'm literally working my butt off in Tae Kwon Do. Typical for the course, Basia took one lesson, quit and is now happily dating the instructor. They have a complicated history, but jeez, these days, who doesn't?

"I *am* dating Lars."

My eyes widened. "You're going to date both of them? At the *same* time?"

"Why not? I'm not under a mutually exclusive contract with either one."

"B-but...do they know that?"

"Yes. Don't worry, Lexi, I can handle them both."

"Wow." I let it hang at that. What else could I say? In terms of dating etiquette, I knew less than diddly, whereas Basia was the master. Besides, I was secretly in awe that she could juggle two guys.

For a few minutes, we sat there in silence until I blurted out, "I'm not sure I know what I'm doing. Do you think Finn really likes me?"

"Of course, he does."

"Because?"

"Because you're *you*."

"That's not providing the boost of confidence I was looking for."

"What do you want me to say? Are you the prettiest, savviest girl Finn has ever dated? Not likely. But that's a good thing. He's probably had his fill of that. A guy like him wants someone genuine. So, I beg you to stop trying to analyze it to death. It's not math, which means it's neither linear nor logical. Now, I believe the reason we're here is to get you an evening gown."

Before I could protest, she practically dragged me toward Nordstrom's.

"When you relax, and are in your comfort zone, you're actually quite pretty, Lexi. Having an inner glow is all about being self-confident, poised and comfortable with your body and sexuality. It would help to start practicing ways to exude your femininity in the real world."

"I don't know what you're talking about."

"Do you want to impress Finn or not?"

I let out a deep breath. "All right. Inner glow. Exude my femininity. How hard can that be?"

"You can do it. You have lots of wonderful qualities."

"Such as?"

"You're loyal, intelligent and funny."

That didn't sound very feminine to me, more like a beloved pet. I tried not to be more depressed. "Okay. And that affects my inner glow, how?"

"You need to build on that so you can loosen up and go with the flow a bit more. Take more chances in life and love. Let's decide right now that tomorrow night with Finn will be the start of a new, feminine, sexy you."

It was a heck of a pep talk, so I kept trying to imagine my element while we browsed around the gown section.

Basia chose gown after gown for me to try on, and I attempted to keep a happy face as I donned one after the other. I didn't like any of them, mostly because they were in girly colors like peach, luscious lemon and butter cream. Instead of feeling gorgeous or in touch with my feminine side, I felt ravenously hungry. But I gave it my best shot.

Had I been alone, I would have picked a long-sleeved black sheath that I saw hanging on a fifty-percent-off rack. When I made one small suggestion about it, Basia nearly had apoplexy, saying that I needed color to stand out in a crowd and to brighten up my apparently lackluster complexion.

After trying on gown number twelve, I no longer cared about my inner glow or if I was feminine. I was seriously cranky, hungry and ready to kill someone with my bare hands. I decided I was pathologically unsuited to clothes shopping.

"What am I wearing now?" I snarled, parading around in a strapless gown.

"It's a Gucci in dark Victorian teal." She fussed with some ties at my waist. "Isn't it beautiful?"

"No. Why can't I buy a black gown?" I kept tugging on the bust. I didn't have enough boobs to hold it up and it kept gapping open like a toothless fish every time I breathed or moved.

"Do you want to look acceptable for Finn or do you want to look fabulous? Remember your new mantra—exude an inner glow."

She stepped back from me and squinted critically. "No, this one won't work either. Try this one." She grabbed another gown off the rack and handed me a sleeveless, greenish gown with spaghetti straps.

Just the thought of spaghetti made my stomach growl

and I tried to remember if any of the food-court restaurants sold pasta.

"Remember the mantra," she said, apparently seeing my upper lip form a snarl of protest.

"Oh, all right, all right," I snapped as I marched back to the dressing room. "I'm focusing on my freaking inner glow. What color is this gown anyway? Pee-pee-green?"

"English-yew-green," she said, rolling her eyes. "It's the rage in Paris this fall."

"I'm not wearing anything French. It goes against my politics."

"Lexi."

"Oh, okay."

Trying to act like a team player, I tried on three more gowns and then decided I really couldn't take it anymore. The next gown would be a winner, whether I liked it or not.

"I think I've found the one."

I cracked open the dressing room door and Basia handed me a slinky, blood-red gown with a low-cut back and leg slits practically up to my butt. Then I turned it around and saw the plunging neckline.

"Are you nuts?" I stared at the gown on the hanger.

Basia laughed. "Lexi, you have a body that can carry this off. Just try it on. It's Moroccan-red."

"I suppose that means this is the latest rage in Morocco."

"At least it's not French."

I tried it on and the gown fit like a glove. That's not a turn of phrase. It really fit like a glove. A tight glove. The tag said the material was silk and spandex, but I'd never heard of the two of them together in an evening gown. Then again, I'd never shopped for evening gowns before, so what did I know? Of course, I couldn't breathe and walking was difficult, but there was no question my inner glow would be on display for all to see.

"Oh, it's perfect," Basia sighed as I opened the door and tottered out. "Finn will have a heart attack when he sees you in this."

"If I don't die of asphyxia first." My voice was wispy because the dress squeezed my lungs, not to mention what little boobs I have, together. It created the illusion of cleavage and that was the best thing that had happened to me all night.

"It's a good thing you don't need to wear a bra with that."

"I don't need to wear a bra with anything. Still, thanks for reminding me."

Basia tugged on the material near my right boob. "Oh, don't be so cranky. It's stunning. One look at you in this and Finn will have only one thing on his mind for the rest of the evening."

Since there was no way I was going to put on one more gown, I let Basia talk me into buying the dress. Considering how little actual material the gown was made of, I sure paid a heck of a lot for it.

Then, of course, I had to buy a pair of sexy, red shoes that Basia picked out. At first I protested because the heels on the shoes put me well over six feet two, but Basia said they were delicate and gave me toe cleavage. All the talk of cleavage made me giddy, so of course, I bought them, too.

As we lugged my purchases out to the car, I hoped I'd done the right thing by buying such a daring gown. It was a huge step out of my comfort zone, but I knew exactly squat about dating, so I had to rely on the expertise of others. I only hoped it would all turn out right. One way or the other, I'd know if it had paid off in less than twenty-four hours.

Chapter Four

Basia had just helped me pile my purchases in the trunk
of the Miata when my cell phone rang. Basia slammed
the trunk shut for me so I could answer my phone.

I flipped the phone open. "Hello?"

"Hey, Lexi, it's me." The sound of Finn's lilting Irish
voice made my heart skip a beat. For some reason, the
brogue seemed to come out more when we talked. I
hoped it was because he knew it was a serious turn-on
for me, but more likely it was because he was worried
and wasn't expending any effort to keep his accent neutral. Actually, that worked for me, too, because I liked
the idea that he felt comfortable around me.

"What's up?" I said.

"How are you feeling?"

"I'm fine. Really. Thanks for asking."

"You up to hearing what I discovered today?"

"Of course." I leaned back against the car and then
mouthed to Basia that I was talking to Finn. She made
kissy noises with her mouth and I rolled my eyes.

"I just finished talking with Michael's father, Gene
Hart," Finn continued. "Gene spoke very highly of
Darren. It sounded like he considers him a second son.
He's known Darren since the two boys became close

friends in college. Then, of course, he provided much of the start-up capital for their company. He says Darren seemed to change after Michael's unexpected death."

"Change how?"

"He said Darren had become paranoid."

"Paranoid? He used that exact word?"

"He did."

I considered for a moment. "Paranoid of what?"

"That someone was out to get him."

"Paranoid enough to do a disappearing act?"

"Possibly. But something else is bothering me. Gene didn't seem all that worried that Darren had vanished."

"You think maybe Darren let him in on his plans?"

Finn paused. "No, I don't think so. I think he just considers it something Darren might do to get himself together."

"He didn't seem worried in the slightest? Did you tell him about the note?"

"I did. That seemed puzzling to him, but he couldn't offer any insight. Unfortunately, he'd never heard of you and couldn't imagine what would make Darren issue such a peculiar SOS. Of course, he's more concerned now, but had no substantive information that could help us clear any of this up."

"Great."

"Cheer up. There is a bit of good news."

"Such as?"

"I have the key to Darren's apartment."

"That *is* good news. Where'd you get it?"

"Gene gave it to me."

"What is Michael's father doing with a key to Darren's apartment?"

"Who else would Darren give the key to? Gene is practically his surrogate father."

It still didn't make sense to me because there was no way I'd ever give the key to my apartment to *my* mom. Perish the thought. But, hey, different keystrokes for different folks.

"Okay. Can I come with you when you look through his place? I'm hoping to come across his transcripts from Georgetown or something else that might jog my memory about him."

"I thought about doing it right now. Are you game?"

"I'm always game," I said. "Give me the address again."

He told me and I committed it to memory. Since it was in Virginia, out near Dulles Airport, I figured I'd need about forty minutes to get there.

"I'm going to grab something to eat," Finn said, "so I should get there about the same time. I'll meet you in the parking lot."

"Perfect," I said. "See you then."

I snapped the phone shut and slipped it in my coat pocket. Basia raised an eyebrow as she took a sip of her soy latte.

"A late-night rendezvous?"

"Yes, but unfortunately not the kind that you're implying. He's got a key to Darren's apartment."

"What about the key to your place?"

"Surely you jest. We haven't even officially had a date yet."

She chuckled. "So, be bold. Give him your key tomorrow night."

"I've got a bad feeling about this whole date thing. I don't think it's going to work out."

"Of course it will. You're just as desirable, in your own way, as the supermodels and actresses he usually dates."

"That *so* doesn't make me feel better."

She grinned. "Sorry, I couldn't help myself. It's just way too much fun to yank your chain. Seriously, you need to relax, Lexi. Finn wants to be with you and not some supermodel. He likes you precisely because you aren't interested in his looks or money. He's attracted to your intelligence, kindness and wit, and I'd venture a guess it's the same on your side. Right?"

I nodded. "Okay, you're right. Can we just stop talking about Finn now, please? I'm already on the verge of a nervous breakdown and the date isn't even until tomorrow."

She patted my arm. "You'll do fine. Now go meet with him and be yourself. That's what he likes best about you."

I wasn't thrilled with that assessment, but what else could I do? As I climbed into the car, Basia added, "Whatever you do, don't tell him about the gown. Every girl needs to keep a surprise up her sleeve."

"Um…the gown is sleeveless."

"Turn of phrase. You know what I mean."

"I just hope he likes surprises."

"All men like surprises. Especially those that involve cleavage."

"I don't have cleavage," I protested. "It's just an illusion."

"Luckily for women, just the suggestion of cleavage is enough for men."

"I hope you're right," I said, slamming the door and starting the engine. I waited until she climbed into her car and waved as I drove off.

While stopped at a red light, I double checked the directions on the map and then headed south on the interstate, toward the Dulles Toll Road. I found Darren's place in just under thirty minutes. He lived about a mile from Flow Technologies, which apparently made his commute quite comfortable. He didn't have to face crazy drivers, road rage and bumper fumes on a daily basis like I did, but everyone has a cross to bear and a crappy commute happened to be one of mine.

I saw Finn already standing in the parking lot, leaning against his dark green car and sipping what looked like a cup of coffee. I pulled into the empty spot next to his and hopped out of the car.

He pulled me into a one-armed hug, kissing the top of my head. "You made good time."

"So did you."

He studied my face. "Are you sure you're okay after what happened in the garage today? He didn't harm you in any other way?"

"No. Just scared the living daylights out of me. No sweat, really. After our last adventure together, I think I'm getting used to attracting psychos. I'll talk to the police in the morning."

He didn't look happy, but didn't argue. "So, what do you think?" He motioned toward the apartment complex with his coffee cup. It looked to be about fifteen floors and had pleasant landscaping. The building was lit up and you could see right into several people's apartments who had either neglected or not wanted to pull the curtains. Most places seemed to have balconies and I could see several bicycles and small tables placed upon them. The parking lot was also nicely maintained and well lit.

"This is where Darren lives?"

Finn nodded. "It's a pretty nice place."

"What floor is he on?"

"Thirteenth."

I looked at him in surprise. "I thought most apartment buildings skipped the thirteenth floor. Bad luck and all."

Finn just shrugged, but it seemed like a bad omen to me. "Are we going in?"

"Not yet. There is something else I'd like to fill you in on."

"Okay," I said, pulling my coat closed and buttoning it up against the cool November air. I had forgotten my gloves, so I stuffed my hands in my pockets and leaned next to him against the car. I could see puffs of my breath.

"I obtained the police accident report on Michael Hart's death," he said.

"And?"

"He apparently swerved to avoid a car that veered into his lane. They never found the driver of the other car."

I fell silent, considering that. "Do you know any more details?"

"It was early evening about two miles from here. There was one witness, an elderly woman, who was driving behind Michael and said a dark sedan coming in the opposite direction veered sharply into the path of Michael's car. She guesses that maybe it was a drunk driver. When Michael went off the road, the other car didn't stop. She dialed 9-1-1, but it was too late. He'd been killed instantly upon impact."

"She didn't get a look at the license plate or the driver?"

"Neither. The dark-colored sedan is the only detail she could remember."

"Great."

"Lexi, there is something else. Gene Hart didn't have much good to say about Niles Foreman and the other investors."

"Somehow, I'm not surprised. Did he say why?"

"He didn't much approve of their cutthroat approach toward handling the company."

I didn't either, but then again, I didn't know squat about running a business. "Did he elaborate on what he meant by cutthroat?"

"No. Unfortunately, Gene was rather tight-lipped when it came to discussing his personal feelings for the group."

"Does he still have any shares in the company?"

"Yes, a small amount."

I sighed. "That's probably why. Still, I don't get it. Why come to us? If Niles and his buddies are so worried about recovering their investment, why don't they hire an insurance investigator to track him down and to heck with the cryptic note about me?"

"My guess is they don't care about the twenty-five million dollars in insurance money at this point. As it stands now, Darren's ideas are potentially worth a hundred times that. Besides, Niles wants this investigation to be discreet so that they don't frighten off the shareholders."

"Yeah. Great."

To my surprise, he reached out and put an arm around my shoulders. "Hey, don't sound so grim. You got us our first case."

"It's not exactly what I had in mind."

"Me neither. But I'm starting to expect the unexpected when it comes to you." Did he sound happy about that or was that wishful thinking? "Come on, it's freezing out here. Let's go in."

I wanted to stay, leaning against his warm, hard body, but my nose was frozen and my ears had started to burn from the cold. "Sure, I'm ready."

We walked up to the doorway entrance and Finn

keyed in a code. We took the elevator to the thirteenth floor and walked down a burgundy-carpeted hallway. Finn stopped at apartment number 1307 and tried the key. It worked, so he stepped in and flipped on a hall light.

I gasped. It was evident, even from Darren's foyer, that the place had been tossed. Papers, books, cushions and clothes were scattered everywhere as far as the eye could see.

"Not good." Finn walked farther into the living room area and turned on another lamp. I followed close behind, looking at the mess strewn about. I'd just had my apartment tossed a few months back and it sucked, not only because it was a serious personal violation, but it took me a heck of a long time to put everything back in the right spot.

"Stay here." He motioned me back with his arm. "Let's make sure we don't have any unexpected visitors still here."

"Are you armed?" My heart started pounding.

He shook his head and then pressed a finger to his lips. I stood in the doorway, my hand clutching the cell phone in my pocket. If I heard even the slightest unusual noise, I was calling 9-1-1.

To my relief, Finn reappeared moments later. "The place is empty, but someone did a pretty thorough job of ravaging it."

"Shouldn't we call the police?"

"How do we know he doesn't live this way?"

"Oh, please. No one lives like this. Not even me."

Finn nodded. "Okay, I agree. But before I bring in the police, I'll have to clear it with Niles first." He pulled out his cell phone and pushed some buttons.

I shrugged. "Well, while you're doing that, I'm going

to look around. Although I'm not sure what I'll be able to find in this disaster."

"Start in the living room and I'll check in the bedroom." Finn disappeared down the hall still holding the phone to his ear.

For a moment, I stood in the living room and looked around. It was small but comfy. Darren had a huge plasma television set flanked by a decent stereo, but neither appeared to have been touched by the intruders. The walls were bare except for two posters. The first hung directly over a handsome wooden desk that had been pushed up against the wall next to the sliding glass door out to the balcony and contained a photograph of Einstein beneath which was the phrase "The Only Real Valuable Thing is Intuition." The other poster was positioned over the television and had words only, contrasting white against black: "Your Opinion, Although Interesting, is Irrelevant." I sniggered. Well, at least the guy had a sense of humor.

The desk seemed a sensible place to start to look for anything of interest, so I gingerly stepped my way across wayward cushions, DVDs and other assorted junk. A computer had apparently once sat on the desk because there were several cables snaking up to the desktop and a printer/fax still stood on an adjoining table. But there wasn't any computer in sight. I checked under the desk and around it and even took a quick peek into the kitchen, but I didn't see anything.

I didn't know what kind of computer Darren had. If it was a laptop, it could be that he had taken it with him when he vanished. If he had a desktop computer, my first bet was that the people who ransacked the place had stolen it.

I knelt and opened the small door on the table where

the printer sat. I switched it on and put a piece of blank paper in the slider. Pushing the redial button, I watched to see where Darren had sent his last fax. To my disappointment, the number for Flow Technologies came up. Nothing too exciting about that.

I began to methodically search through the papers on and around his desk. There were several research articles on the floor, most containing technical jargon beyond my understanding. I flipped through the drawers looking for bank statements, bills, credit-card receipts or anything that might clue us in to his current whereabouts. *Nada.* Most likely, he kept all that information on his computer, which is exactly what I did. It cut down considerably on the paper clutter.

I couldn't find an address book or even a calendar, although I suspected someone as technology-minded as Darren would probably keep the info he needed on his computer or phone. I was sitting on the floor, looking through some research articles when Finn stepped into the living room.

"Did you find anything interesting?"

He held up a manila folder. "Some papers from Georgetown University, including transcripts. I also found a box with some mementos inside. But more importantly there is a sticky note on top of the box with the initials L.C."

I stood and took the box from him. "What? It's got my initials on it?"

Opening it up, I saw some assorted trinkets inside. Nothing jumped out at me. Yet.

"Okay," I said. "I'll take a more careful look at this stuff later. The transcripts will be useful. Did you reach Niles on the phone?"

"I did. He was surprised we were here. I told him

we got the key from Michael's father. He already knew about the apartment getting tossed, but he said he wants to keep it under wraps for the time being. No police, not just yet."

"Nice of him to fill us in on this. Why didn't he happen to mention it before?"

"He didn't think it relevant."

"Jeez, his concern for his employee's welfare is really touching."

"Niles is a paying client, Lexi. Don't make this too personal."

"Unfortunately, it became personal the moment I saw my name on that note," I snapped.

Finn didn't reply and instead resumed his search around the apartment. I wanted to apologize for making it seem like this mess was all Finn's fault, but I didn't know how to do it gracefully. I chalked it up to mental exhaustion after an emotionally draining day.

We looked around for another hour, but found nothing else useful. Darren's answering machine was blank and we couldn't find a scrap of paper or any hint of where he might have fled. I suspected the missing laptop held any clues we might need and wondered if it were safe in Darren's hands or with whoever had searched the place before us.

"Well, I don't think we're going to find anything else of interest here," I yelled from the kitchen, replacing several pots and pans back into the cabinet and then stretching.

Finn strolled in, rifling through the phone book. "I agree." He set it down. "I do have a couple more leads to follow, if you're game."

"Tonight?" I glanced at my watch. It was nearly eleven o'clock.

"No, tomorrow. I'm done for the evening."

So was I. After the trauma of the garage and then the grueling gown search, I was pretty much a walking zombie. "What do you have in mind?"

Finn pulled out a piece of paper from his shirt pocket. "I found out that Darren and Michael liked to hang out at a place called the Lighthouse Cyber Café. Ever hear of it?"

"Sure, it's a regular hangout for the university kids. The place makes a mean double cheeseburger and has the best fries in town."

"I thought we might venture in, ask around and see what we can find out."

I smiled. "You need me to walk the walk, and talk the cyber lingo, right?"

"Is it that obvious?"

"Nah," I lied. "You're a natural tech head."

He grinned. "It opens for lunch at eleven thirty. We'll check it out and maybe even have lunch there."

"Gee, a trip down memory lane *and* a double cheeseburger. I can't wait."

Careful to leave everything as we'd found it except for the box of mementos and the Georgetown transcripts that I now carried, we locked up Darren's apartment and returned to the parking lot. Finn held open the car door for me as I climbed in and turned the key in the ignition.

He leaned down, so I opened the window. "Thanks for coming out so late," he said. "Especially after what happened to you today. I know it's selfish, but I wanted to see you for myself, to make sure you were okay."

I gave him a cheerful smile. "Well, as you can see I'm just peachy." Embarrassed as soon as the juvenile words left my mouth, my cheeks heated. I closed my eyes knowing if there were a firing squad nearby, I would be shot immediately for crimes against conversation.

When I dared to open my eyes, Finn was climbing into his Jag. Sleek, gorgeous car—sleek, gorgeous man. As he drove off, I groaned and banged my head against the steering wheel. I'm sure he'd never met a bigger dork. All I needed was to give him more reasons to dump me before we ever went out.

It was nearly midnight by the time I got home, pulled on my pajamas and got into bed. Despite the worries I'd had that day, I'm certain it took me all of three nanoseconds to fall asleep.

Unfortunately, once I was in la-la land, I dreamt I rode around in a sleek green Jaguar with Darren Greening in the passenger seat while a pickup truck filled with gun-toting Navajo Indians chased after us. I evaded the Indians until I came to a fork in the road.

Unable to decide which way to go, I screeched the car to a stop and hopped out. That's when I realized I wasn't wearing any pants, but stood there in the middle of the road in my panties and a T-shirt. When I turned around to face the wrath of the armed Indians, I saw only Finn standing there, hissing at me with the same noise Neck-Snapping Man had made. I woke up with a start amid a tangle of sweaty sheets.

One thing was certain. You can bet I wasn't going to ask anyone to interpret *that* dream for me.

Chapter Five

I couldn't go back to sleep after my Freud-on-drugs dream and decided to head for the office early. I made my usual morning swing by Dunkin' Donuts for a cranberry-orange muffin, a caramel latte and a Diet Coke from the refrigerator cooler. Once at the office, I munched on the muffin while sorting through the emails Jay and Ken had sent me on Darren Greening. I methodically eliminated all emails containing identical information and when I was finished, I was pleased that my employees had done such a thorough job. I had boatloads of stuff to review.

Before I delved deeper into that, there was something else I wanted to do first. I hauled out the shoebox Finn had found at Darren's apartment with my initials on top and set aside the transcripts from Georgetown for later. I started to go through the box, carefully cataloguing each item on a piece of paper. I took out the first item and scrawled on the paper, *high school ring, sapphire*. A close inspection of the engraving indicated that Darren had gone to Thomas Jefferson High School for Science and Technology in Alexandria, Virginia—just a hop, skip and a jump from where I sat in Crystal City. TJ is a special high school, mostly for kids gifted in science and technology, and the competition to get in is fierce.

I then removed from the box a small National Honor Society pin also from TJ; three first-place blue ribbons from various science fairs; a blank postcard of the planet Mars bought at the Smithsonian Air and Space Museum; a well-worn rabbit's foot on a key chain; and a signed snapshot of a very proud Darren, who looked to be about in his mid-teens, standing with the so-called "Fathers of the Internet" Bob Kahn and Vinton Cerf. But other than a small dust ball in the corner, that was it for the contents of the shoebox. Nothing leaped out at me except perhaps the rabbit's foot. Weird as tech geeks aren't usually superstitious.

I gently returned all the items to the box and picked up Darren's Georgetown transcripts. I had brought a copy of my transcripts as well and I laid them out side by side on my desk. It took me about thirty minutes to go through and carefully compare. When I finished, I leaned back in my chair and tapped my pencil against the desk in frustration. Although we were both undergraduate students at GU for the exact same years, not once had we taken a class together. Sure, we'd taken similar courses, even from the same professors, but never at the same time.

Crap. It looked like a dead end.

I took a sip of my long-cold latte and then set the transcripts and box aside. I swiveled my chair toward the computer and logged on to the STRUT website that Elvis and Xavier had told me about yesterday. After reading and agreeing to the site treatise (no flaming, no patronizing, and discussions of technology only, please), I became a STRUT member. I logged in to the chat room with the screen name CryptHead. For about an hour I followed the chat, but avoided all attempts by others to get me to join in. This was complex stuff and I needed more time to familiarize myself with the material. Instead, I scanned through the archive of old messages, and read some comments about Darren's controversial paper. Nothing mind-blowing and I couldn't find any messages that were obviously from Darren. Of course, he likely would have been using a screen name, too, but nothing leaped out at me. I'd have to think about it some more.

I set my elbows on the desk and rubbed my temples. There had to be *some* connection between Darren Greening and me. Why couldn't I see it?

As I sat there morosely, my gaze fell on Darren's article, "The Dangers of Nanotechnology." I picked it up and read it all the way through again, this time slowly. Most of it was over my head, but it vaguely reminded me of something. But what? I racked my brain, but came up empty. Nonetheless, there was something about it that seemed significant. Sighing, I put it aside and started methodically plowing through the data Ken and Jay had sent me.

I'd been at it maybe a little more than half an hour when Finn rapped on the door. When I looked up, he smiled at me and my pulse went all aflutter. Jeez, I really had it bad for him.

"Hard at it already, are you?" he asked.

He looked amazing as usual in a crisp white shirt, navy pants and a red tie. His coat was draped over his arm. I didn't want to think about how I looked with bloodshot eyes, boring gray slacks and flat hair.

"Come in and have a seat. I think I'm getting a clearer picture of Darren Greening."

He took me up on my offer and sat down in one of the chairs. "That's good to hear." He set his coat aside. "Have you had a look at the transcripts, then?"

"Yep, but unfortunately, no dice. We took similar classes at GU, but never together."

I could see Finn was disappointed. "What about extra-curricular activities? Could your paths have crossed there?"

"He didn't have any that I could find. And for that matter, neither did I. So, I guess that connection is out." I tried not to look embarrassed about my lack of activities, social or otherwise.

"None at all? No sports, no clubs, no outside interests?"

"None whatsoever. It's called the Geek Syndrome. The computer is your one and only connection to the outside world, your entire social life, and well, for lack of a better comparison...a companion."

He fell silent for a moment. "I see."

I knew he didn't really, but now wasn't the time for a psychiatric exposé. "I know it's pathetic. Don't say it."

"Hey, I didn't intend to. And it's not pathetic. It's just different, that's all. Intriguing."

The flush crept up my neck. "Right. Anyway, what's important is that we still don't have a connection. Unfortunately, I didn't see anything else of interest in his box either."

Finn loosened his tie. "Well, it was a long shot. But if none of this is working out, tell me why you think you have a clearer picture of him."

I filled him in on Darren's connection to STRUT, gave him a copy of the controversial paper Darren had

posted to the website and explained the twins' evalua-
tion of what it all meant in terms of scientific progress.

Finn listened, his expression thoughtful. "So, you
think that Darren Greening disappeared because he
might have been worried about how the world might
use his technology."

"I don't know. I suppose it's a plausible theory. I'm
a bit shaky on understanding how his technology could
be widely misused, if it's indeed something that could
also potentially serve the needs of earth. I mean, think
about the staggering implications of energy nanotechnology. How incredible would it be if we didn't need to
mine the ground and pollute the air for our energy?"

"Incredible, indeed. However, Niles told us there are
many people who wouldn't want Darren's energy-pro-
ducing nanotechnology to come to fruition. Oil-rich na-
tions, for starters."

"True. But why run and hide? Why not figure out
ways to protect the technology? And why hide from
your investors, the people who, besides you, have the
most at stake?"

"I don't know."

"Worse, why drag me into this? I'm all for protecting
the environment, and even more in favor of ending U.S.
dependence on foreign oil, but I'm neither a nanotech-
head nor an energy specialist. I can't even remember
meeting this guy. What's the connection?"

"You'll figure it out, Lexi."

While I appreciated his confidence, I wasn't certain
I shared it. I ran my fingers through my hair wearily.
"I think I need a more thorough understanding of energy-related nanotechnology. In fact, that reminds me
of something I wanted to ask you. What are the chances

that Niles and the rest of the trio would let me in to Flow Technologies for a look at Darren's work space?"

Finn stood up and stretched. "I can't see why they wouldn't if you think it might bring us closer to Darren. I'll give Niles a call this morning."

"Thanks."

"By the way, the police will be here at ten o'clock to get your statement."

"Oh, great." I wasn't looking forward to reliving that incident, but knew it was necessary.

Sighing, I turned back to the monitor and cruised back over to the STRUT website. I logged in to the chat room as CryptHead again, and this time I saw there were two people actively chatting with about four others observing. Of the two chatting, one was called RawMode and the other Grok. I assumed RawMode came from the hacker term meaning a mode that allows a program to transfer bits directly from an I/O device. Grok was taken from a novel I'm nuts about, *Stranger in a Strange Land* by Robert A. Heinlein. In the Martian language, Grok meant, "To be with one."

After a few minutes, they tried to get me to join in.

Grok: Hey, CryptHead. What brings you to our humble domain? Haven't seen you here before.

I needed information, so I took the plunge. Typing quickly, my fingers flew over the keys. That was one plus about being a geek—excellent typing skills. If this information-security job didn't work out, I could probably get a job as a secretary. Except I had sucky phone skills and people annoyed me.

CryptHead: I'm a STRUT virgin. It's my first time here. What are you guys talking about?

RawMode: I.E.

If memory served me correctly, I.E. stood for Information Ecology. I wasn't well versed in the subject, but at least I knew the basics. Sort of. Unfortunately, Mr. Terlittle's T&A course (Technology and Anthropology) at Georgetown, where I had supposedly learned said basics, had been a real snoozer. He was fond of his pointer and slides, which meant a good portion of the class was taught in the dark. That also meant most of his students slept through his lectures, myself included. However, some vestiges of knowledge must have somehow seeped into my brain because I seemed to recall that I.E. represented people, values and technologies intermingled in the environment. Maybe I could keep up with them after all.

CryptHead: Down with monoculture!

I was sure a slam against monocultures was the war cry for I.E. supporters.

RawMode: Ha, ha. You still in high school, dude?

I grimaced. Okay, so maybe I should have stayed awake a little more in Terlittle's class, but I still hoped it would be enough to get me chummy with these guys so I could ask them if they knew anything interesting about Darren Greening.

CryptHead: Okay, guess I'd better 'fess up. I.E.'s not my prime deal, but I did take a course on it at GU.

I figured it couldn't hurt to advertise my GU connection in case Darren logged on and went through the chat records and put two and two together as to my identity. I presumed he was afraid to contact me directly but that wouldn't preclude him from logging on under an assumed name and getting a message to me somehow via a live chat. It was a long shot, but one worth pursuing. To my relief, it seemed that the GU connection had broken the ice.

RawMode: GU? Cool. You had Terlittle? Heard he's a zoner.

CryptHead: Yeah. Can't believe you've heard of him. You go to GU, too?

RawMode: Nah, went to MIT. Met the zonehead at a conference. Impressed. NOT!

CryptHead: Likewise. You go to GU, Grok?

Grok: Nope. I'm from MIT, too.

CryptHead: Where you guys operate now?

RawMode: Me—at a pharmaceutical company in Boston, making drugs from RNA molecules.

I didn't have a clue what that meant. Already I felt way out of my league and began to understand why the

twins liked to hang out here. Still it didn't seem fair that
I was an outcast even among my own people. I tried hard
to fit in anyway.

CryptHead: How about you, Grok?

Grok: I'm into AI.

Jeez, artificial intelligence. Things were getting
worse. I was in seriously exalted company and now I understood why they laughed at my pathetic understanding
of information ecology. I just hoped that for the rest of
the chat they wouldn't, like, ask my opinion on anything.

RawMode: So, how about you, CryptHead? What's your
deal?

CryptHead: INFO Sec now, but a former IT drone and
cryppy.

No one wrote anything for a moment and I watched
my cursor blinking, wondering what I'd done to spook
them. Then I followed their train of thought: cryppy =
cryptanalyst = NSA = government = people not to be
trusted. I waited, but when no one typed anything, I
wrote:

CryptHead: What? You guys got something against
cryppies? I'm no poser and I don't work for Uncle Sam.

What that really meant was I was not a government
InfoSec guy pretending to get chummy with potential

hackers or troublemakers in cyberspace so I could bust them later. To my relief, I saw Grok answer.

Grok: So, how many distinct ciphers can you generate with no restrictions on shifting the alphabet?

Jeez, they were testing me.

CryptHead: 400,000,000,000,000,000,000,000,000

Grok: Impressive.

RawMode: Welcome, dude.

CryptHead: That's Dudette to you.

Grok: Ooooh, we are not worthy, geek princess. You know, I thought about crypto myself. Maybe still will someday. What brings you to our site?

CryptHead: I've got friends who frequent here. We got into a gabfest about the dangers of nanotech. They said I should read an article posted here by a dude named Darren Greening.

RawMode: Yeah, I remember that. Last month I think. He's some east coast techhead or something. Said molecular replicating assemblers and thinking machines pose a fundamental threat to humans.

RawMode: Machines of Destruction.

CryptHead: Whoa.

Grok: Yeah, fully sentient machines, but without constraints.

CryptHead: Created using nanotech?

RawMode: On target. Some dudes are crying that since the development of cognizant, self-replicating machines is inevitable, scientists need to fully understand the technology to ensure a benign application.

Heavy stuff, but not new. That had been the gist of what I'd understood from Darren's paper. Still it seemed odd to me that a man who founded a nanotech company and dedicated his life to furthering nanotechnology would have such a sudden change of heart.

CryptHead: You guys agree with that?

Grok: Course we agree. We're here on the site, aren't we?

Like, *duh*, Lexi. "Think before you type, knucklehead," I muttered to myself.

CryptHead: So, you know anything else interesting about this Greening dude? Does he frequent this chat room? Maybe I could ask him directly about this stuff.

RawMode: Couldn't say if he comes here. It's not like we use our real names anyway. For all you know, I could be Darren Greening.

That stopped me cold. I thought for a minute before I resumed typing.

CryptHead: So, are you?

RawMode: Nah. Hahahaha.

I rolled my eyes. Jeez, two geeks with a sense of humor. A dangerous combination. On any other day, I might have been amused, but not today.

CryptHead: So, how close do you think we are to creating these self-replicating thinking machines?

There was a long pause and I stared at the blinking cursor, wondering what they were thinking. Maybe I had asked a few too many pointed questions. Nonetheless, I waited patiently and finally saw a reply.

Grok: Some say we're already there, geek princess. Beta form, of course.

Now that shocked me. Even at a beta or testing stage, creating conscious beings using nanotechnology was astounding. I wondered whether this was a factor in Darren's decision to disappear. But what did sentient machines have to do with the nanotech energy production that Darren was working on?

Whatever the case, these guys had given me a lot to think about. I wasn't sure this was what I logged on hoping to find, but it was enough for now and I didn't want to put them off by being too pushy or curious.

CryptHead: Well, thanks, dudes. Gotta go. Hope to see you here again soon.

RawMode: Come back anytime, crypt princess.

I logged off and then leaned back in my chair. Jeez. Machines of Destruction. It sounded spooky…no, surreal. I took a sip of my Diet Coke. As mind-boggling as all this might be, I was getting paid to figure out how, if at all, any of this information applied to Darren Greening, and for that matter, to me. And frankly, right now, I was seeing diddly as far as a connection between the three of us.

I took an aspirin to ward off the headache that had started behind my right eye and washed it down with more Coke. It was perfect timing because shortly thereafter, a Detective Mastory came into my office and interviewed me about the neck-snapping man in the garage.

I spoke to him for about ten minutes, but he didn't have any more of a clue than I did about who had attacked me. I had done my civic duty and the D.C. police would do exactly nothing to track him down on my behalf.

I readjusted my office temperature, got some coffee and read through more of the info that Ken and Jay had sent my way about Darren, Michael and Flow Technologies. Nothing leaped out at me. In fact, nothing at all was coming together for me in terms of a big picture. And a good, big picture was what I really needed right now.

About eleven-thirty, Finn stopped by my office to ask whether I was ready to head out to the Lighthouse Cyber Café. I'd almost forgotten about it, but just the mention of the place made my stomach growl in anticipation of a thick, juicy double cheeseburger. I grabbed my coat, putting it on in the elevator as we headed to the underground garage where Finn's Jag was parked.

"Did you reach Niles?" I asked as the elevator dinged and we got off.

"I did. And we're all set for a visit tomorrow morning."

I looked over at him. "Tomorrow? Why not today?"

"They're supposedly in meetings all day."

"Like I need them peering over my shoulder the whole time. I guess that means we're not permitted to look at the space without their supervision."

"Apparently not." I saw the corner of his mouth tighten. "Will that put a cramp in your style?"

"Do I have a choice?"

"No."

"Well, there you have it."

It was clear he was annoyed and, for that matter, so was I. For a bunch of guys supposedly worried sick about their star employee, they weren't making things all that easy for us to find him.

We climbed into Finn's Jag and pulled out of the parking lot. Traffic wasn't too bad as we made our way into Georgetown.

I glanced at Finn. "Did you have a chance to read Darren's paper yet?"

"Yeah, but it was complex. I did pass it on to Ben though."

"Good thinking." Of the three of us, Ben was probably the most likely to understand the nuances of nanotechnology.

I directed Finn to the Lighthouse Cyber Café, but we drove around for another fifteen minutes until we were able to snag an empty parking space on M Street. Luckily Finn was an ace parallel parker and easily squeezed his car in between a pickup and a minivan.

"My parents live just a few streets over that way," I said to Finn, shoving my bare hands into my coat. I'd forgotten a hat and my ears were burning from the cold.

He pulled his collar up against the wind. "You told me that they live in Georgetown. Do you visit often?"

"*Often* is not the operative word."

"It isn't?"

I love my parents, but sometimes they drive me crazy. My mom, a former Miss Teen USA and Miss Colonial Blossom, hates the fact that I am not into clothes, big hair or lawyers who aspire to be politicians. She constantly ambushes me with blind dates with catastrophic results. Unfortunately, my lack of looks and a wealthy husband at age twenty-five is a perpetual horror to her. To my growing dismay, she has now made it her life's mission to find me a husband, which doesn't make my parents' house a particularly inviting place to visit these days. In fact, if it weren't for my parents' wonderful chef, Sasha, and his amazing food, they'd probably only see me once every couple of months.

Finn opened the door to the café. "Well, maybe I'll meet them someday."

My heart skipped a beat. I knew my mother would approve of Finn, especially since he's a lawyer and the heir to a billion-dollar fortune. But I wasn't about to tell her and subject Finn to a full-out assault by a mother highly skilled at urban matchmaking.

I stepped across the threshold and into the café. It was more like a pub that had been turned into a cozy student hangout with warm wood paneling and dim lights. Like any respectable pub, it smelled of smoke and beer. A bar of old polished mahogany stretched across the left side of the wall and the rest of the room was crammed with tables and booths. Pretty much everyone seemed to have a laptop or electronic device of some kind. Most people wore earphones while they worked to block out the music blaring over the speakers.

Since it was lunchtime, the café was packed with students sitting, talking and milling about. There were no tables immediately available, but I noticed a young couple leaving a booth in the back corner. Using well-practiced moves, I quickly swept across the room and snagged it right from under the noses of what looked like three rowdy frat boys. One of them made an obnoxious comment to me, but they acknowledged fair play by moving instead toward the bar.

I looked over my shoulder and saw Finn still standing by the door. He looked utterly out of place here in his expensive wool coat and fancy Italian shoes. He had probably never frequented a place like this nor had he likely ever had to snag a table in his life. I had a sinking feeling that I was in for Hurt City big time if I continued to have fantasies about this guy.

But now we had work to do. Standing on tiptoe, I waved him over and he smiled as he made his way through the crowd to me. We slid in on opposite sides of the booth and Finn shook his head as he shrugged out of his coat.

"Nice move. I thought those guys might actually fight you for it."

"Nope. One look at me and they knew I meant business."

"You're serious."

"Darn right. You don't grow up with two older brothers and not learn how to defend yourself."

He laughed. "You never cease to amaze me, Lexi."

"I sincerely hope you mean that in a good way."

"I do, lass."

I liked it when he called me *lass*. It seemed intimate and sexy—almost a pet name. Of course, it was probably just wishful thinking on my part. All the same, when he talked to me like that, I forgot all about our fundamental differences and my tummy went all warm and fuzzy.

"Hi, I'm Brandy." A young girl stepped up to our table and took out an order form and pen. "I'll be your waitress for the day. Do you need a menu?"

Brandy looked to be about nineteen, thin with blond hair tied back in a ponytail. She wore jeans, a white T-shirt and a green apron tied around her hips. Clearly a student working for extra cash. She openly eyed Finn in appreciation and when he smiled back at her, she blushed red to the roots of her hair. This *always* happened when we were out together, and I tried to swallow my annoyance.

"I highly recommend the double cheeseburger and fries," I said to Finn.

He nodded. "All right. That works for me."

"Make it two," I said to Brandy and then pulled Darren Greening's photo out of my bag. "Before you go, would you mind looking at this picture and telling me if you've seen this guy in here before?"

She narrowed her eyes at me. "What are you, a cop?"

"Nope."

"Then what?"

Finn reached across the table and touched her arm. "Brandy, we could really use your help. We think this boy might be in trouble and we're trying to find him. Would you be so kind just to let us know whether you've seen him here before and when?"

Finn's voice was low and seductive and it worked wonders on Brandy. Her eyes widened and I thought she might just melt all over him on the spot. Finn snuck a glance at me and I rolled my eyes. The corner of his lips twitched.

"You know, you look familiar," Brandy said to him, her eyebrows crinkling together. "Have we met before?"

Only in the pages of *Celebrity Focus* magazine, I thought, but wisely held my tongue.

"No, I'm sure I'd remember," he said.

She shrugged. "Well, I guess it can't hurt to look."

She took the photo, angling it toward the light. Then she shook her head. "Can't say for certain. We get a lot of his type in here. You can ask Rudy or Alan behind the bar, I guess. They might know, although Alan has been working here for only a couple of weeks. Of course, you can always check with the manager, Jody Hansen. She's got an office in the back." She jerked her thumb toward a small alcove, which also housed the restrooms.

"Thank you, Brandy," Finn said. "You've been so helpful." She beamed as she left, shaking her hips for his benefit.

"Do you want me to talk to the guys at the bar?" he asked.

"I know Rudy. I'll talk to him. You take Jody."

We left our coats at the table so our booth wouldn't get stolen and went our separate ways. I squeezed up to the bar and waved to get Rudy's attention. He stood barely five foot five, all muscle with bulging biceps, a thick chest and no neck. His eyes registered surprise as he saw me, but he smiled.

"Take over for a moment, Alan," he called over the music to the other guy behind the bar who nodded.

"Well, if it ain't Lexi Carmichael." He came around the bar to greet me. His voice was deep and throaty, the result of decades of smoking.

He pumped my hand. "How are you, girl? It's been some time since you've come in here. Now you're all grown up."

"That's nothing new. I've always been taller than you."

He laughed good-naturedly. "You still at the NSA?"

"Hey, where'd you hear I worked at the NSA?" I said with mock indignity. "That's classified."

"Ain't nothing classified in a bar."

I grinned. "Well, if you must know, I'm working for a new, private computer security firm in Crystal City."

He whistled. "Moving up to the big time, now are you?"

"Some might see it that way."

"So, what brings you here?"

"Hopefully, some info," I replied, raising my voice to be heard over the music. I handed him a photo of Darren. "You ever see this guy in here before?"

Rudy squinted at the picture and then turned back to me. "Didn't make you out as Darren's type."

"So, you *do* know Darren."

"Sure. He and his friend Michael used to haunt this place until they graduated a few years back. Came in often enough that we were on a first-name basis. They've visited a couple of times since, but I heard they started some big-wig tech corporation, and I haven't seen either of them for some time."

"Oh. You ever see them in here with anyone else?"

"Like who?"

"I don't know, a girlfriend or some other guys?"

Rudy rubbed his hand over his forehead. "Not once. And since you asked, I think those boys only had eyes for each other...if you get my drift."

"What drift?"

Rudy sighed. "They *liked* each other, kid."

"And your point would be?"

"For God's sake, Lexi, I think they were gay."

I looked at him in surprise. "Gay?"

Rudy shrugged. "Don't know for sure. Just a bartender's hunch, that's all. You'd probably know better. You understand his geeky type better than I do. In most ways, you *are* his type, Lexi."

"Am I supposed to take that as a compliment?"

Rudy snorted. "You kids nowadays can't see beyond your computer monitors and texting all the time. Not that I'm complaining, mind you. Turning this place into a wireless café was the best idea I ever had. Still, imagine my surprise when a smart girl like you is sitting over there with a pretty boy toy like that."

"Rudy, jeez, when have I *ever* had a boy toy?"

Rudy laughed. "Knew you had it in you. You're just a late bloomer."

"Yeah, really, *really* late."

"So, is he your toy?"

I put my hands on my hips. "First, Finn is not a toy. Second, why are you so interested in my love life all of a sudden? Jealous?"

"Maybe," he said, but I knew he was yanking my chain.

"You're such a lousy liar. You've got it way too good with Jackie. You two still together?"

"Eighteen years. So, that guy ain't your boyfriend?"

"Well, not yet. Right now, he's kind of my boss."

"Your boss? Haven't you heard of sexual harassment?"

I held up a hand. "Trust me there is no harassment. And there is definitely no sex…yet. But there is still hope."

He eyed me for a moment. "So, that's how it is. You be careful with a guy like that, especially if he's writing your paycheck."

I sighed. "I know, I know. I can't tell you how many times I've already heard about the horrors of dating someone you work with. Knowing my luck, it's highly unlikely to work out anyway. But I'm not here to talk about my love life or current lack thereof. Let's get back to Darren. Do you have any idea where on the net he liked to surf when he was in here?"

Rudy grunted. "Lexi, you know how many customers I get in here in one day? The places they go, the places they've been? You think I remember? Besides, I'm no net cop. People go where they want as long as they're of legal age and it ain't porn. Got blocks on that. Otherwise, I don't care."

I let out a breath. "I know that. Look, Rudy, I don't know if you've heard, but Michael Hart is dead and I think Darren might be mixed up in some pretty bad trouble. He's asked for my help, but now I can't find him. If you can remember anything about Darren, it could really help me out."

To Rudy's credit, he looked shocked. "Michael is dead? How did the kid die?"

"Car accident. I think."

Rudy raised one of his famously bushy eyebrows. "You *think?*"

"It's a long story. Just help me out here. Please."

He sighed. "You swear you aren't with the police."

"I swear. Cross my heart."

"Or the government?"

"Not anymore."

He looked over his shoulder to make sure no one was listening to our conversation, which was ridiculous because I didn't see how anyone could overhear us with all the noise in the bar. I saw Finn return from the back area and sit down at the booth. He caught my eye and I nodded slightly to indicate I'd seen him.

"Okay, so maybe I know what Darren liked to do. He played a lot of GURPS," Rudy said. "GURPS Robots in particular. He was a king or something. Not that I understand what that means, but he liked to brag about it."

If I remembered correctly, the GURPS Robots game let you play at being a robot—from nanobots to megabots. You could become a cyborg, android and even a biomorph. It wasn't exactly up my alley, but, I wasn't judgemental. I filed that information away to check out later.

"Thanks, Rudy." I dug out one of my brand-new business cards from my purse. "You think of anything else about Darren or if you happen to see him, will you give me a call?"

"Sure, Lexi. I hope you find Darren. He's a good kid. And mind my advice on the pretty boy."

"Sure."

When I returned to the booth, Finn was squeezing mustard over his French fries. I looked at him in disbelief.

"Jeez, that's sickening. Mustard? Is that a European thing?"

He laughed. "No, I just don't care for catsup." He eyed the cheeseburger. "Now, how am I supposed to eat this heart attack on a plate?"

"Let me show you how Americans do it." I shook the catsup bottle and poured a generous amount across my fries and burger. I smashed the bun down on top of the burger and managed to get my hands around it.

"Like this." I took a bite.

"Jesus, Joseph and Mary," Finn said, eyeing me with something akin to wonder. I saw him glance at his fork and knife in indecision before leaning over and picking the burger up with his hands. He took a small bite and chewed thoughtfully.

"Well?" I asked.

He grinned and I saw a smudge of mustard on his mouth. He looked so darn adorable, I couldn't believe he was sitting here with me.

"It's the best bloody burger I've ever had," he said. "What do they cook it in?"

"Grease. Hope you made out a will."

He rolled his eyes and took another bite. "So, did you find out anything useful from the bartender?"

"You first," I insisted, taking another bite.

He set down the burger and wiped his mouth and hands on a napkin. "I didn't get anything from the manager. She says she doesn't remember the kid and doesn't give a fiver about the customers so long as they pay and don't cause trouble. She wouldn't give up any more information on a customer without a subpoena. She's a bit of a sleeven."

"A what?"

"Sleeven. What you Americans might call a tough cookie."

"She must be if you couldn't charm her."

"So, what did you get from the bartender?"

I dabbed at the corner of my mouth with a napkin. "Rudy thinks Darren and Michael might have been more than just friends."

"Pardon?"

"Rudy thinks they were gay. But I'm not convinced. I mean, why didn't they have an apartment together? They were, after all, two consenting adults."

Finn still looked startled by my revelation. "Did you say gay? As in homosexual?"

"Of course. What did you think I meant—happy?"

"No need to be caustic. It's just when I'm with you, I want to be certain."

"Oh. I guess that's fair. Anyway, I don't see how it would matter if Darren and Michael were gay. Darren certainly didn't have to worry about disapproval from his family since he didn't have any, but I suppose Michael might have."

"And don't forget that Darren considered Gene Hart as something like a surrogate father," Finn added.

"Not to mention, he held the purse strings, at least at first, for Flow Technologies." I dipped a fry into some catsup and took a bite. "Anyway, I can't confirm whether it's true or not, and at this point, I can't even say if it's relevant. Still, it's something to add to the mix. I also found out that Darren likes to play GURPS."

"Lexi, would you mind speaking English, please?"

"Speaking in acronyms is a bad habit of mine. Sorry. GURPS are Generic Universal Role Playing Systems. They're online games—virtual worlds. Cool stuff. I'm a recovering addict. But given current circumstances, I might just have to become active again to check this out."

We finished up our lunch and Finn insisted on paying, claiming company business. We drove back to the office in Crystal City mostly in silence, both of us thinking about what we'd learned. As Finn parked the Jag, he said, "I'll round up Ben and let's meet in the conference room in fifteen minutes. We'll lay out what we know so far."

"Okay. Maybe he has some new insight on Darren's paper."

Fifteen minutes later, we all sat around the conference table with our notes spread out. Finn filled Ben in on what we'd discovered at the café and I spelled out everything Finn and I'd learned up to that point.

Ben told us he'd discovered that Darren hadn't used his credit cards or made any cash withdrawals in the past ten days, well before he disappeared. However, two weeks before he vanished, he had withdrawn fifteen thousand dollars in cash.

"So maybe this was a planned disappearance," I said, leaning back in my chair. After the burger, I felt like unbuttoning my slacks but it would have to wait until I wasn't in mixed company.

"Perhaps," Ben commented. "But we've got no other paper trail and his car is missing."

That surprised me. "His car is missing?"

"Yes, and I don't like the fact that his apartment was searched. For what purpose?"

"Clues to his whereabouts?" Finn suggested.

Ben shrugged. "But by whom?"

Finn frowned. "Niles Foreman?"

I shook my head. "Why? I can't believe that Niles and

his buddies would trash the place. Search it, perhaps, but why the mess? It implies desperation."

"And urgency," Ben added.

"Besides why not tell us they'd been through the place?" I was pretty much just thinking aloud. "Or offer us the key, for that matter?"

Finn ran his fingers through his hair. "You're right. It doesn't make sense."

Ben looked at me pointedly. "What about your connection?"

I shook my head. "*Nada.* Not even an educated guess. I have no idea why I'm even a player in all this. Did you get anything useful from your nanotech connections?"

"Not yet," Ben replied. "I've got several calls in and am waiting to hear back."

"Anything about Darren's paper raise any flags?" Maybe we'd gotten lucky.

"It's hard to say without really understanding exactly what he was working on," Ben said. "But if we look at the big picture, I suppose some could consider Darren's technology threatening on a larger scale."

"Threatening? How so?" Finn asked.

"Well, let's put the facts on the table," Ben replied. "Darren was working on energy replacement using nanotechnology. Let's speculate that perhaps he has actually come up with a way to make oil obsolete."

I whistled under my breath. "That would be huge. No, that would be *beyond* huge."

"It would be a colossal step in the field of nanotechnology," Ben agreed. "But that's not all. Creating a new energy replacement would be revolutionary enough, but that is not all that is at stake here. *If* Darren has indeed accomplished the impossible, our entire world will change."

"In what way?" I asked.

Ben leaned forward, his elbows splayed on the table. "Because theoretically, it would then be only a matter of time before atoms will be able to be manipulated to make anything we wanted."

"Anything?" Finn didn't look like he believed it.

"Anything," Ben replied. "Let's consider the consequences. If humans become able to replicate whatever we need or desire, including food, energy and material goods, what happens to our way of life? How does culture and society progress? What would happen to the global market if everyone can have anything they want for nothing?"

His words were so astounding that Finn and I just stared at him with open mouths.

Ben stood up, seemingly oblivious to the bomb he had just dropped on us. "This is all speculation, of course. We need to get more detailed information on exactly what Darren was doing at Flow. Then perhaps we can better understand what's going on."

"I'm going to check out his work space tomorrow," I managed to say, my mind still reeling.

"Good. And hopefully I'll have heard back from my sources."

Without another word, he exited the room. Finn and I watched him. Then Finn rose and shook his head.

"Why couldn't we have got a simple case for our first assignment?"

I felt a stab of guilt even though the reasonable part of my brain reminded me I shouldn't blame myself. "I'm sorry," I blurted out anyway.

He looked at me, and his expression softened. "I'm not blaming you. I feel fortunate to have you on the team. Besides, don't you believe that everything happens for a reason?"

I did, but that belief was more based in science than mysticism. "Yeah, I do. Thanks for the support."

He gathered his notes. "Ben's given us a lot to think about."

I nodded. "I'll take another look at the archives on the STRUT site and continue to work my way through the emails Ken and Jay sent me."

He nodded and put his papers under his arm, heading for the door. He paused at the exit. "By the way, I'll pick you up at seven."

Jeez, with all the excitement, I'd forgotten about the date. I felt my nerves jangle, but I managed a smile. "Sure. See you then."

He leaned against the door. "I'm really looking forward to getting to know you better outside work and in a situation where we aren't in immediate danger of losing our lives."

"That sounds great."

He left and I sat back in the chair, closing my eyes. OMG. A *real* date with Finn. He wanted to get to know me, the genuine, geeky, awkward me. I only hoped my social inadequacies wouldn't interfere with what I hoped would be a truly memorable night.

Chapter Six

After work I went straight home, took a shower and washed my hair. I slathered myself with lotion, wrapped my wet hair in a towel and slid into my bathrobe. Taking a deep breath for courage, I reached under the sink for my rarely used makeup box. Applying makeup was a skill I'd never mastered, much to the never-ending dismay of my beauty-queen mother. I'd once seen a makeup artist on a morning news program say the most important areas of the face to address were the eyes and the lips. So, I swiped on some mascara and added lip gloss and hoped for the best.

I quickly blow-dried my straight hair, combing the flyaway strands down. It hadn't been cut in some time and I realized it reached nearly down to the middle of my back. Leaving it loose, I squeezed into my red gown. Once in I seriously considered scotch-taping my nipples to the material but I'm chicken when it comes to physical pain, so I let things lie where they were and hoped for the best.

Going into the bedroom, I donned a pair of dangling red earrings and a ruby ring my dad had given me on my sixteenth birthday. I preened for a while in front of the body-length mirror, thinking I didn't look half-bad. A curvy hourglass figure would have been perfect for this dress, but we are who we are. Nonetheless, I felt a bit drafty with all the cleavage showing, so I found a shawl my grandma had given me eons ago and wrapped it around me. I was afraid to eat or drink anything in case I popped out of the gown, so I stood motionless in my living room, leaning against the wall until I heard Finn buzz from downstairs at ten minutes after seven.

I let him in and he arrived at my door a minute later looking stunning in a three-piece navy suit with white shirt and blue-and-gold tie. He smelled heavenly, too, wearing some kind of sexy, musky, masculine cologne.

He looked at me inquisitively and I knew he was curious as to why I was clutching the shawl around my neck. But I was too chicken to reveal my outfit yet, so I just smiled brightly.

"Sorry I'm late. I had to wait for the driver."

"Driver?"

"It's a surprise." Just then his cell phone rang. He fished it out of his jacket pocket and previewed the number. "Do you mind if I take this? I'll be just a moment."

"Of course not. Go ahead."

He gave me a grateful smile and then stepped into my kitchen and began talking. I retrieved my coat and slid it on over my shawl, feeling awkward and shy. I wished I had bought the black sheath gown because now I'd be feeling a lot more safe and comfortable. On the other hand, I did want to capture Finn's attention and keep it, just like Basia had suggested. I needed to remember that tonight was the start of a more sexy me. I just had to concentrate on exuding my inner glow and femininity. I could do this.

I inhaled a deep breath, which wasn't easy in my gown, just as Finn hung up and opened the front door.

"All ready?"

"Ready steady." I winced inwardly. Time to upgrade my conversational skills, too.

I set the alarm and we headed downstairs. When we got to the parking lot, I saw a black stretch limo.

"You hired a limo?" Like it would have been a real burden to take his Jag.

"It wasn't my idea. The gallery owners insisted. I hope you don't mind."

As if I'd mind riding in a limo. If the truth be known, I'd never ridden in a limo before, but I didn't want Finn to think I'm utterly unworldly, so I didn't mention it. The limo driver, dressed in a natty black suit complete with a hat, stood by the car and held open the door for us.

"Good evening, madame."

What did I say? Good evening, *monsieur?* I just stood there staring at him like an idiot.

"After you," Finn said, putting his hand in the small of my back and giving me a gentle push.

Easier said than done. I very, *very* carefully climbed in and half sat, half lay on the seat. The last thing I needed to do was asphyxiate myself before the date even started. Finn climbed in and sat beside me on the plush leather seat. Trying not to look like a kid in a candy store, I glanced around at our luxury surroundings. There was a bar, a television, a telephone, a stereo and a small refrigerator. A chilled bottle of champagne and two glasses sat on top of a crystal platter on the bar.

"This is nicer than my apartment," I muttered in spite of my intention to appear sophisticated.

Finn smiled as he poured me a glass of champagne. "I'm glad you like it."

He handed me the champagne and settled back against

the seat. I took a sip and then cradled the glass, thinking maybe I should pinch myself. Could it be possible that I really was sitting here with the most gorgeous guy on the planet in a black stretch limo, sipping champagne?

"Where is the gallery located?" We were headed into D.C.

"Not too far from the Hilton Hotel in northwest D.C."

The Hilton is now best known as the site of John Hinckley's botched assassination attempt on former President Ronald Reagan. I figured it would take us about thirty minutes to get there. That meant thirty minutes of lounging in serious luxury while drinking what I was sure was expensive champagne. It also meant social conversation, at which I happen to be lousy.

I tried to hide my nervousness by chatting with Finn about as many non-consequential issues as I could think of. As we talked, I gratefully noticed that he steered clear of topics like code and nanotechnology. I sensed that tonight he wanted to separate work from play, which was just fine with me.

After a while, my nervousness dissipated and he poured me another glass of champagne. I was feeling rather giddy and I wasn't sure whether it was from the champagne, the lack of air to my lungs because of my skin-tight gown or the fact that for once in my life, I was sort of holding my own in small-talk conversation.

Eventually we lapsed into silence and Finn pulled something out of his pocket and began fiddling with it.

"A Rubik's Cube?" I asked in surprise.

He nodded sheepishly. "I do it sometimes to relax."

"Relax? You're not nervous." I paused, suddenly uncertain. "Are you?"

"A little."

Maybe he was giving a speech at the party tonight or receiving an award. That kind of stuff would definitely make me anxious. His nervousness wouldn't have anything to do with me. He'd dated tons of beautiful women a lot more sophisticated and worldly. Comparatively speaking, I was a plain Twinkie compared to the usual double-fudge cupcakes he usually accompanied.

But what if he was worried what people might think of me? I imagined them whispering behind their wineglasses, shaking their heads and clucking their tongues, wondering what a gorgeous guy like Finn was doing with an ugly duckling.

Why in the world had I thought I could pull this off?

Resisting the urge to chew my fingernails, I tried to calm myself while watching Finn turn some of the faces on the Rubik's Cube. He was doing it all wrong.

"I've been stuck in this one place," he said. He moved some more of the panels, making it worse. "I can't seem to get out of it."

"Need some help?" I offered.

"Sure."

I took the cube and quickly fixed it so that he had about six moves to finish it.

He stared at me for a moment and then back at the cube. "That's amazing." He flipped the last panels into place. "You do that all from memory, don't you?"

"Maybe," I said. "I just see it somehow."

He smiled at me and I swear I saw desire in his eyes. Holy cow, had I somehow just turned him on by doing the Rubik's Cube?

"What do you mean that you can see it?" He slid closer to me.

His thigh pressed against mine and I could feel his warm breath on my cheek. Yep, I'm sure sparks ignited.

"It's just visualization. Like in chess. I can usually see at least three or four moves ahead."

"Fascinating." He nuzzled my ear. "Did I happen to mention I love a woman with a quick mind?"

His voice sounded husky, sensual and very Irish. Every nerve in my body stood at full attention. At the same time, I made a mental note to buy a half dozen Rubik's Cubes and place them strategically around my office and apartment. Maybe I'd stuff one down my bra for good measure.

"Ah…it's nothing, really," I said. "I can show you how to do it, if you'd like."

He moved his lips to my neck and kissed me there. "I'd like that," he murmured, his mouth hot against my skin.

My body was on fire. Finn's lips were taking their time moving up to my chin and I knew he'd be seriously kissing me any moment. What if I disappointed him? What if having a quick mind couldn't make up for a horrible lack of kissing experience? I also wasn't sure where I should put my hands. Should I put them around his neck or his shoulders or would either of those be too forward? I didn't want him to think I was too easy. But then again, I had no idea how to play hard-to-get.

What I needed was the proper protocol here. Why hadn't I researched methods of kissing before? Then I could memorize all the steps and apply them as the situation arose. Jeez, how did people figure this stuff out without Google? I sincerely hoped the answer wasn't instinct because it was painfully clear I had none.

I was saved from any decision where to put my hands because the limo abruptly pulled to a stop in front of a curb. To my enormous disappointment, Finn stopped nuzzling my neck and looked out the window.

"Sorry," he breathed. "We're here, lass." He reached across me and opened the door.

I tried to calm my breathing and act casual, like good-looking guys kissed my neck every day. I wriggled to the door, trying to figure how to get out without ripping or falling out of my spandex-squeezing gown. Thankfully, the driver gallantly stepped up and stretched out a hand.

"Careful now, madame," he warned.

Like, *duh*. What did he think I was doing?

When he saw me just sitting there trying to mathematically calculate the safest move, he grabbed my hand and pulled hard. I guess he had some experience at rescuing spandex-clad women from limos because, to my great relief, I exited the limo with dress intact and Finn following close behind. He took aside the driver and slipped him something.

Finn had just rejoined me on the curb when a stocky man with blond-streaked hair tied back into a ponytail came out to meet us at the curb. A cigarette dangled between his lips and he was dressed in a black suit with a white turtleneck and tennis shoes.

"Well, Finn, ye ole dog." He smacked Finn hard on the back. "Bloody good to see ye, mate. How's the form?"

"Just grand, Colin. And you?"

"Brilliant," he said and then his gaze settled on me. He gave me a long and thorough perusal and then grinned. "Who's the lass?"

"Let me introduce you to Lexi Carmichael," Finn said, his hand still resting in the small of my back. He pushed me a little bit forward. "Lexi, this is Colin Kelley, owner of the Shamrock Gallery."

I noticed that Finn's voice had immediately changed to a full-blown Irish lilt upon our arrival and it made me smile. "It's nice to meet you," I said to Colin.

To my surprise, Colin snatched my hand and pressed it to his lips for what I thought was an inordinate amount of time. "So, an American lass," he murmured against my skin. "That's a surprise."

I wasn't so sure what was surprising about that, but before I could say anything, Finn spoke up.

"Colin and I go way back." He extracted my hand from Colin's lips. "We've been friends since primary school."

Colin glanced with amusement at Finn. "Has it been that long?" He eyed me while taking a long drag of his cigarette and blowing it out the side of his mouth. "Finn was the favorite o' the nuns, ye know, whereas I was the black sheep. But if the truth be known, Finn was always the instigator o' trouble."

Finn laughed. "Don't pay him any mind, Lexi. Colin is the master of exaggeration…among many other things."

Colin stared at me for a moment longer and I got the distinct impression that he was trying to figure out what a guy like Finn was doing with a girl like me. I didn't blame him; I wondered the same thing myself. All the same, I shifted uncomfortably on my feet until Colin abruptly took my arm.

"Now why are we standing out here jabbing in the draft?" He pulled me along with him. "Come in, ye two, and take the weight off yer feet."

Colin led us into the gallery and a blast of warm air. I took one look around and my mouth fell open. The building looked rather ordinary from the outside, but on the inside, the two-storied building had been architecturally redesigned to form one great room with vaulted ceilings, glass beams and a striking green marble stair-case. A gorgeous crystal chandelier hung from the center of the room nearly touching the outstretched hand of an enormous, stunning white marble statue of a nude maiden sitting by a fountain. The fountain was real and sprayed water lit by a background rainbow of colors. But the sight that shocked me the most was the sea of black and white that filled the gallery. My heart dropped to my feet and stayed there.

"Are those priests and nuns?" I asked Finn, my voice sounding strained and squeaky.

Finn glanced at me. "Oh, did I forget to mention that proceeds from tonight's gala are to be donated to Our Lady Queen of Ireland Parish?"

Boy, did he ever.

"Um… I guess it must have slipped your mind." A nun passed by me and smiled.

Finn shrugged. "Here, Lexi, let me take your coat."

I stood frozen to the spot. I was dressed to kill in a sinfully low-cut gown and he wanted me to take my coat off in front of an army of God's servants? I started to hyperventilate. I was going to kill Basia. I *knew* I should have chosen the black gown on the half-price rack.

"I… I…just…"

Finn slipped out of his coat as a young woman with spiked black hair, a nose ring and a stud in her lip arrived and quickly took it from his hands. I didn't miss the look of pure appreciation she gave Finn or the look of disdain she gave me.

Finn tugged impatiently at my coat and I realized I couldn't wear it all evening. Thank goodness, I still had my shawl. Finn helped me slip off my coat, while I made certain that one hand clutched the shawl tight around my chest. Finn looked at me a bit strangely but I pretended not to notice. I heard the studded girl give a snort at my death clutch, but she took off with our coats anyway.

"Would you like me to carry your shawl?" Finn asked gallantly.

"Actually, I'm a bit cold," I said even though the room was well heated.

Colin introduced us to an elderly couple and went off to speak to someone. Finn captured a couple of flutes of champagne. Somehow, I managed to hold my drink, keep a death clutch on the shawl and smile until my cheeks hurt. We mingled for a while until Finn excused himself to speak to someone and I was left alone. As I stood there at a loss, a jolly-looking priest with a shock of black hair, red cheeks and the hint of a belly beneath his priest's attire approached me.

"Ye're looking a bit lonely," he said. "I'm Father Mulrooney, one of the priests at Our Lady Parish." I judged him to be a bit over fifty, with a warm smile and eyes crinkled with laugh lines. "I'm mighty pleased to make your acquaintance." He stuck out a pudgy hand. Since I was holding the glass in one hand and the shawl in the other, I couldn't shake his hand. So, I just smiled brightly until he dropped his hand.

"I'm Lexi Carmichael. Finn's uh…colleague. We work together at X-Corp."

Father Mulrooney nodded. "O' course, ye do. I noticed ye the minute ye arrived. Ye know that Finn's our guest o' honor tonight. He's a dear one to us, that lad. He's been very generous with his time and money to support the parish."

"That's wonderful."

"Personally, I love the lad as if he was me own son."

"Well, he's very lucky then."

"So, how long have ye known our Finn?"

I thought back. "A few months or so." I didn't see how useful it would be to tell him that we had met under life-threatening circumstances involving handcuffs, terrorists and guns.

"And ye say ye work with him. That's in the office, right?"

Jeez, where else would I work with him? "Yes. In the office."

The priest put an arm casually about my shoulders. "Ye know, lass, none o' us would ever want to see Finn hurt in any way at all. Do ye know what I mean?"

Whoa, was it getting hot in here or was it just me? I really, *really* wanted to take my shawl off, but I didn't dare. On the other hand, I suppose seeing my cleavage might distract the father from a line of questioning that was starting to feel increasingly like the Spanish Inquisition. However, a part of me had this horrible feeling that Father Mulrooney could already see right through my shawl to the exposed flesh beneath. Undoubtedly, he had made me out to be loose, a tart or perhaps even Jezebel herself, planning on leading Finn down the slippery slope of perdition.

"So, what is it *exactly* ye do at Finn's company?" the priest continued.

I ignored the thin sheen of wetness now forming on my upper lip. "I'm the Director of Information Security." When I got a blank look, I added, "Computer stuff."

To my relief, his eyes lit up. "Computers? I love computers. God, computers and crossword puzzles—those are my passions. I also like gin rummy. Do ye play?"

"Don't even think about it," I heard Finn say, coming up behind me and putting a hand lightly around my waist. "She is unbeatable at rummy. Utterly unstoppable. I've never seen anything like it."

Finn was referring to the time I beat him forty-six games in a row, letting him win the forty-seventh so that he could salvage what was left of his pride. I smiled modestly.

"It's nothing, really. By and large, the game of rummy is a mathematical equation. Elimination, deduction and a little luck are really all it takes to win consistently."

"Och, be still my beating heart," Father Mulrooney said, clapping his hands together in delight. "You've found a gem, my lad. Can I borrow the lass from ye sometime?"

When Finn narrowed his eyes, the priest smiled. "There's an extra round at the rosary said for yer soul, plus a votive candle lit every Sunday. 'Tis a generous offer, if I do say so myself."

Finn frowned. "Sounds more like a bribe."

Father Mulrooney beamed. "Watch now how ye consider the motives o' a man o' the cloth."

"Well, if the shoe fits…"

The priest chuckled. "Be a good lad, would ye, and go fetch a wee dram for an old man. I think I might be failing a bit."

"He just wants to be alone with you," Finn whispered in an overly loud voice to me.

"Don't worry. I can hold my own."

Finn wagged a finger at the priest. "Go easy on her. I'll be right back."

As soon as Finn left, the priest whipped a pen and a crumpled piece of paper out of his pants. He smoothed out the paper on a nearby table and looked up at me hopefully.

"Would ye mind helping me a bit on this puzzle, lass? I would be mighty appreciative."

I looked over his shoulder to the paper. "You carry a crossword puzzle around with you?"

"Aye. What better way to keep the mind sharp? Will ye help me?"

I guess I had gone from Jezebel to schoolmarm. "Sure. What do you need?"

"A five-letter word for licorice flavoring."

I thought for a moment. "Anise."

Father Mulrooney jotted down the word. "Dead on!"

"Now how about a five-letter word for pottery from Japan?"

"Imari."

He looked at me in surprise. "Aye, it fits. How do ye do it so quickly, lass?"

"I'll let you in on a little secret. It just so happens crossword puzzles are one of my passions, too. I did the puzzle this morning."

The priest chuckled. "Why ye truly are the full shilling. At last Finn has found himself a true cracker. How unexpected and wonderful."

Before I could figure out what the *heck* he'd just said to me, Finn returned, carrying a drink for the priest.

"Thanks, lad," the priest said, taking the drink from Finn. "I'm away now. But I'll be seeing *ye* later." He winked at me and then hurried off into the crowd.

"What was that all about?" I asked.

Finn watched the priest as he crossed the room. "You didn't just help him with a crossword puzzle, did you?"

"Why? Is that a cardinal sin?"

"Sort of. He has a daily bet with Sister Aileen on who can finish the *Washington Post* puzzle first. I think you just won him twenty-five dollars. It also means you'll be his friend for life."

"Wow." A priest who drank, bet and obviously had a great fondness for his parishioners. How come I'd never had a priest like that when I was growing up? "He called me crackers. Should I be offended?"

Finn laughed. "It just means he likes you. You've made quite an impression on the father."

I wasn't so sure, but I could hardly argue when half the time I had no clue what these people were saying to me. Social conversation was hard enough for me, and tonight, I had to do it in a foreign language. It was just my luck.

Eventually dinner was announced and Finn and I were seated at the head table with gallery owner, Colin Kelley, and some other distinguished-looking people. Somehow, I was not surprised to see Father Mulrooney finagle a seat next to me. He leaned over close and immediately started telling jokes. I couldn't help but be completely charmed.

It wasn't easy eating and keeping my shawl tight around my neck, but I managed. I know Finn, among others, thought I was acting strange, but there was nothing else I could do.

Salad and soup were served first and Colin got up to introduce one of the featured artists for the night. The man talked on about Irish art, culture, and history, interspersing lots of accolades for Finn's support—which I learned was a generous twenty-five thousand-dollar donation.

I was a bit dismayed when dinner was served and I

saw a steak, baked potato and vegetables on the plate. I wasn't sure how I'd be able to keep my shawl tight around my shoulders and cut my meat, so I'd have to be inventive.

While one of the speakers droned on, Father Mulrooney tapped my elbow and then surreptitiously pulled out a bottle of steak sauce from beneath the table. As my eyes widened, he put a finger to his lips.

"I can't eat a steak without it," he whispered.

Everyone else's attention at the table was on the speaker, so no one noticed the priest pouring it over his steak. With a grin, he handed it to me.

"Go on, lass."

Since I didn't want to appear rude, I took it. Without thinking, I did what I always did to a bottle—I shook it vigorously, not realizing the lid wasn't on tight. To my horror, it flew off the bottle with the force of a speeding bullet and hit the father just above his forehead. I gasped in shock as his hairpiece flew off and landed directly in the soup of the woman sitting next to him.

I'd also spilled steak sauce down the front of my shawl. Before I could move, a nun who must have witnessed the entire horrid chain of events, quickly came up behind me and whipped the soiled shawl off my shoulders.

"Dinna worry," she said as I felt a huge draft and realized I had just been revealed in all my glory. "I'll have it back to ye in a few minutes. Ye go ahead and eat, dear."

The room fell silent and even the speaker on the podium looked over at us and lost his place. As if in slow motion, I turned my head to look at Finn who was now staring at my near-naked bosom, his eyes wide and his mouth hanging open in stunned amazement. My face flushed hot and I tried to think of something, *anything,* to say to get every eye in the room off me.

"I'm...ah, really, *really* sorry about your hairpiece," I whispered to Father Mulrooney, wishing the floor would open up and swallow me whole. This was the most embarrassing moment of my life and I wanted nothing more than to vanish in a puff of smoke. But I was frozen to the chair.

The priest was utterly speechless, but he managed to tear his gaze from my bosom to the location where his hairpiece had landed.

"Ach...ah...'tis o' no consequence, lass." He retrieved his soggy hairpiece from the soup dish and shook it out. "In fact, there isn't a soul in the room who doesn't know o' my vanity. I've been meaning to get rid o' it for some time. Perhaps this is a sign from God that now is the time."

I didn't think my mortification could go any deeper, but it did. "Oh no. I think it looks great on you. I mean, I didn't even know it was fake."

I winced as the words fell from my lips. Could I have said anything more stupid? Why hadn't I just kept my mouth shut? I closed my eyes. My face burned so hot, it was like I'd been sunburned in the Caribbean.

Thankfully, about this time, the speaker at the podium cleared his throat and began speaking again. I didn't dare take another glance at Finn. No way was I brave enough to withstand the horror in his eyes now that the shock had worn off. Instead I slid down in the chair as low as I could and pushed around the food on my plate, managing some small talk with Father Mulrooney. He seemed to have recovered far more quickly than I and had resumed telling jokes. Still, the evening crawled by so slowly I thought it would drag on into infinity and beyond.

Finally, dinner ended and the nun returned my clean shawl. I felt relieved to be covered again, but the damage had been done.

When I stood up from the table, I glanced at Finn, but his face was completely neutral. My heart sank and I had a knot the size of Texas in my throat.

Finn took me by the elbow and whispered in my ear. "Would you like to go?"

Oh, boy, would I ever. "If that would be all right with you."

"It is."

Finn began his good-byes, and Father Mulrooney, now sporting a shiny, bald head, came over and enveloped me in an embarrassingly big bear hug.

"Finn has my number if ye want to visit the church sometime."

I'm not sure if he said that to be nice or, since he'd seen for certain the way I was dressed, wanted to save me from boiling in the deepest pits of hell.

"Thanks. And I am really, *really* sorry about your hairpiece."

He laughed. "'Twill be the talk o' the parish for a good week or so and then Mrs. O'Shea will have a new bout o' indigestion and that will be that. Don't ye worry about it, lass."

Amid a chorus of cheerful farewells, we headed out to the limo where I feared the most dreaded part of the night was waiting. I'd be alone with Finn for at least thirty minutes and would certainly face either a stony or awkward silence. As we climbed in, I could feel my body trembling.

After the driver pulled away, Finn spoke first. "So, did you enjoy yourself tonight, Lexi?"

As weird as it seemed, up until the hairpiece disaster, I really *had* enjoyed myself.

"It was great. The people were the best—so interesting and friendly. I'm just sorry that I ruined it for you."

"Ruined it? What are you talking about?"

Was he going to force me to relive it? "Well, I shot Father Mulrooney's toupee into a bowl of soup and I dressed like a…a ho. I didn't mean to embarrass you in front of your friends."

Finn looked at me with a puzzled expression. "You dressed like a *what?*"

I sighed. "A lady of the evening. I understand completely if you never want to see me again. I just want to say in my own defense that I didn't know there were going to be people of the cloth here tonight or I never would have worn anything so risqué."

He frowned. "You looked gorgeous tonight. Extremely sexy. In fact, it's probably a good thing you wore that shawl around you all night or we would have stayed at the party for all of five minutes."

My mouth dropped open. "I looked…sexy?"

"Dead on. For the love of God, Lexi, didn't you see how several of the other ladies were dressed? Many of them had outfits far more revealing than yours."

I guess I had been so obsessed with my own insecurities, I hadn't even taken a good look around the room. "There were people dressed worse than me?"

"*You* looked amazing."

I still couldn't believe my own ears. "Amazing? So, you don't think I look like a hooker?"

He laughed. "No, of course not."

Basia was right. I did need to bring out my inner femininity more. The good news—Finn liked the outfit. Basia *did* know what she was talking about.

"But what about Father Mulrooney's hairpiece?"

"What about it? Lexi, he was playing you. That hairpiece isn't held on with more than a clip. Do you know how many times it has fallen off? It makes for good fodder in the church and the father loves being the center of attention. Frankly, in my opinion you've made a new friend for life."

I sank back into the plush seat, feeling hopefully optimistic. Maybe the night hadn't turned out as badly as I had thought.

"Thanks for making me feel better."

"No, I thank *you* for being such a breath of fresh air in my life."

He leaned toward me, his mouth inching closer to mine. Just before his lips touched mine, his cell phone rang.

"Darn me luck." He paused a moment before pulling the phone out of his pocket and checking the number. "Bugger it. I'm sorry, Lexi. I have to take this. It's my da. He's in Rio tonight."

"It's okay," I said, still a bit giddy from the fact that he really liked me and had thought I looked hot in my gown. Things were definitely looking up.

Finn said something about an investment transfer and then smiled at me. I got a warm feeling in my stomach and it stretched all the way to my toes. I had a strong feeling some serious kissing was in my immediate future. I just hoped Finn wouldn't talk long because if I had too much time to think about it, I might have a nervous breakdown.

Since I wanted to be prepared, I took the opportunity to reach into my coat and pull out a breath mint. I popped it in my mouth, figuring it couldn't hurt to have fresh-smelling breath for the forthcoming neck-fest. Saying something about a spreadsheet, Finn reached over and slid a hand beneath my coat and rested it just above my knee. His fingers squeezed lightly. I started to breathe like a racehorse, suddenly terrified I would hyperventilate and pass out before things could move forward.

Just then, the limo hit one of D.C.'s famous potholes and Finn and I were jolted back in our seats. The breath mint slid down the back of my throat.

I tried to cough, but no luck. I leaned forward, shaking my head, trying to dislodge it, but it stuck tight. Trying not to panic, I tugged on Finn's arm, but to my horror he only smiled, slid his hand up my thigh and kept talking.

I shook my head and pointed to my throat, trying to make a gagging sound.

He kissed my neck. "Patience, lass," he whispered to me, covering the receiver. "I'm looking forward to it as much as you. I'll just be another minute."

In another minute, I'd be dead. My life began flashing in front of me. Unfortunately, all that kept playing was me sitting semi-naked in my red gown in front of a sea of nuns and priests who—despite Finn's arguments to the contrary—looked at me aghast. I sincerely hoped this lapse of fashion judgment wouldn't affect my chances to get into heaven.

Desperate and knowing I'd regret it if I lived, I abruptly yanked the phone from Finn's hand and tossed it across the limo. Then I grabbed myself around the neck and stuck out my tongue.

Finn looked at me in shock and then concern. "Have you gone mad?"

I rolled my eyes and then stuck a finger down my throat. My vision swam and I saw two Finns.

"Are you choking?" I heard him say.

I nodded furiously, certain my face had turned blue.

Without another word, he pulled me onto his lap. His warm hands slid beneath my coat to a spot in the middle of my body, just below my breasts. He yanked upward once, doing the Heimlich maneuver as firmly as he could.

Nada.

He did it again and again, but nothing happened. By now, I was feeling faint. Blackness was crowding out my vision. Perhaps sensing brute force was in order, Finn braced his feet against the opposing seat and pushed so hard the breath mint popped out of my mouth like a cork from a champagne bottle, hit the window with a crack and fell to the floor. I took one gasping, greedy breath of air and promptly threw up on the television set.

I collapsed to the seat, staring in horror at the mess in the limo. "Oh, no," I moaned. "This isn't really happening. No one can possibly be this unlucky."

Finn just sat, clearly in shock, when we heard the driver's voice come through on the speaker.

"Are you all right back there, sir?" he asked.

Finn blinked, apparently coming to his senses. "We're fine, thank you."

"I… I just threw up in your limo." Sometimes, my intellect frightens me.

"It's okay," Finn said with amazing calmness. "It'll clean up. Are you all right?"

"I don't know. I may have to move to China."

Just then Finn's phone rang. He didn't make any move to get it.

"Aren't you going to answer that?" I asked.

"No."

"What if it's your dad?"

"He can wait until I get you home safely. I think I'd better keep an eye on you."

Feeling weak, I sat back against the seat and closed my eyes until the limo pulled up to my apartment building.

"I'd ask you up, but under the circumstances..." I said.

"Understood completely. At least let me walk you to the door."

He gallantly got out and walked me to the entrance. I keyed in the code and he carefully kissed me on the top of my head, so as possibly not to get any throw-up on him.

"Good night. I'll see you in the morning."

I walked up the stairs glumly. Not at all how I envisioned the night ending. Trying not to dissolve into tears, I opened the door, unset and reset the alarm. My vomit-covered coat landed on the floor of the hallway.

Once in the bedroom, I pulled off my gown and laid it on the bed. I took off my earrings and ring and then grabbed a T-shirt and a clean pair of panties. I seriously needed a shower.

Standing under the hot spray, I let it pound me, all the while crying in big, gulping, noisy sobs. I let myself wallow in self-pity for a good fifteen minutes before soaping up and getting out. Numbly I brushed my teeth, got dressed and combed out my hair.

On my first date with Finn, I'd dressed like a hooker and been on display for priests and nuns to see, hung up on his father *and* tossed my cookies all over a limo. That had to be some kind of record. He'd *never* ask me out again and I didn't blame him. I'd completely blown it.

Feeling like I was going to cry again, I stepped out of the bathroom, carrying my dirty underwear. I promptly dropped it and shrieked. Sitting on the corner of my bed was the sexiest and most dangerous *uberhacker* to ever walk the face of the earth.

"Slash!"

He smiled, his black eyes sliding down the length of my body and back up again. I wished I had chosen a floor-length flannel nightgown instead of the barely-covering-my-butt T-shirt, but I hadn't expected guests.

"What are you doing here?" I had no idea how long he'd been here and if he'd heard me sobbing my heart out in the shower.

"And hello to you, too," he said, amused. "Did you miss me? I'd have come sooner, but I had to go out of the country for a while."

Slash works for the NSA and is considered so proficient at what he does he is followed around the clock by his own personal FBI detail. He's an Italian/American ultra-secret hacker, but he also carries a gun, has a black belt in karate, hangs around military commando types and has never *ever* revealed his real name to me.

I frowned. "Don't you ever ring the bell? Must you always bypass my alarm?"

He feigned hurt, but his eyes gleamed. "I thought you found my electronic prowess enticing."

"What if I had someone in here? You know, a hot date or something."

He looked around. "But you do not."

"I was speaking theoretically. At least consider it might be a possibility."

"There's no one here but me."

I sighed, realizing arguing would get me nowhere. "Look, tonight is really not a good time."

He reached out, gently took my hand and sat me down beside him on the edge of the bed. "What's the matter, *cara?*"

He always calls me *cara,* which means "darling" in Italian. I wanted to tell him to leave, but instead, I hiccupped a small sob.

"I think I'm having a quarter-life crisis."

"You? Impossible."

"Why is that impossible? Do I really give the impression that my life is perfect?"

"Of course not. You are not anywhere near perfect, but that's what I like best about you." He lifted my hand to his lips and kissed the knuckles. His mouth was warm, hard and sexy.

I couldn't figure out how to comment on the backhanded compliment, so instead I said, "What do you want, Slash? I'm not in the mood for games."

"Would you believe me if I said I came just to see you?"

"No."

"I am deeply wounded that you question my motives," he said spreading his hands. "And I am especially jealous. Dare I ask who got to see you tonight in this heart-stopping gown?" He held up the dress and eyed it appreciatively. "Although he apparently did not fully value the look of you in it or else he'd be here now."

I snatched the gown out of his hands. "That's none of your business."

"Ah, but you are my business, *cara*."

"Why are you really here?"

"If you must know, your name has come up in the highest circles of the U.S. government…again."

I looked at him in disbelief. "The U.S. government? That's crazy. Why would my name come up? I'm not working for the NSA anymore."

"Why are you looking for Darren Greening?"

"Hey, how do you know about Darren Greening?"

He laughed. "Do you so quickly forget, *cara?* I work for the NSA."

I exhaled a deep breath. "Look, I'm not at liberty to discuss Darren Greening. Company confidentiality and all."

"Ah, but we all work for the government in one way or the other." He leaned closer, practically radiating heat. "Don't forget, the NSA knows how to get back those it wants. Our arms are always open to you."

He trailed a hot finger along my jawbone and down my neck, stopping on my shoulder. I shivered when he smiled.

"None of us wants to see Darren get hurt. We know he is missing."

"I don't want him to get hurt either. He seems like a good kid, just running scared."

"What's he scared of?"

"Don't you know?"

"Ah, the dance of nondisclosure," Slash said. "We are on the same side, *cara.* To prove it to you, I will go first in a show of good faith. We think Darren is in danger."

"I completely agree. Especially since I've been the recipient of said danger."

Slash lifted an eyebrow. "Explain."

I filled him in on what had happened to me in the garage. When I finished, Slash swore under his breath.

"Where was Shaughnessy?"

"In his office. He couldn't have possibly anticipated that I'd be accosted in our own office garage."

Slash rose and started to pace. "What else do you remember about this man?"

"Other than he was extraordinarily large, strong and seemed to have an expertise in snapping necks?"

He shook a finger at me in warning. *"Cara."*

"Okay, okay. Not much. I didn't see his face at all. He wore gloves and had an accent. Slavic, I think. I can't swear to it. Like everyone else he seemed convinced that I would know where Darren is. Lucky for me, he believed me when I said I didn't, which by the way, is the utter, absolute truth."

Slash sat back down on the bed next to me, taking both of my hands in his and setting them on his lap. "You be careful from now on. I insist on it."

"Don't worry. I'm making it a top priority. So why is the U.S. government interested in Darren?"

"Energy-replacement technology. Need I say more?"

"He works in the private sector."

"For now. I can't say more now, *cara.* But we will share more information soon, I assure you."

He stood and walked over to the desk in my bedroom. A tall, thin bottle stood next to my laptop computer.

"Where did that come from?" I asked.

"It's a gift from me to you. It's a very special bottle of wine."

"That's really nice of you. But I've got a whole case in the kitchen that will take me ten years to drink. In fact, you can take some, if you'd like."

Finn had given me a case of his family's excellent Irish label a few months ago as part of a deal we had made.

Slash snorted contemptuously. "Shaughnessy's wine?" He crossed his muscular arms against his chest. "I assure you, *cara,* mine is far superior in every way—aged, robust and much, *much* more experienced."

Suddenly I wasn't so sure we were talking about wine anymore. "Okay. So, what's the occasion? It's not my birthday and it's not yet Christmas."

"It's to be saved for a special time."

"Like what?"

"Like the time we first make love."

Huh? He wanted to make love…to *me?* Okay, clearly I was doing *something* right on the feminine front, minus the hurl-fest in the limo, of course. But dealing with Slash was like handling a live grenade. and I didn't have a clue how to react to this statement. So, I did what I always do when I'm faced with a socially unclear situation. I asked for clarification.

"Isn't that just a bit presumptuous?"

"Not even in the slightest."

Before I could ask him to clarify *that,* he walked over to the bed and yanked me to my feet. I opened my mouth to say something but he used that opportunity to give me a searingly hot open-mouthed kiss that left me breathless and without a single coherent thought in my brain. When he finally released me, I nearly slid to the floor. I barely had time to register any of this before he exited the bedroom without another word, disappearing from my apartment as silently as he had come.

I took a step backward, collapsed onto the bed and lay there in what I'm certain was a partial coma. I don't know how long I stared at the ceiling before rolling to my side and looking at the bottle of wine next to my laptop.

I still couldn't wrap my mind around this. Slash wanted to make love?

To me?

Could this night get any stranger?

I glanced at the clock and saw it was twenty minutes after twelve in the morning. My life was a mess and I desperately needed someone to talk to.

I picked up the phone and speed-dialed Basia's number. After two rings, the phone was answered.

"Hello?" a sleepy voice said.

I frowned, confused. "Xavier? Oh, I'm sorry. I must have dialed your number instead of Basia's…" I stopped talking, a feeling of dread creeping over me.

"Lexi?" I heard him say, sounding more awake. "You want to talk to Basia? She's right here."

I thought I might just drop dead of a heart attack. Basia was sleeping with Xavier? Was the Earth still round? Did a donut still have a million carbohydrates? Did I just throw up in a limo? What was going on in my life?

"No, no. Don't wake her. Jeez, never mind. I'll talk to her in the morning."

Before he could say another word, I hung up. Holy cow, I couldn't take any more unexpected excitement tonight. I lay completely still on top of the covers, staring at the digital clock and watching the time slip past. Eventually I closed my eyes and fell asleep with the lights on. It wasn't an elegant ending to the evening, but at least it put me out of my misery for the night.

Chapter Seven

I had a throbbing headache when the alarm went off at six o'clock, so I pushed the snooze button four times before dragging myself out of bed. Stumbling into the bathroom, I gulped down two aspirin with tap water before getting dressed. I brushed out my hair, securing it in a long ponytail at the nape of my neck with a hair clip. Makeup consisted of lip gloss.

Running late, I had to forgo my regular stop at Dunkin' Donuts and instead, grabbed a banana and a Diet Coke on the way out of my apartment.

Somehow, I made it to work on time and was shocked to see a single red rose lying across my keyboard. A small white card lay to the side. I picked it up and read "Thanks for an unforgettable evening. Finn."

I was torn between being happy with the gesture and insecure about the message. No doubt last night had been unforgettable, but that wasn't necessarily a plus. On the other hand, I got the feeling that Finn was trying to make light of the whole debacle. In any event, giving me a rose had been very thoughtful of him. and I appreciated it more than he would probably ever know.

I filled a paper cup with water from the fountain and put the rose in it, propping it up against my window.

I'd just sat down in my chair and turned on my computer when Basia bounced into my office, all sunshine and smiles.

"So, how was it last night? Details, details, details."

I leaned back in my chair. "You first. I call you at nearly one in the morning and Xavier answers the phone?"

Basia ran her fingers through her short bob and sat down. "Well, yes. Wow. How shall I put it—who knew that a geek could be so astounding in bed?"

I winced. "Jeez, Basia. Way too much information for me."

"See, I told you Xavier is like a brother to you."

"Okay, I'll admit that. But did you have to sleep with him?"

"What are you—my mother? It was sweet, spontaneous and quite good sex. What's wrong with that? We're both consenting adults."

I sighed. "I know. It's just I think Xavier has fallen hard for you and I don't want to see him hurt. Are you going out with him again tonight?"

"No, I happen to have plans with Lars."

"How are you going to keep that from Xavier?"

"I'm not keeping anything from him. He knows."

"And?"

"He's taking it better than you."

"You're like…double-dipping. Isn't that illegal?"

Basia laughed. "Not in my book. Don't worry, I can handle it. Now speaking of sex…please tell me you finally slept with Finn last night because I seriously think it's you who needs a big-time roll in the hay."

"For heaven's sake, Basia, it was our first real date."

"And your point would be?"

I sighed. "Okay, if you really must know, there was no sex. As of this morning, the notch on my bedpost remains at exactly one entirely forgettable encounter."

She rolled her eyes. "Oh yes, the college geek. From your description, I would barely classify that as a sexual encounter."

"Hey, I lost my virginity, didn't I?"

"You don't even remember his name."

"Neither one of us should have had the mystery punch at the post-lecture computer party."

She exhaled a breath. "You're utterly hopeless, Lexi. Sometimes I really do worry about you. I seriously hope there is a good reason why you didn't sleep with Finn last night."

"Maybe he didn't ask."

"Maybe he did and you turned him down."

"Maybe I asked and *he* turned *me* down."

"Maybe you should know that in the history of mankind, there hasn't been a guy on a date who has ever turned down free sex with a half-naked woman in his limo."

"Maybe he didn't like the way I hurled all over it."

Basia stopped. "You did *what?*"

I gave her the brief version of the night's events and when I finished, her face had paled considerably. "Oh, Lexi, that's the most horrible, heart-breaking date story I've ever heard."

Whatever improvement there had been in my mood since I saw the rose from Finn vanished in a puff. There was a long painful pause and then Basia broke out laughing. "I'd have paid good money to see Finn administer the Heimlich maneuver on you in that gown," she choked out between laughs.

"Basia! You're not helping."

"Sorry," she said, trying to swallow her laughter. "But it looks like the night wasn't a complete loss." She glanced pointedly at the rose. "From Finn?"

"He said the night was, um, unforgettable."

Her laughter bubbled up again. I narrowed my eyes.

"What?" She wiped away tears. "Don't give me that look. You *do* know how to make an evening unforgettable. Don't get so worked up about it. I think Finn is crazy about you. A little mix-up with the gown and some projectile vomit isn't going to change that."

"Stop. I beg you. This *really* isn't making me feel any better. What I need is some help with sex. I don't have a clue what I'm doing."

"Okay, let's get serious then. There is clearly more work to be done."

"What kind of work?"

"Work on your sexual confidence."

"How do we do that?"

Basia stood. "Come on, let's go get some coffee and I'll explain it to you on the way."

The thought of coffee appealed to me even if learning about my sexual confidence didn't. My headache had subsided, but I still felt some niggling pain behind my eyes. Caffeine might provide a bit of the perk I so desperately needed this morning.

"All right." I stood and picked up my mug.

"Overall, I think you took an important step last night," Basia said as we walked down the corridor. "You showed Finn a feminine side of you he hadn't seen before. Try to focus on the good parts of the evening. He did say you looked hot."

"How helpful is looking hot if I don't know how to

follow up? I think guys can tell when a woman is inexperienced."

"For some guys, sexual inexperience is a real a turn-on. They like to be in charge."

"What if Finn isn't one of those kind of guys?"

"Every guy is like that to some extent. Either way, I'm betting you're a fast learner. With an IQ like yours, good sex should be a walk in the park. Xavier is my case in point."

I couldn't help it, I winced. "I sincerely hope you're right."

"Have I ever steered you wrong?"

"How about last night?"

"A technical miscalculation. You learned an important lesson. Get more information ahead of time."

"Yeah, thanks, Einstein."

She smiled at a young guy who passed us in the hall and looked at her with open appreciation. "Now, an important question, although I think I already know the answer. During that one pathetic sexual encounter of yours, did you ever experience the Big O?"

"Big O?"

"Orgasm."

I looked at her in horror. "Jeez, Basia, keep your voice down. Do we have to talk about orgasms in the middle of the hall?"

"No one will hear us."

"Right," I muttered as we walked into the office kitchen. To my relief, it was empty. "Well, if you must know, I've never had the Big O, but I think I was close when Slash kissed me last night."

"Slash?" She stared at me. I remembered I hadn't

given her the details about his late-night visit, so I quickly filled her in.

She arched her eyebrow. "And you accuse me of double dipping?"

"I'm not double dipping. I'm not getting *any* sex."

"Then don't even think about Slash. He's got *bad news* written in big neon letters across his forehead. An enormous no-no."

"Oh, I see," I said, picking up the coffee carafe and pouring some in my mug. "It's okay for you to date two guys at the same time, but not me?"

"We are *not* talking about dating just any two guys. One of those two guys is Slash. In dating terms, Slash is like a wolf and you're the paralyzed rabbit in his thrall. He should be considered forbidden—off limits. You've got to trust me on this, Lexi. He is the kind of man trouble you *really* don't want. On the other hand, you've got a lot in common with Finn. You both are turned on by technology, are highly intelligent and have the same sense of dry humor."

"I have dry humor? As opposed to a wet humor?"

Basia rolled her eyes at me before picking up a Styrofoam cup. I poured some coffee into it for her. We both tipped a ton of creamer in our coffees and stirred them with a swizzle stick. I sipped mine as we headed for one of the small round tables in the kitchen corner.

"Okay, look, I think I have a good idea." Basia sat down.

"I don't think so," I said, joining her. "No offense, but look where your help got me last night."

"My *help* gave you the one highlight of the evening. Finn loved the gown."

"Before I threw up on it."

"You know what I mean."

Before I could reply, Finn's secretary, Glinda McBain, strolled into the kitchen. She wore a tight ivory blouse that strained across her generous bosom and a fitted dark green skirt with matching green pumps. Long red hair fell artfully around her back and shoulders, and her makeup looked professionally applied. She caught me staring and shot me the finger.

My lips curled into a snarl. We had despised each other since the first time we had met a couple of months ago, mostly because we both had the hots for Finn. Usually we made a point to avoid any possible chance encounters. But this morning I was cranky and her gesture had me spoiling for a fight.

"Isn't Glinda the name of a witch in *The Wizard of Oz?*" I said.

Basia followed my gaze. "Yes, but the good witch."

"In my opinion, a witch is a witch. If the shoe fits, wear it."

Basia snickered and Glinda strode over to our table. "What are you looking at, Carmichael?" she said in a low throaty voice, a trace of Irish lilt evident. "Trying to get some tips on how a real woman dresses?"

"Too bad I don't need to dress like you to get Finn's attention."

It was a direct hit because Glinda flushed red to her roots. She leaned down, tapping a blood-red fingernail on the tabletop. "Do you honestly think I worry about you being any kind of competition? Let me make something clear. You don't have a prayer with Finn. You're not the kind of woman he needs."

"And I suppose you know the kind of woman he does need?"

Glinda laughed contemptuously. "Of course, I do. I

really don't like you, but I am generous enough to share a little advice—woman to woman. Give up on Finn. You'll only get hurt and badly."

"You wish."

"In fact, I do. So, if you want to ignore my advice, then go ahead and keep on believing you have a chance with him. Just don't say I didn't warn you."

"You're a real piece of work," I said with a disgusted shake of my head.

"And you have absolutely no idea who Finn is, because you don't know him like I do. Our families have been friends since we were both in nappies. I grew up with Finn in Cork and we share the same culture, history and background. How do you think I got this job here at X-Corp? Finn's mother. Even she knows we're meant to be together. So, here's the stone-cold truth, sweetheart. You're nothing more than a distraction, an oddity to Finn for the time being. I respect the fact that a man like him needs to sow his oats and experience different kinds of women. Even women like you. But in the end, when he comes home—it will be to me."

"Ha! Maybe you don't know Finn as well as you think," I bluffed. "Maybe I find it amusing that you're so jealous."

Glinda tossed her head and a sea of perfect curls rained around her shoulders. "Me? Jealous of *you?* That's nothing short of absurd. I'd never be jealous of someone so…how do you Americans say it, geeky."

With a choking noise, I leaped from my chair and hurled myself at her. Basia seized my arm and pulled me back just as I grabbed a fistful of Glinda's blouse at the collar. Glinda shrieked and tried to rake her nails down my cheek.

"Have you both gone certifiable?" Basia hissed, pulling us apart and stepping in the middle. "As much as the men in the office might enjoy seeing the two of you trying to pull each other's hair out while rolling around on the floor, we do have a modicum of decorum to maintain here."

Glinda glared at me and I'm sure I was about to throw myself at her again when Finn unexpectedly walked through the door. All of us froze in place.

"Well, here you all are." A frown crossed his face, as if he realized he'd just interrupted something. "I wondered where everyone in the office had disappeared to."

To her credit, Glinda recovered first. "I was just fixing your coffee, Finn *gra*," she said, hurrying over to the coffee pot. I hadn't missed the familiarity with which she said his name and the little Irish endearment. I gritted my teeth and tried to smile as Finn addressed me.

"Are you ready to head out to Flow Technologies?"

"Ready when you are."

Glinda brought Finn his coffee. "It's just how you like it, Finn," she said, batting her eyelashes at him.

I wanted to throw up.

"Thanks, Glinda," he said, smiling. She tossed a smirk of victory over her shoulder at me as she sashayed out of the kitchen.

Even though I tried to squelch it, I still felt cranky and jealous. I was definitely having a PMS morning and I needed to cool it. At work, Finn was my boss, not an object of heated desire. I tried to remember that as we headed for the garage and climbed into his Jag.

"I saw Ben this morning," Finn said, putting the Jag into gear. "He said to ask Niles about their new partnership with NanoLab Industries."

"NanoLab Industries? Who are they?"

"Flow's manufacturing partner. Flow develops the technology and NanoLab works on mass producing and distributing the final product."

"Meaning the energy replacement."

"Yes."

"Do we know anything else about them?"

"Not much," Finn said. "Ben is still working on it."

"Good," I said and we lapsed into an uncomfortable silence. I figured I should thank him for the rose, but I wasn't sure how to do it.

"Um… I found the rose this morning," I finally said. "It was really nice of you. Especially after…well, what happened."

"You were the star of the evening. I enjoyed being with you and showing you off to my friends. I had fun."

"Even though I hung up on your father and hurled all over the limo?"

He chuckled. "There's never a dull moment with you, Lexi. Truthfully, I had a good time. There is no pretense, no games. But most of all, I like being with you."

The warm, fuzzy feeling began spreading in my stomach. "I like being with you, too, Finn. By the way, I forgot to mention I'd be happy to pay for the clean-up of the limo."

"Forget it even happened."

"That's top on my list of things to do today."

He laughed. "See, I have to work hard to stay one step ahead of you."

The tension broken, Finn turned on the radio to the local jazz station and I tapped my foot in time to Louis Armstrong until we arrived.

Flow Technologies was in a brand-new building just off the Dulles Toll Road, not too far from Darren's apartment.

The industrial-looking building was a bit of an oddity in an area full of high-rise, dazzling architectural structures with unusual shapes and lots of glass windows. Flow Technologies was a long one-storied complex, painted silver and surrounded by an electric fence. Someone had designed the building to curve slightly in order to form almost a semi-circle. In front of the building stood a huge fountain that even in November sprayed water high into the air and down over two magnificent glass dolphins. A guard stood at attention at the entrance to the parking lot and stopped us, checking with Flow to make certain we were permitted to enter before letting us in.

We pulled into the visitor area and parked the car. As we walked toward the entrance of the building, I tossed a penny into the dolphin fountain for good luck. Finn smiled, so I tossed in another one for him. Inside, the receptionist made us wait in an area with real plants and lush leather armchairs while she checked with someone to announce our arrival. I noticed with interest two armed guards patrolling around the building. I guess Flow considers its secrets well worth guarding.

Niles came out to meet us. He wore a badge around his neck and handed two visitor badges to Finn and me. He led us to a locked wooden door and slid an electronic card from his pocket and then placed his palm on a nearby screen. The door beeped and he pulled it open.

"Tight security," Finn commented as we passed through and into a stark white hallway.

"Yes," Niles said. "It's a necessity in our business. Industrial spying is rampant."

We walked down the hall as Niles explained how the office was divided into several sections.

"To the right is the Materials Division," Niles explained as we stopped at a fork in the hallway. "That is where work is done on self-organized nanostructures. To the left is the NanoDevice Division where our scientists are conducting research on new materials, processes and instrumentation. Straight ahead is the Biomolecular Division where Darren spent most of his time exploring new systems and concepts based on self-assembled or single molecular manipulations at nanoscale."

"Cool," I murmured. I glanced over at Finn and saw he was completely clueless so I gave him a reassuring smile.

We continued down the long corridor. Somehow just the sheer size of Flow Technologies surprised me. I guess I'd kind of thought of Flow as a small, tight company. I should have realized creating something as mind-boggling as an energy replacement for oil would take a lot more space and equipment than two kids could manage, even if they were geniuses.

We walked past a highly guarded area, including a security guard armed with a stun baton.

"Hello, Richard." Niles nodded. "Richard is standing in front of the specially designed Clean Room—an experimentation lab designed so that there are less than ten micro-inches of floor vibration throughout the lab complex. This ensures optimum performance from ultra-sensitive equipment, including an electron-beam lithography system and a scanning electron microscope. Would you like to check it out?"

Since I didn't see how I would understand much I saw beneath a scanning electron microscope, I asked instead, "Can we have a look at Darren's office?"

"Certainly. It's this way."

We bid good-bye to Richard and headed not too far from the Clean Room to a large office. A multifunctional desk stood pushed up against a wall upon which sat a computer with an extra-large flat panel display. Shelves took up nearly every other inch of wall space and were crammed with books, reference materials and manuals. A framed poster with a black background and white lettering hung over the computer desk and read simply: Your Village Called, Their Idiot is Missing. I couldn't help but snicker.

I sat down in his nice leather swivel chair and placed my fingers over the keyboard. It took me two strokes to realize the computer was password protected.

"Anyone know his password?"

Niles shook his head.

"Who's your IT guy?"

"Our what?"

"Computer guru."

"Oh, that would be Jonah Miller. Shall I bring him up?"

"That would be helpful."

Niles lifted the telephone receiver on Darren's desk and punched in a couple of digits.

"It would also be helpful to see Darren's personnel records," Finn added.

Niles nodded and then spoke into the phone. "Mary, please find Jonah Miller and ask him to come to Darren's office at once. Also, I need a copy of Darren's personnel folder. Bring it immediately."

After he hung up, Finn asked, "What can you tell me about NanoLab Industries?"

Niles raised an eyebrow. "They are our manufacturing partner. Their headquarters are located about five miles from here. They're a new company, but come highly recommended."

"They've agreed to manufacture and distribute a product not even created yet?" I asked.

"Based on Darren's prototype and theoretical work in progress, yes," Niles replied. "It's not an uncommon practice."

"When did you enter this partnership?" I asked.

Niles thought for a moment. "About three weeks ago. We haven't finalized the details, but it's a done deal."

That would be a week before Darren disappeared and I wondered if there was any significance to that. But before Finn could ask anything more, an older woman with a severe bun and sensible shoes arrived with Darren's personnel file. About a minute after that, a young, thin guy wearing an ID badge around his neck hurried into the room.

"I'm Jonah Miller. What do you need?"

"Access to Darren's hard drive," I explained, vacating Darren's chair.

He looked over to Niles for confirmation. When Niles nodded, he sat down in front of the monitor and starting logging on using administrative privileges.

"That's weird," he said after a moment.

"What's weird?"

"It isn't letting me on."

His hands flew over the keyboard and then paused. Nothing happened. He started typing again and I could see he had abandoned attempts to get on as an administrator and was now trying to log on as a regular user. That apparently failed, as well.

"What's going on?" he muttered.

"What's wrong?" Niles peered over his shoulder.

"For some reason, I'm being denied access to his account. That's highly irregular."

"Why didn't you notice this before?" Niles said, his voice icy.

"I don't make a practice of surfing around in other people's accounts unless I'm specifically asked."

"Can you access the drive or not?" Niles asked.

"Yeah." Jonah stood. "I just have to go to the server room and reset the user password for Darren."

"What does that mean?" Finn asked, clearly bewildered by our techno-talk.

"It means he's going to erase and then reset Darren's password, logging on with a new one as if he were Darren himself." I glanced at Jonah. "Mind if I tag along?"

"If it's okay with the boss."

Niles waved his hand impatiently. "Go ahead."

"All right, we'll be back in a few minutes," Jonah said.

I followed Jonah to the server room. He sat down at a terminal and started typing. Within minutes it was clear that this approach wasn't going to work either.

"I don't get it," he said, pounding the desk in frustration. "Why isn't it working?"

"Because he hacked it."

Jonah looked up at me incredulously. "What did you say?"

"I bet Darren hacked it. He cut you off on purpose."

"Why in the world would he do that?"

"Good question. How well did you know Darren?"

Jonah shrugged. "Honestly, not well at all. He was nice enough, I guess, but a little strange. High-strung is maybe a better word. I talked to him a couple of times about some computer stuff and he was knowledgeable. But he didn't seem the hacker type to me."

I wondered if Jonah thought I was the hacker type.

Guess I wouldn't tell him. "Did he hang with anyone at work?"

"Only Michael Hart," he answered. "They were as tight as brothers until the accident. Or maybe they were something more."

"Like what?" I asked even though I knew what he meant.

"You know…boyfriends," Jonah said, his face reddening slightly. "Not that I care. What people do in the privacy of their own bedrooms isn't any of my business."

I happened to agree with that statement. "So, what happened after Michael died?"

Jonah shrugged. "Darren became all withdrawn and weird."

"Weird how?"

"He didn't talk to anyone. He'd just walk past you in the corridor, staring off in space, muttering to himself. He spent a lot more time locked in his office than in the labs after that."

I didn't see how I could get any more useful information from Jonah, so I flicked my thumb toward the door. "All right, let's go break the bad news to the others."

Jonah stood and I could tell he was troubled. "This isn't your fault," I said, trying to make him feel better. "It's hard to protect from an inside hack, especially one coming from someone with as many privileges as Darren. Since everything else seems to be running smoothly, it looks like the hack wasn't malicious. Just paranoid."

Paranoid. There was that word again. More and more, it seemed to be an accurate description of Darren Greening.

Niles and Finn were waiting for us. Finn was looking through Darren's personnel folder and Niles sat in

Darren's chair, his hands folded in his lap, his face impassive.

"So?" he asked Jonah, rising from the chair.

"I'm sorry, sir. He must have hacked into the network and removed himself from the group."

"What?"

"It's a very unusual happenstance," I added.

"Are you saying you can't access his hard drive?"

"As of right now, that's what I'm saying."

"I don't understand how he could lock out his own IT guys," Finn said.

"Most likely Darren stole the administrative password," I offered. "Then he removed the domain administrators and users from his group and created his own local account. His drive information and account would then be accessible to him and him alone."

Niles's face flushed an angry red. "Why would he do this?"

I shrugged. "I don't know. The winning supposition of the moment is paranoia."

"From what?" Niles asked.

"It's hard to say. To me, an action like this really does scream fear. As if Darren felt he could trust no one."

"That's absurd."

"Perhaps, but that's where we're at."

"So, the bottom line is that we have no way of accessing his hard drive," Finn restated, bringing us back to our current dilemma.

I sat down in Darren's chair and tapped on his keyboard. "Yes, unless we get lucky and guess the password to his local account. Frankly, the odds of that are astronomical. Darren doesn't strike me as the type to use his birthday as his password. But since we have no other choice, I suppose I could give it a shot."

Niles strode over to the window and looked out, his lips pressed tightly together. "How long will it take?"

"Probably forever," I said. "I can't hack it, Mr. Foreman. I can only guess at Darren's password."

"Then do it. This situation is intolerable. I've got something I have to take care of right now. I'll be back in a few minutes."

With that, he stalked out of the office without a backward glance. Jonah made a slicing gesture across his own neck and then followed.

Finn and I exchanged glances. "Niles looked pretty upset," I said.

"Yes, but frankly I wonder why Niles hasn't tried to access Darren's drive before this."

I tapped my finger against my chin. "Personally, I think he did."

"What?"

"Look, nothing about Niles smacks of inefficiency. And if my star employee bolted into Neverland, you can be sure, the first thing I'd do is check out his computer files. But my guess is Niles wanted to go about it quietly, so at first, he didn't involve Jonah. I bet he hired some outside consultants who had no luck."

"But why the secrecy? Why not tell us?"

"Heck if I know. Clearly Niles has his own agenda."

"So, what now? You think he's hoping we can figure a way to get in?"

"Well, it was *my* name on Darren's cryptic note after all," I murmured, swiveling back in the chair. "If I were Niles, I suppose, at the very least, I'd give me a try. Can I have a look at Darren's folder?"

Finn handed it over, shaking his head. "I'm going to look through the papers in Darren's desk. Maybe we'll get lucky and find something useful."

"Go for it." I sincerely doubted it and was certain Niles had already been through the place with a fine-tooth comb. But maybe he didn't know what to look for. Then again, I didn't know what to look for either.

I thumbed through Darren's file, disappointed to see it contained only standard information, nothing remotely exciting or revealing. And as much as I doubted that Darren would be stupid enough to use his birthday as a password, I didn't have many other options to try.

I typed in his birthday in as many different ways as I could think, then his phone numbers, social security number, middle name, mother's name, father's name and every combination of his personal data that I could manipulate. Nothing worked. Taking a breath, I tried *STRUT, nanotechnology, energy, oil and Earth.*

Nada.

Not willing to give up yet, I thought about his personal effects in the shoebox. I typed *Einstein, rabbit's foot, Thomas Jefferson High School, Mars,* and *Michael Hart* in a multitude of combinations. I even typed the word *paranoia,* but came up empty. I spent another ten minutes manipulating all that data some more in as many normal and weird ways that I could imagine, but still came up with nothing.

"Crappola," I whispered in frustration and, just for the heck of it, typed in that word.

Nothing.

I expelled a frustrated breath and pressed my hand to my forehead. "What are you about, Darren?"

"No luck?" Finn was still going through the papers in Darren's desk.

"None, and frankly I think this is a lost cause. He probably used a mixture of nonspecific letters, symbols and numbers. That's what I would do if I were him."

"Then think like him."

There you have it. Wisdom dispensed from a lawyer.

Sighing, I leaned back in the chair and closed my eyes. I needed to put myself in Darren's shoes. If I were paranoid and had just hacked into my own company's network to create my own safe haven, how would I protect it?

I linked my fingers behind my head and thought. I guess it would depend on why I created my own account. If I wanted complete and utter secrecy, I would use a case sensitive, nine-digit password. Then it would be nearly impossible to crack. Since I presumed that was the whole reason Darren eliminated administrative access to his computer, I couldn't see how I'd have any success pursuing this avenue of investigation. He obviously didn't trust anyone, *ergo,* he didn't want anyone to be able to see what he had on his drive.

Then why did he name me in that note?

My mind flitted to Darren's Navajo coded message. *SOS,* it had read. A universal cry for help. A cry of one geek to another.

Suddenly, a weird sensation came over me. I abruptly sat up and started typing, my fingers flying over the keyboard. I tried half a dozen manipulations and then stopped when I heard the computer working.

"Finn, I'm in," I said in disbelief.

Finn dropped the papers and rushed over to my side. "You're a bloody genius, Lexi. What was the password?"

I looked up at Finn, feeling a bit dazed. "My name

as it appeared in Georgetown's yearbook the year we graduated."

"You mean to say the password was *Lexi Carmichael?*"

"Well, um...not exactly."

His brows drew together. "So, *what* exactly?"

I sighed. "Lexi *"Zorch'* Carmichael."

"*Zorch?* Do I dare ask?"

"Well, in hacker language, it can mean a lot of things. In my particular case, it referred to luck or brownie points."

"Bugger it, Lexi. Would you mind speaking English?"

"I'm trying," I protested, lifting a hand. "Let me put it this way, some of the other students may have considered me—in a tiny way—a bit of a teacher's pet. They sometimes said things like, "'Maybe Lexi could help me increase my quota of *zorch* with Professor Colby' or "'I ran out of *zorch* for the programming exam.' It was a joke. Lots of computer-science students had nicknames. I don't know why, but somehow my nickname stuck."

"*Zorch.*"

"Look, forget the *zorch*. The point is he used my name as a password on his computer at work. This is getting totally creepy."

I accessed Darren's hard drive, somehow not all that surprised to discover it had basically been wiped clean. There was no smoking gun, no blinking message for me and no encrypted or coded file. Nothing. I might as well have not guessed the password.

"It's clean," I said to Finn who was still peering over my shoulder. "Nothing of interest here."

In fact, the only possibly useful items left on Darren's drive were his email address book and the bookmarks in his internet browser. I glanced through his address book and noticed he had my home email account listed in his book.

"He's got my personal email account address," I said, shaking my head. I quickly emailed both files to my account for a closer perusal later and then sat back. I rarely gave out that address, mostly just to my parents and close friends.

"That is peculiar."

"Peculiar?" I repeated, my voice going up a notch. "Darren Greening uses my name as a password and has my home email account listed in his personal address book. But to my knowledge I've never met this guy nor received any kind of correspondence from him. What's the connection I'm missing?"

"I'm certain we're getting closer to finding that out."

But I didn't share his confidence. I needed a lot more data.

"How are you doing on the paper search?"

"Nothing," Finn said. "All the research materials are on nanotechnology and energy. It's all Greek to me. But I've got one more drawer to go. Maybe I'll get lucky."

I thought for a minute. "You know, at our initial meeting Niles mentioned that they had brought in a new guy to replace Michael Hart. Do you know who he is?"

Finn nodded. "Yes. A guy named Evan Chang. I talked to him on the phone. He didn't seem to know anything useful."

"Maybe I could talk with him."

"Niles might not approve of you wandering about the hallways alone."

"You think I should call for his approval first?"

Finn sighed. "No, I don't think it's necessary and frankly, I'm not crazy about the way he is hovering. I'll cover for you if he comes back while you're gone. I'd like to finish up here."

"Okay. Any idea where Chang's office is located?"

Finn slid his finger down a laminated piece of paper taped beneath Darren's phone. "Room 1604. Think you can find it?"

"Of course, I can. If I get lost, I'll just ask directions."

"Just don't get shot by security."

"I think it would be wiser to hope I don't touch something and blow us up by accident."

Finn chuckled as I left the room. I wandered down the blinding white hallway looking for Room 1604. It took me all of two minutes to find it and I didn't even have to ask for directions. The door was open and someone sat typing at a computer, his back toward the door. I cleared my throat and he swiveled around.

"Can I help you?"

He was young and Asian, dressed in jeans and a tucked-in button-down shirt. His white lab coat was open and a couple of pens were shoved upside down in his pocket. His glasses had been pushed up on the top of his head.

"Hi, I'm Lexi Carmichael from X-Corp." I waited to see if there was any flicker of recognition of my name in his eyes. Nope. Nothing. "Are you Evan Chang?"

"Yes." He stood and adjusted his glasses on his nose. "What can I do for you?"

"We were hired by your company to locate Darren Greening. I wondered if I could ask you a few questions."

"I already talked to someone from X-Corp. I don't know where Darren is. It's not like we're friends or confidants. In fact, we're barely colleagues. I think he resents me, at least in his mind, for trying to take Michael Hart's place."

"Well, essentially wasn't that why you were hired?"

"I was hired because I'm a good scientist and a careful researcher. I never wanted to take Michael's place in Darren's life."

"Is that what he thought you were trying to do?"

"Probably. He certainly hasn't yet had a kind word for me."

I thought for a moment. "Tell me a bit about your background. What did you get your degree in?"

"What does that have to do with Darren's disappearance?"

"Just humor me."

He shrugged. "I've got an undergraduate degree in molecular chemistry and a MS in biochemical engineering, both from MIT. I also took several graduate courses at Penn State in nanoscience and nanotechnology. I'm currently working on my PhD there."

"So getting a job at Flow was a big step up for you."

"Well, yeah, sort of. Look, I'm not going to lie to you. Darren is brilliant. The glimpses of his work that I've seen are breathtakingly revolutionary. He's poised to make scientific history and I don't mind admitting that I'd like to be a part of that. But the guy is completely nuts. He's been extremely difficult to work with in my short time here."

"So how is it that you became interested in Michael's old job?" I asked. My question seemed to catch him off guard. Curiously I saw a flicker of uneasiness in his eyes, replaced quickly by indifference.

"A friend heard about the opening and thought I'd be a good fit. I interviewed and got the job. A lucky break for me, I guess."

He was lying to me. But why?

"So, you have no idea where Darren is right now?"

"He could be on the far side of the moon for all I know. But frankly I wish he were back here now. Working without his guidance, bizarre as he may be, is near impossible."

I thanked him and made my way back to Darren's office. Niles waited there with Finn and looked angry with me.

"Why didn't you wait for an escort?" he demanded.

"Sorry. I didn't touch anything."

Niles seemed to calm down. "Finn told me that you got on to Darren's hard drive."

"Yep, I got a lucky break. But it's essentially wiped clean."

"By Darren?"

"My gut says yes. But I haven't figured out why."

"Well, if you do, you will let us know, won't you?"

His voice was slightly sarcastic and I resisted the urge to return the favor. "You'll be the first to know. Especially if you let us take the hard drive back to X-Corp. If there is something interesting here, we can find it. It may take time, actually a lot of time, but it can be done."

Niles narrowed his eyes. "No."

"No? Finding out what was on this hard drive might lead us to Darren."

Niles waved a hand. "No, you can't take the hard drive back to X-Corp. Sorry, but it wouldn't be secure enough. You can work on it here."

I looked up at Finn. "I guess we can send Ken and Jay to work on the drive around the clock. Who knows, maybe they'll get lucky like I did."

Finn nodded. "All right. We'll be in touch."

Niles showed us out and we returned our badges at the security desk.

"Any luck with Darren's papers?" I asked Finn as we climbed into the Jag.

"None whatsoever. It was a colossal waste of time. Any success with Evan Chang?"

"I don't know. I have to think about it. There's something about Chang that didn't add up for me, but I can't put my finger on it just yet."

"I'm curious about NanoLab." Finn put the Jag into gear and then pulled out of the parking lot. "I'll see what Ben has dug up when we get back."

We drove the rest of the way back to X-Corp in relative silence. Finn parked the car in the garage and I was just about to get out when he put a hand on my arm.

"Are you free for dinner on Friday night?"

Was he serious? "Are you sure you want to risk another date with me?"

"I wouldn't ask if I weren't."

"Okay, then I'm free."

"Don't you want to check your social calendar?"

"Ha, ha. What time?"

"Seven o'clock?"

"Just don't bring a limo," I warned, climbing out of the car.

"Only if you promise not to empty the contents of your stomach in my Jag."

"You drive a hard bargain, Shaughnessy."

"I call them as I see them, sweetheart."

"It's a deal."

He grinned and the day started looking a whole lot better. I hummed a tune and a little spring crept into my step as I headed back to my office.

Chapter Eight

Hours later, I headed for home. I had time to nuke a TV dinner and eat it before changing into my karate outfit and tying a spanking new yellow belt around my waist. I'd broken a wooden plank with my naked foot to earn that belt and I was proud of it.

I wasn't feeling much like breaking anything tonight, including a sweat, but I wanted to see Lars before his date with Basia. I drove to Anderson's Karate Studio in Laurel and hopped out of the car. I warmed up doing the usual pretzel stretches and then faked ten push-ups. Lars seemed to be in a good mood, probably in anticipation of his forthcoming date with Basia. Unfortunately for his students, it meant we had to run extra laps around the studio and do fifty extra push-ups. I was sweating like a pig and class hadn't even officially started yet. We practiced some routines and kicks and then sparred for about twenty minutes. I got paired with a fifteen-year-old kid with glasses. He beat the crap out of me.

I headed to the water fountain where Lars stood alone. "So, I hear you have a date with Basia tonight."

He smiled. "Want to come along?"

"Ha, ha. What are your intentions?"

His smile stayed in place. "Are you sure you're old enough to hear?"

"Look, I have the right to know. She's my best friend. I don't want to see her get hurt."

"Don't worry, Lexi. She's in good hands."

He held up huge hands that I knew were licensed killing machines. It didn't make me feel all that better. But it wasn't like I could say any more. They were adults and I just hoped they used protection.

I grabbed my equipment bag and slung it over my shoulder, heading out into the cool November air. I had almost reached my car when a figure stepped out of the shadows and nearly collided with me.

"Lexi?"

"Xavier? You scared the living crap out of me. What in the world are you doing here?"

Xavier stood with both hands shoved into jacket pockets, no hat on his head. He jerked a gloveless thumb toward the karate studio. "Checking him out."

I leaned back against my car. "Jeez, you're not going to start stalking him or anything, are you?"

"Of course not. I'm just sizing up the competition, which, by the way, happens to be undeniably formidable."

Trying to cheer him up, I said, "Contrary to popular belief, size isn't everything." Like I'd really know. Oh well, friends say what friends must.

"Well, he must be really good at karate."

"He owns the studio. He's a millionth degree black belt or something. You weren't thinking about trying to take him on, were you?"

"After seeing him, no. He could snap me in two like a twig. Well, I wanted to see him and now I wish I hadn't. I'm depressed."

I looked at him in concern. "You aren't going to go all postal now, are you?"

"You're not making me feel any better."

I sighed. "Look, Basia really likes you. She wouldn't have slept with you if she didn't. Take heart in that."

"But it wasn't good enough or she wouldn't be seeing Lars."

"It isn't all about sex for a woman, although she did say it was amazing with you."

He perked up. "She said that?"

"She did. Come on, get in my car and let me turn on the heater. I'm freezing."

We climbed into my Miata and I started the ignition, letting the car warm up before I turned on the heater.

"So, if Basia likes me and thinks the sex is great, why does she want to see Lars?" Xavier looked miserable.

"Maybe she just doesn't want to commit to one person right now. Basia is sort of a free spirit."

"Do you think that means she'll never want to commit?"

"Jeez, Xavier, you're asking relationship advice from the wrong person. Practically speaking, I know squat about matters of the heart."

"Well, you are a woman, right?"

"I'm insulted by that question."

"I meant it as a statement of fact. You are a woman, and therefore, you know in general what women want."

I thought that over. "Well, that's true."

"What *do* women really want from a guy? Please, be a friend and enlighten me."

I tapped my chin for a minute, letting the wheels in my head spin. "Okay, Xavier, you want to know what women *really* want?"

"Please, I'd be beyond grateful."

"Okay, you asked for it. A woman wants a man who takes the time to see the *real* her. To look beyond the fact that she may not have big boobs or be as socially competent as other women. And fashion, he shouldn't care a thing about fashion. A guy should like a woman whether she's in a simple black sheath gown or a low-cut red hooker dress. In fact, looks shouldn't matter at all. He shouldn't be attracted to women who have nicely manicured fingernails and gorgeous red hair that looks like a flame-colored waterfall cascading down a curvy body. Oh, and I think women wouldn't mind having a guy who could cook, clean, vacuum, iron, squish spiders and put the toilet seat down. Yep, I think that just about covers it."

For a minute, Xavier just looked at me with his eyes wide, his mouth open. Then he cleared his throat. "Um, actually, Lexi, I was thinking of something I could buy Basia online."

"Oh. Um, in that case, jewelry or expensive chocolate would work."

"Great." He put his hand on the door latch. "Thanks, Lexi. I feel better already. You're a good friend."

Make that an *idiot* friend, I thought. "Sure, anytime. And, let's keep this little talk just between the two of us, okay?"

He hopped out of the car and gave me a thumbs-up sign.

On the way home, I decided to stop by the county library and pick up a couple of books. I slid into a chair and surfed the computerized catalogue to see what might help me understand men-women relationships better. I jotted down the numbers and easily rounded up all three of the books I wanted: *Men are from Mars, Women are from Venus* by John Gray, *The Secret to the Big O* by Claudia Morner and *Deciphering the Kama Sutra* (illustrated) by Marina Bhutra. Lucky for me, there aren't many sexually clueless people in my neighborhood. I was headed for the check-out line when I ran directly into Slash.

"Aaaaaak," I yelped. "What are you doing here?"

"You think I never visit the library?"

"You're following me."

"*Si,* in a manner of speaking. What have you got there, *cara?*" He eyed my books.

"Nothing." I hugged the books to my chest. Unfortunately, the *Kama Sutra* book was on the bottom, featuring a handsomely illustrated picture of a couple embracing in a very interesting, not to mention complicated, position. Slash looked at me and lifted an eyebrow.

"They're for a friend. A neighbor. She doesn't get out much. What do you want?"

He took me by the elbow and led me to a small table in the back of the library surrounded by bookshelves. "I want to talk to you."

"You couldn't wait until I got home to break in?"

"I enjoy seeing you in different venues."

"Very amusing. What's up?"

"Michael Hart's death was no accident."

"I agree."

Slash studied me for a moment. "Do you think it was a hit-and-run?"

"Yes, but I'm not sure the hit was an accident."

"It wasn't."

"Are you sure about that?"

"We did a little investigation of our own."

"We, meaning who?"

He just smiled and I didn't know if he referred to the NSA or the entire federal government, whom he seemed to have at his every beck and call.

"The police did an investigation and ruled it an accident," I pointed out.

"The local police don't have *our* resources."

There it was again, the oblique reference. "So, why did you rule out accident?"

"There was a dent in the driver's side of his car, above the rear tire. The paint flecks recovered came from a dark-colored sedan, just like the one the witness said she saw."

"That doesn't prove it was intentional. The driver might have fallen asleep at the wheel or been drunk or something. The witness said the sedan swerved unexpectedly."

"True. But the swerve could have been intentional."

"Could have wouldn't hold up in a court of law."

"We traced the paint and then ran simulations of the accident on where and how the offender's car would have been hit based on the point of impact. Then we canvassed mechanics within a fifty-mile radius to track down the car. We got lucky and came up with a winner."

"You know who did it?"

"Not yet. The car was registered to a person known to be deceased for six years with a bogus address. He used cash for payment. But it is only a matter of time before we track him down."

"Remind me never to underestimate the power of the NSA."

"Moreover, it wasn't the first so-called accident Michael had survived."

"It wasn't?"

"He'd been attacked in what was eventually considered a mugging gone bad a couple of weeks earlier. He would have been dead, but the mugger's gun jammed."

"I don't get it. Why all the effort? If they wanted Michael Hart dead, why not just take him out with a sharpshooter?"

"Because it had to look like an accident."

"Why? I'm not following you here. Why would someone want to kill Michael Hart?"

"To have direct access to Darren Greening? To interrupt his work or drive him over the edge? Make him paranoid? Control his work or report on his progress?"

"If someone wanted to end or interrupt Darren's work, why bother with Michael? Why not go straight for Darren?"

"It could be for any number of reasons. They don't want to kill him, just monitor him."

"You mean someone is trying to steal his work? As in industrial spying?"

"Possibly."

I narrowed my eyes. "Why is the U.S. government really so interested in Darren Greening?"

He was silent.

I thought a moment. "Okay, I can play the speculation game. Darren is our ticket out of Middle Eastern problems. That must mean he's a lot closer to the energy-replacement fuel than I thought. You've been monitoring his progress."

"Yes."

"Whoever started this has succeeded in interrupting his work and making Darren paranoid."

"If that was what they intended. Somehow, I don't think they intended for him to bolt."

"I don't blame Darren for being paranoid, but who is he running from?"

"We're not sure yet. We're doing our own research into NanoLab Industries."

"The manufacturing partner."

Slash nodded. "Yes."

I let out a deep breath. "Okay, even if I buy all this, why the heck am I mixed up in all this? I'm sure I don't know Darren Greening. Why send an SOS to me—a person he's never even met?"

"Psychologically, it makes sense. In fact, *you* make sense. You would be a good person to have on his side. When you are forced into a position of not trusting anyone, you've got to rely on people you don't know, people who aren't familiar with your patterns or habits or style. Only those completely unconnected to you or your problems are the most trustworthy."

Slash sounded like he was speaking from experience. "But why *me?*"

"Why not? You're in a good position to help him. You have strong connections in both the government and private sector. You're a hacker like he is and you have similar mindsets—a kinship of sorts."

"But I'm hired by the very people he may not have reason to trust."

"Yes, but at *his* command," Slash reminded me. "Regardless, there must be a link between the two of you, *cara*. I'd advise you to figure it out and soon."

He pressed a kiss against my cheek and then headed for the exit. I watched him go, wondering why I let him come and go in my life in such an unpredictable way.

I went to the circulation desk and checked out the books, telling the librarian that the books were for a neighbor. She didn't believe me, but at least it allowed me to save face. I drove home and checked the messages on my phone. I had one from Basia who told me a gift would soon arrive and be sure to accept it, and one from my mother asking me if I'd come for dinner over the weekend. I headed for the shower, trying to think of a good reason why I couldn't go to my parents' for dinner. I knew full well my mother had another blind date set up for me and I wasn't even remotely in the mood for suffering through it.

I took a shower, pulled on a pair of panties and a T-shirt even though it was only nine-thirty and got the Mars-Venus book to read in bed. I was headed there when the doorbell rang. Surprised, I looked out the peephole and saw a young blonde woman I didn't know standing there. She held a large black purse, which looked kind of like a doctor's bag.

"Can I help you?" I said without opening the door.

"My name is Ursula. Basia Kowalski sent me."

"Basia?"

"Yes, she said she'd call and tell you I was coming."

I thought for a moment. Basia *had* said on the answering machine that she was sending a gift. Could this woman have it?

"Just a minute." I hurried back to the bedroom and pulled on my ratty white-and-blue robe. I unarmed the alarm and unlocked the deadbolt, cracking open the door.

"Okay, you can hand it over," I said.

"Hand what over?"

"The present."

Ursula laughed. "I *am* the present, darling."

"What?"

"Can I come in?"

"Um. No offense, but I don't understand what's going on here."

"Basia sent me to give you a little instruction on sexual confidence."

My mouth dropped open. "I… I don't know what to say. Look, I'm terribly sorry but there appears to have been some kind of mistake. My door doesn't swing that way. In fact, it barely swings at all. I mean, I'm not *that* kind of girl…"

Ursula laughed again. "Open up, darling. I'm not here for what you think. I'm an exotic dancer. I'm supposed to give you some tips on loosening up and learning more sensual tricks to get your man. I can see I'm not a moment too soon."

"Oh."

"So, can I come in?"

I opened the door. "Sure, I guess."

Ursula stepped across the threshold and slipped out of her coat. She was clearly braless beneath a tight white tank top. A pair of super snug black shorts hugged her butt. Handing me her coat, she strolled into my living room like she owned it. "Where's the stereo?" she asked, pulling a CD out of her bag.

I trailed after her, still holding her coat. "Look, Ursula. I know Basia means well, but I really think this is a bad idea."

"There's nothing bad about understanding your sexual prowess as a woman. It's empowering and feminist. Get on board the new millennium train, honey."

She snatched the coat from my hand and threw it across the room where it landed on the couch. "Relax. I'm just going to show you some moves. But first, I want to set the mood with some music."

Before I could say anything, she spotted my stereo. Walking over, she slipped her CD in and turned up the volume. A sexy, grinding beat thrummed through my living room.

Ursula started to sway her hips. "I'm a stripper." She ran her hands over her curves. "My job is to entertain and entrance men, to make them forget about their daily ho-hum lives and permit them to fantasize about whatever they want."

Despite my reluctance, I was intrigued. "It sounds like a monumental task."

She laughed. "I think I'm going to like you, Lexi."

"You'll probably change your mind about that because I think…" Before I could finish my thought, she grabbed my hand and pulled me into the center of the living room. My leg bumped against the coffee table and I winced.

"No thinking," she warned. "Just feeling. Dancing is a form of expression. Dancing provocatively is a tool of empowerment. You told Basia you wanted to improve your sexual confidence, so I'm here to help you do that."

I gulped. "Okay."

She started swinging my arm back and forth and then, with astonishing speed, she untied the belt of my bathrobe and yanked it open. As I gasped in shock, she eyed me in my T-shirt critically.

"Hmm…you have the right body for a stripper, although it would have been nicer if the girls were a bit bigger."

I looked down at my chest and flushed. I tried to pull my hand away, but she held on tight.

"However, you have amazingly long legs," she continued. "Extremely sexy and excellent for dancing. They are your best feature, so we'll play them up. Your hair is nice, too. Long and naturally wavy, but it requires a bit of a sexier cut and some soft blond highlights."

"I'm *so* not dying my hair."

Ursula clucked her tongue softly. "Female empowerment requires putting your best assets front and center. You do want to make a good impression on this new guy of yours, don't you?"

Just the mention of Finn had me wavering. "Well, yes, but…"

"Then no buts. Do as I say. Act as I act. Remember I'm here to help you."

I heaved a deep breath. I had nothing to lose. Besides, what could be the harm of dancing a little in the privacy of my own living room?

"Okay, I guess I can give it a try."

She smiled, showing pretty white teeth. "Excellent. Now, you need to feel the beat of the music. Close your eyes. Sway to the rhythm."

I closed my eyes and started to move back and forth on each leg. However, instead of feeling sexy, I felt incredibly sleepy.

She jarred me awake with a shove on the shoulder. "You're not a robot, Lexi. Loosen up a bit. Lose your insecurities and start feeling comfortable in your own body."

Easier said than done. I tried to loosen myself up by imagining I was a limp noodle. Unfortunately, I wasn't sure it improved my swaying ability. When I cracked my eyes open, I saw Ursula staring at me, a look of shock on her face.

"This is going to be a challenge," she said.

Walking over to the stereo, she turned it off. Then she

steered me to the couch and we both sat down. "We're going to have to try a different approach," she said. "I think in your case, we have to start with your mind."

"Thank goodness," I said with feeling.

She leaned back on the cushions and considered me for a moment. "We are going to create an alter ego for you."

I raised an eyebrow. "An alter ego?"

"Yes. Someone who is you, but not you. A fantasy inside a fantasy. It can be anyone from Mary Poppins to Marilyn Monroe. You can study this person, watch films of them and safely become that person in your own mind because none of it's real. And if it's not real, there are no inhibitions and no insecurities. You can do what you want, be what you want."

It kind of scared me that she was making sense.

"Okay. So, who should I be?"

She tapped her long fingers on the top of her thigh, her brow furrowed in concentration. After a full minute she said, "Pussy Galore."

"No way." I'm a huge Bond geek and *Goldfinger* is one of my favorites.

"Yes way. She owns a flying circus of sexy female pilots and is Goldfinger's accomplice in the plot to rob Fort Knox. She and her female pilots plan to spray a gas over the area to immobilize key personnel and then steal the goods."

"But Bond seduces her and points out the error of her ways."

Ursula laughed. "Exactly. She had skills and a brain. But she's extremely sexy. I think you might connect to her."

I thought it over. "Guess there could be worse choices."

Ursula patted my leg. "Now, that's the spirit. Here's your homework. Rent the film. Watch it several times. Pay special attention to the way she talks and acts. Memorize her habits, the way she flicks her hair, bats her eyelashes and presses up against Bond. These are visual clues that let Bond know that she's attracted to him. We'll incorporate these mannerisms into your dance." She stood up and took her coat from the couch. "See you tomorrow evening. I can't say exactly when, but it will probably be late."

"How much is this going to cost me?"

"It's a present from your girlfriend. And, honey, even if it wasn't, I'd consider it my duty to womankind to help you out."

I wasn't sure if I should be flattered or worried, so I just hurried to the door and let her out. After she left, I set the alarm and leaned back against the door.

Settling one hand on my hip, I drawled in as sultry a voice as I could manage, "Hello, James."

Then, in my best James Bond voice imitation, I replied, "You? I must be dreaming."

Chapter Nine

Sex appeal or not, I still had to earn a living. Driving to work the next morning, I rehashed all I'd learned about Darren Greening. Unfortunately, I felt no closer to figuring out why he'd fingered me in the note, why I'd been accosted in the parking garage and what it all meant in the bigger scope of things. Upon arriving at the office, I poured myself a cup of coffee and started to go through the info Ken and Jay had emailed me about Darren. Both guys were spending the day at Flow Technologies, digging around Darren's wiped-clean hard drive in the hope they could find something I'd missed in my cursory search.

Ken had taken the initiative and tracked Darren's online presence from the office for the twenty-four hours prior to his disappearance. Not surprisingly, it indicated Darren had spent about four hours online in the STRUT chat room. I made a note to visit again to see if I'd missed anything.

I also got an email from Ben saying he'd been digging into Flow's manufacturing partner, NanoLab, but nothing had jumped out at him yet. After my third cup of coffee, I gave Darren's analysis on the dangers of nanotechnology another thorough read. This time around,

I began to understand how worried he really was about the potential dangers of future manufacturing practices. I read it again slowly and took notes. I had taken so much time, it was after noon when Basia entered my office and sat down.

"So, how'd you like my present?" She crossed her legs and gave me a Cheshire Cat smile.

"You're inventive." I took my glasses off and put them on the desk. "I'll give you that."

"True. So, how did it go?"

"She might charge you extra."

She laughed. "I'm sure I'll get my money's worth. Do you think it will work?"

"Well, she's starting with my mind."

"Smart girl."

"And she's insisting on giving me an alter ego. Bond girl, Pussy Galore."

She clapped her hands in delight. "Oh! I can't wait to see how this turns out."

"I'm glad you're so positive because I've got a bad feeling about this."

"You wanted help, so I delivered. After all, that's what friends are for."

"Jeez. I'd hate to have any enemies."

After she left, I decided I needed a fourth cup of coffee and maybe something chocolate to substitute for lunch from the vending machine. I slipped a couple dollars' worth of change in my pocket and headed for the break room. On the way down, I ran into Finn, who looked glad to see me.

"Oh, there you are, Lexi. I was just coming to see you."

"About what?"

Taking my hand, he pulled me toward a nearby utility room. "About this."

He opened the door and motioned me inside. Stepping in, I looked around. The tiny room was barely bigger than a closet and had some metal shelving units with three of our spare printers, an extra computer used for data storage and assorted boxes with various cables, cords and wires.

"You want me to set up another printer?"

To my surprise, he stepped into the room behind me and closed the door. I turned around and found myself pressed up against him.

"No printer. I'm going to steal a kiss."

I blinked in astonishment. "Steal?"

He lifted his hand and tucked a stray strand of hair behind my ear. "I adore you. It's just a turn of phrase, Lexi. I'm not really going to do anything without your permission. It's just I've gone barmy thinking about you all morning and I hoped one kiss would give me a moment's peace to get my mind elsewhere. But I couldn't figure out a way to stroll into your office, devise a pretext to lean over close enough to plant one on you, so then I remembered this closet and…" He let the sentence trail off and his cheeks reddened. "Listen to me. I've completely mucked this up. I sound like a randy teenager."

Since I could totally relate to his embarrassment, I stepped up against him and cupped his warm cheeks with my hand. Without a word, I kissed him gently on the lips, letting my mouth linger just a bit because he tasted like tea and honey.

"There. No stealing necessary. You really went barmy? Over me?"

He slid his arms around my waist and I put my hands

against his chest. I could feel the thump of his heart beneath my palms.

"Straight up. It's driving me mad. I've never really had to use my brain to impress a woman before. In the past I've been able to rely on my other, um, assets."

"Good looks, charm and money?"

"Not necessarily all of those, nor in that order, but yes."

"Hmm. Money and looks are superficial, not to mention overrated. Charm and wit, not so much. Good thing you've got those things in abundance."

He smiled. "That's exactly what I like best about you, Lexi. No games. It's the real deal with you. You say things like they are."

"Why would I say it any other way?"

"Why, indeed?" He lowered his head to kiss me and I instinctively prepared myself for a hungry assault. Instead his mouth was gentle against mine. Just then I realized that despite his past sexual conquests, and I assumed there had been many, he was thinking of me and my comfort zone. That knowledge along with the exquisite and soft caress of his lips created a powerful web of dreamy seduction.

"There," he murmured against my mouth. "That should do me for a little bit. Thank you."

I sighed with contentment. "No, thank *you*. Really."

My knees must have been a bit wobbly because I shifted in his hold and my elbow hit the corner of a metal unit. I yelped in pain and warning as a box above us teetered and fell, raining cables and wires.

For a moment, we just stared at each other in disbelief before bursting out in laughter. The sound froze in our throats as we heard someone in the hall.

"What was that?" A voice. Male.

Finn carefully reached over and locked the door. A second later, someone pulled on the handle, shaking it a couple of times.

"Guess it didn't come from here. It's locked."

"Probably nothing," I heard a female reply.

We waited in silence until we didn't hear the voices anymore.

Finally. Finn pressed his fingers to his forehead. "I'm going to have to fire myself. Ravishing a female employee in the utility closet."

I stared at him. "You, uh, *ravished* me?" It sounded so...amazing. Lexi Carmichael, a ravished woman. What would Basia think of me now?

Finn held up a hand. "Well, technically we were just kissing."

My dream bubble burst. "Oh, right." I hoped I didn't sound too disappointed.

Finn ran his fingers through his hair and pulled out a thin black wire. "Regardless, that still doesn't let me off the hook. I apologize for putting you in this situation."

"Um, I don't believe you heard me complaining."

Smiling, he reached over to pull a red cable out of my blouse. It had snagged in the material and when he tugged harder, two buttons popped off my shirt.

I stared at the gap and the bra clearly visible beneath it. "Uh oh."

Finn sighed. "Well, now you are technically ravished. Sorry."

Hooray! I'd been ravished after all. "Hey, no sweat. I'll fix it. I think."

"I believe there's a first-aid kit in the kitchen."

"Are you suggesting a bandage?"

"A safety pin. Or you could ask the boss to let you off early."

"He'd never go for it. He's a real tough guy."

He laughed, kissing my cheek. "Go home and get decent. I still can't believe I just did this."

"Me neither. But I'm glad you did."

"And I'm bloody thankful for that. I'm also glad we'll have more time to spend together on Friday. It's a special day for me, you know."

"It is?"

He straightened in his shirt. "It's my birthday."

"Your birthday? Really?"

"Really. Look, Lexi, I know that sometimes you're uncomfortable spending a lot of time out on the town with other people, so I thought perhaps you'd enjoy an evening with just the two of us. I'd like to fix dinner for you at my place, if that's okay."

"Seriously? You cook?"

"A decent linguine with clam sauce. Sound good?"

"Sounds amazing. You are a man of many talents."

"Ah, and I've yet a few up my sleeve."

Pulling the gaping part of my blouse together with one hand, I tried to smooth down my hair with the other.

"How do I look?"

"Fantastic, sexy, kissable."

"Bet you say that to all the girls."

"Bet I don't."

Giggling like two kids, we picked the rest of the wires and cables off each other. I finally insisted that Finn leave the closet so I could pick the rest of the mess up. There was no way we could do it with both of us crammed in there and besides, I knew where everything went.

It took me about ten more minutes to pick up the cables, rearrange them and arrange myself into a semi-presentable state. Thankfully, I managed to slip out of the office without anyone noticing my missing buttons. I had the security guy walk me to my car and then I drove home, changing into jeans and a long-sleeved baby-blue T-shirt. While pulling my hair back into a ponytail, I gave the Zimmermans a quick call. Elvis answered.

"Hey, Lexi," he said. "What's up?"

"Can I come over? Or are you guys in the middle of something?"

"The door is always open for you."

It took me about five minutes to get to their house. Elvis came to the door before I rang the bell. He wore jeans and a sky-blue sweater. We almost looked like twins.

"What brings you to our humble abode?" he asked, leading me to the computer control room. I shivered at the cold air when I took off my coat so Elvis fetched the blanket from the back of a chair and wrapped it around me.

"I wanted to ask your opinion on GURPS Robots. You ever play?"

"Sure," Elvis said. "But Xavier is better at Robots than me. I'm more into the GURPS Fantasy, like you."

Yeah, like me *before* I had to force myself to go cold turkey. I'd been spending too much time in the fantasy world and needed to pull out.

"Did someone say GURPS Robots?" Xavier walked into the room. "Hey, Lexi. Glad you're here. I wanted to show you what I bought Basia."

He walked to his desk and picked up a small box and something flat wrapped in tissue paper. Bringing them both over, he handed me the box first. "Open it and tell me what you think."

I opened it, temporarily blinded by the bling. "Holy cow. Are all those diamonds?"

"It's a tennis bracelet. Think she'll like it?"

Before I could answer, he'd unraveled the tissue on the other gift, revealing a pair of edible chocolate underwear protected by a sheer plastic wrap. "You said chocolate, so I thought she might like these, too. Well, at least *I'll* like them."

For a moment, I just stared stupidly at the gifts. It was sure nice of him to buy her stuff, but heck if I knew if it was appropriate.

"That's interesting."

Apparently, it was the correct reply, because he happily gathered everything up and replaced them on his desk. "You're a good friend, Lexi. Thanks for cheering me up the other night."

"My pleasure."

He sat down in front of a computer. "So, I hear you want to play a little GURPS Robots."

"I'd rather watch you, if that's okay. I want to observe and think, not get involved in the play right now."

"Okay. Want to start from scratch?"

"Yeah, I think that would be best."

"Do you want to be a nanobot, megabot or a biomorph?"

I considered for a moment. "Nanobot."

Elvis and I stood behind him, looking over his shoulder as he logged on and in. "Okay, give me a sec to create the settings."

"Appreciate it."

For the next forty minutes, we watched as Xavier

played. He interacted with androids, biomorphs, cyborgs and a slew of other characters. I took notes, trying to figure out the world building. It wasn't as hard as I expected, but I wasn't sure what my point was in having Xavier play the game. Rudy had said Darren spent a lot of time on GURPS Robots, so maybe it was significant. On the other hand, Darren was a lonely geek like me and this could have been nothing more than a fun way to pass the time. How the heck would I know?

It wasn't until I saw a passing reference to "Master-Nano" that something clicked for me.

"Wait," I said, bending over Xavier's shoulder. "Can you check the profile for MasterNano?"

Xavier found the profile, but as expected, there was no personal information. MasterNano was clearly the reigning king of all nanobots in GURPS Robots and he had amassed an impressive nano-kingdom with slews of servants and citizens. However, in terms of personal information, we got zip. It was all fantasy in GURPS and there was no way the person behind MasterNano was really named Si Borg who lived on Mars Street in Roswell, New Mexico. But there was that Mars reference again and it bugged me.

"Can I sit? I'd like to hack into the profile and see if I can't get the real name and location of MasterNano."

The room fell silent and I exhaled a deep breath. "I know what you're thinking and it's okay, guys. I can do this. I *want* to do this."

"I thought you'd gone legit," Elvis said. It was sweet how he was almost protective.

"Yeah, for seven hundred and thirty-nine days." I'd become a *former* hacker once I'd started working at the NSA.

I had liked my job and wanted to keep it, so I'd given up hacking altogether, even for recreational purposes.

"I'm getting off the wagon starting right now for two reasons. One, I'm not in my office at X-Corp and here I will be absolutely untraceable. And two, it's our first case and somehow it's all connected to me personally."

Elvis gave me a thoughtful stare. "It's not necessary, you know. I'll do the hack for you."

"I appreciate that more than you will probably ever know. But this is my case, so it should be my hack. Besides, it's not a malicious hack—not that I ever did those, um, much. Anyway, I have to do this."

The room was silent.

I paused, pressing my fingers against my temples. "Okay, okay, who am I kidding? You two know me better than anyone in the universe. I'm doing this because I *want* to."

With that, Xavier quickly vacated the chair. "Your throne, geek queen."

"Thanks," I said, sitting down.

Elvis leaned over my shoulder as I got started. "You think MasterNano is important?"

"Maybe."

I flexed my fingers and got to work. It made me happy to realize I hadn't lost my finesse in those seven hundred and thirty-nine days. It felt good. *Really* good. It took me about four minutes to hack in and another ten to trace the ID.

"The supposed genuine name is also bogus," I said as the data popped up. "Albert Asstein."

"Ha." Xavier appreciated that one.

"But the ID is interesting."

Elvis peered at the screen. "What do you have?"

"The provider for MasterNano is in Northern Virginia, near Dulles. That's Darren's neck of the woods."

"You think Darren Greening might be MasterNano?"

"Possibly." I tapped my finger on my chin. "Let's look at the last time Master played."

"Scoot over." Elvis squeezed into the same chair with me. "Want a partner?"

"Sure." I gave him some room and he sat, our hips pressing together. "You want the keyboard or you going to give instructions?"

He smiled. "How would you like it?"

"I'll take the keyboard."

"Okay." He gave my ponytail a gentle tug. "Girl's choice."

Apparently bored with our mundane hack, Xavier wandered out of the room. With Elvis at my side it was a super easy hack and in just a few minutes we'd discovered that MasterNano had played yesterday at 11:48 p.m. for a period of sixty-seven minutes. After a while, I let Elvis have a turn on the keyboard. But instead of elbowing in front of me, he reached one arm around my waist, basically hugging me as his fingers flew over the keyboard.

It wasn't long until we discovered that the provider for MasterNano yesterday was not the same as in his profile.

"This one leads to Massachusetts," Elvis said. "Cambridge, to be exact."

"Cambridge?" For a moment, my mind raced until it suddenly came to me. "Cambridge. That's where MIT is."

Elvis shifted in the chair. "What does MIT have to do with anything?"

"Nothing or everything." I leaned back. Elvis's arms

were still around me. He smelled nice, like soap. I felt comfortable and safe resting my head against him.

"Want to illuminate the thought process?"

"The STRUT chat room. I met two guys there. Raw-Mode and Grok."

"Grok as in Heinlein's Martian?"

That's what I loved about Elvis. I never had to explain anything. "Exactly. And Darren had a postcard of Mars in his treasure box. Could be significant."

"Darren has a treasure box?"

"Yeah." The tone of his voice made me decide not to tell him about mine. "Anyway, Grok and RawMode talked to me in the chat room about Darren and his theories on nanotechnology. Grok was from MIT or so he said. Maybe it's a coincidence or maybe it's not."

"Want to check out Grok?"

"We can try." I leaned forward and logged in to the STRUT chat room. There were six other people there chatting but none of them were Grok or RawMode.

"Dang. Can't trace them if they're not online."

Elvis leaned forward, his arms still around me. I watched as his fingers flew over the keyboard. He shifted a bit as he typed so that his chin rested lightly on my right shoulder and his cheek pressed up against mine. Weird, but it felt kind of nice.

I waited until he had finished before asking what he'd done.

"I wrote a protocol to alert me when either RawMode or Grok logs in," he explained. "It'll start an automatic trace. The next time either one logs on, I should be able to narrow the location for you, and if we get lucky, we might even be able to pinpoint it."

"Good idea," I sighed, feeling oddly relaxed. I turned

my head slightly to look at him. "Thanks, Elvis. You're the greatest."

At that moment, I realized my mouth was nanoinches from his. I had a sudden memory of a very nice kiss he'd given me a few months before just as I'd embarked on one of the most dangerous operations of my life. He'd been my pillar then just as he was now, helping me out when I'd really, really needed it.

It seemed as though he was lowering his mouth toward mine when Xavier walked back into the room. Elvis jumped up and I almost toppled out of the chair, managing to catch myself at the last second.

I rose and shrugged the blanket off my shoulders. "Uh, thanks again. You guys rock."

Xavier gave me a thumbs-up. "For you, Lexi, anytime."

"Yeah, you're only saying that because I'm Basia's best friend."

Elvis laughed. "Hey, it helps."

He walked me to my car, no hint that anything might have passed between us. Had I started to imagine things or had my commitment to explore my femininity suddenly started to pay off in unexpected ways?

After I left the Zimmermans', I headed home. The first thing I did was open my laptop and download *Goldfinger*. I watched the movie while eating a dinner consisting of Frosted Cheerios and raisins. I paused and replayed parts of the movie several times to watch Pussy Galore in action and jotted some notes on a pad of paper. Hopefully Ursula would approve.

I made myself a cup of tea and took it into the living room with the *Kama Sutra* book. I started with the chapter on kissing. Just to be on the safe side, I jotted some notes down on that for further review. Because I was curious I read three more interesting chapters on sexual positions, taking an inordinate amount of time to review the large and complex illustrations. Most of the time I think I had the book upside down. Jeez, who knew everything could fit properly when people were contorted like pretzels?

A little after one o'clock in the morning Ursula rang the bell to my apartment. I'd fallen asleep on the couch, right on top of the *Kama Sutra* book. I leaped from the couch and opened the door. She walked in, looking a bit frazzled.

"It's been a heck of a night." She slipped out of her coat. Nothing underneath but a blazing pink bra with rhinestone studs and matching panties. Her blond hair was mussed and her face had tons of makeup.

"Do you ever wear normal clothes?"

"I just got off work. The patrons were crazy tonight."

"Sorry." Was that an appropriate reply?

She grabbed my hand. "So, how are you tonight?" She pulled me into the center of my living room.

"Sleepy."

"That's Lexi answering. I want to hear from the Bond girl."

"Oh. That girl says she's feeling all feminine and sexy."

"That's better. Come on, let's practice moving to the music."

She slipped the CD in the player and I dutifully swayed, closing my eyes and trying to feel the beat. I nearly jumped out of my skin when she grabbed my hips and started shaking them back and forth.

"Move your hips, not your whole body. You look like a frozen cadaver when you rock back and forth like that."

"I'm trying, but this is embarrassing. Finn is just going to laugh."

"This is *not* for Finn. This is for you. The point is that you need to feel sexy and confident. That way you don't have to rely on a man to make you feel that way."

I sighed. "I guess."

"Look. After a few...or maybe a hundred...sessions with me, you should be able to walk across a room naked and with full confidence in your womanly power."

Panic gripped me. "But we're having dinner alone at his place on Friday," I blurted out. "On his birthday."

"Friday? Are you freaking out of your mind? For God's sake, I'm a stripper, not a miracle worker."

"Oh, jeez. I knew this was too good to be true. Isn't there anything you can do?"

She ran her fingers through her hair. "Okay, okay. Calm down. We can figure this out. It's a good thing I made a hair appointment for you tomorrow at five o'clock."

"What?" I screeched. "Forget the hair. This is about sexual confidence."

"Appearance is half the battle. The appointment is at Shay's Hair Salon on Fifth and Main Street. You'd better be there."

"But I need time to process. To mentally prepare myself for a...a hair appointment." I could hardly bring myself to say it.

"If you are going to be alone with him on Friday at his place, there is *no* preparation time. Be there, shut up and let Karen do her magic with your hair. I already told her what I wanted."

"Oh, no. No hair dye."

"Highlights. Subtle. And a bikini wax. That's the deal."

"Bikini wax?" I scrubbed my hands over my eyes. "I'm not planning on wearing a bikini. We're having linguine. This is all moving too fast. I'm going to be a train wreck."

"If you stay calm, we might be able to get you through this. Live with it. It's just hair."

I took a deep breath. Sex appeal was harder than facing down crazed terrorists, and I would know it for certain since I'd already done that.

"Okay. What do I do next?"

"Did you do your homework?"

I nodded. "I watched *Goldfinger* in its entirety and paid special attention to Pussy Galore's mannerisms, behaviors and words. Just as you instructed."

"Good. So, why don't you show me some of what you saw?" She sat on the couch and watched me expectantly.

I closed my eyes and imitated some of the things I'd seen the Bond girl do on the screen. I sashayed across the room, wiggled my hips, flipped my hair and cocked a hand on my hip before purring, "So, how was that, James?"

Ursula looked at me in astonishment. "How'd you do that?"

"Um, I have an excellent visual memory?"

"Now you tell me? Sit down, shut up and watch me. Memorize my every move and gesture, just like you did for the movie. Okay?"

"Okay."

Ursula began dancing. She slid her hands up and down her sides, strutted forward, bent over provocatively and whipped her hair around until I thought it might fly off her head. Lifting one leg high in the air, she slid her hands down it and then twirled around and pretended to hump an imaginary pole. It all seemed pointless, but no more than say, the Ride the Elephant in the Wind position I'd read about in the *Kama Sutra*.

"Okay, you try." She sat next to me on the couch. "Now remember, you are the woman who *will* seduce James Bond."

I stood and went to the middle of the living room. Closing my eyes, I remembered what she had done, in what order and how. I added in the mannerisms as often as I could. I took it step by step and was gratified when she rose and clapped madly when I finished.

"This is a heaven-sent stroke of luck. You're not half-bad when you do that visualizing thing."

"I'm not?"

"Well, the point is I've got something to work with. Anyway, your next homework assignment is to come to the club tomorrow night and watch me and the other girls dance. You'll get to see all the moves and then you can *visually* pick and choose what you think will work to heighten your confidence." She scrawled an address down on a scrap of paper and pressed it into my hand.

"Sounds easy."

"It will be." That's when she noticed the *Kama Sutra* lying open on the couch. "Are you going to visualize that?"

"I'm trying. But it doesn't seem scientifically to scale."

She laughed. "I'm *so* not the voyeuristic type, but I swear I'd pay good money to see you in action."

I shrugged. "I'm not judgmental. Whatever mode floats your code."

Chapter Ten

I got to the office bright and early the next morning. I'd read through my email and was just about to log in to the STRUT chat room when Basia came bounding in.

"I got an excellent progress report from Ursula," she said. "Now, that's the quick study I know."

"We have to work fast. Finn invited me to dinner at his place on Friday. It's his birthday."

"Ooooh. That's the best news I've heard all week. I cannot *wait* to hear the details."

I told her what had happened in the utility closet and she clapped her hands when I told her I'd kissed Finn first.

"I really did spend every penny wisely."

After she left, I sipped my stone-cold coffee and logged in to the STRUT chat room. Just a few people chatting about something off-topic. I didn't have an email from Elvis either, so I supposed neither Grok nor RawMode had made an appearance last night. I was just standing up to go get some more coffee when my phone rang.

"Carmichael."

"Hey, Lexi," said Elvis. "Got some news for you."

"Be still my beating heart."

"I did a little hacking of my own last night. Between the STRUT chat room and GURPS Robots, I came up with something interesting."

I felt absurdly touched that Elvis had spent a considerable bit of his own free, not to mention super valuable, time working on this for me. "Really?"

"Yeah. MasterNano last played GURPS from an ID in the same area as Grok last logged in to the STRUT chat room. Just shot the particulars your way if you want to go a bit more on it."

I felt my heart leap. "That's great, Elvis. You are totally the bomb. I owe you big."

"I'll keep it in mind."

I printed off the info from Elvis, perched my glasses on my nose and paused. To hack or not to hack? I really needed this information and time was of the essence. It would be extremely risky to do a hack right here from X-Corp and even riskier to do it from my own work station. But jeez, it had to be done and *now*.

My mind made up, I gathered the materials and went to a guest office. In the highly unlikely event I got traced, no one could pin the hack directly on me. Nonetheless, X-Corp would suffer, so whatever I did, I'd have to do it perfect.

As soon as I got started, I felt the rush of adrenaline I always got when beginning a significant hack. I couldn't help but savor each stroke, each moment.

"Better than sex, baby." I remembered Finn's kiss in the closet. "Well, maybe."

I spent double the usual effort and time hopping around, making sure I couldn't be tagged. Then, once I felt secure, I started digging.

The digging is the sweet part, the addictive pull. I

loved it and realized just how much I missed it. When I hacked, it was me and the virtual world and no one else.

I wasn't sure how long I'd been at it when I finally found what I was looking for.

"Bingo."

As I had suspected, both internet IDs came from the exact same location in Cambridge.

"Come to Mommy." I zeroed in on a street address.

Once I had the address, it was a piece of cake to find out who lived there. The name hit me like a ton of bricks.

"Dr. Yan Gu. GU. It wasn't Georgetown University at all."

I looked up all the information I could find on Dr. Yan Gu. He'd been a faculty member on staff at MIT for eighteen years, single, no children. Not surprisingly, he taught artificial intelligence and nanotechnology. He'd done undergraduate study at Georgetown University, medical school at Johns Hopkins in Baltimore and doctoral work at MIT. He had an impressive online body of work including eighty-two scientific articles and papers ranging from nanotechnology in medicine, to biometrics and even the future of synthetic chemistry. Another search turned up a popular series of articles on the dangers of nanotechnology. Clearly a kindred spirit in nanothought with Darren Greening.

I printed out a bunch of materials, ready to take them to Finn when an interesting notation caught my eye. I'd printed out an online photo of Yan Gu during his doctoral days at The Johns Hopkins School of Medicine in Baltimore and was startled to see the man standing next to him in the photo identified as Gene Hart.

"Michael's dad?"

Gathering up all the papers, I shoved them into a manila folder and walked down the hall to Finn's office. Glinda prissily informed me he was on the phone, but Finn saw me through his glass window and waved me in. Trying not to gloat too much, I strode past her desk and into the office, shutting the door behind me. Finn finished up his conversation and waved me to a chair.

"What's up?"

"I think this case has blown wide open."

I quickly filled him in on all the details, passing him some of the materials on Dr. Gu. Finn's eyes grew wide at the mention that Gene Hart and Yan Gu might have been acquaintances back at Johns Hopkins University.

Finn jotted some notes on a pad of paper. "I think this requires another visit to Gene Hart. It might be useful to see if we can discover a connection."

"I think Darren might be hiding at Gu's place. But if he has Gu to trust, why does he need me?"

"No idea. You've never met Dr. Gu?"

"Not to my knowledge. I've never been to MIT either."

"Okay. Let's talk to Gene Hart first and then we'll see if we can't arrange a meeting with Dr. Gu. You see if you can find Ben and let him know where we are on things. Ideally Gene can see us right away and we can move quickly on this."

I left his office, smirked at Glinda and headed over to Ben's side of the building. He listened to my rundown and let me know he might have something for us on NanoLab by the end of the day. I'd just left his office when I nearly collided with Finn in the hallway.

He steadied me by grasping my elbow. "Gene can see us now. Let's go."

We walked quickly to the garage and hopped into

Finn's Jag. It took us about thirty minutes to reach
Gene's townhouse in Manassas. We walked up to the
front door but before we could ring the bell, it opened.
"Have you found Darren yet?" His face was lined with
worry as he ushered us in.

Finn shook his head. "No, sorry. But I think we may
be close. That's why we wanted to talk to you as soon
as possible."

"Please come in and sit down."

Gene ushered us into a neatly arranged living room
with two couches placed strategically in front of the fireplace. "Can I get you something to drink?"

"No thanks," Finn said for the both of us. "What we'd
really like to do is talk to you about a possible acquaintance of yours."

"Acquaintance?"

"Yes," Finn replied. "By the name of Yan Gu."

"Yan? What does he have to do with anything?"

"So, you know him?"

"Why, sure. We were classmates at Johns Hopkins.
Then about three, maybe four years ago, he did a special three-week seminar on nanomechanics at Georgetown University. Darren and Michael both took it. The
boys were quite taken by him, so I invited him over to
dinner once or twice. Is this relevant?"

"Maybe," Finn said.

"Did Darren come to these dinners, too?" I asked.

Gene frowned as if trying to remember. "I think so.
I can't be certain."

"You've had no further contact with him since then?"

"No. Should I have?"

"No, it's okay." Finn stood up. "You've been very
helpful."

"Well, if it helps to locate Darren, then I'm happy to have helped."

Finn motioned for me to go past him toward the door, so I did. But I stopped abruptly at a small table with framed photographs, causing Finn to bump into the back of me. Snatching up a frame, I waved it at Gene Hart.

"Who's in this photograph?"

"Why, Michael and me. It was taken about four years ago in front of his dorm at Georgetown University."

Holy crap.

I was such an idiot. I'd expended gobs of time and focus on Darren Greening at the expense of ignoring Michael Hart. At the time, my reasoning had been sound. Michael was dead and Finn had taken care of talking to his father. It had been a colossal mistake on my part.

"Lexi?" Finn touched my shoulder. "What is it?"

I put the photo down gently. "Crap. I get it now. I didn't know Darren Greening, Finn. I never did. But I knew Michael Hart."

Chapter Eleven

"It's a huge technical error," I said as we climbed into the Jag. "I should have checked out Michael Hart myself."

"It's not your fault. Michael was dead and I assigned you Darren Greening. Besides, it was Darren, not Michael, that fingered you in the note. How'd you know Michael?"

"We met at a party following a lecture on nanophotonics several years ago. I think we met only that one time. I didn't remember his name, but I remember his face."

"Do you recall what you talked about?"

My face heated. "Not exactly."

"So, how does your connection to Michael Hart play into things here?"

"I don't know yet. But I remember we exchanged email addresses, which would explain how Darren got it. Give me a bit more time to think about it."

He gunned the Jag through an intersection. "Okay, think hard and fast. As soon as we get back to the office I'm going to see if Dr. Gu is willing to see us tomorrow. We'll fly up there and meet him. I want to know if Gu knows something."

When we got back, I went to my office and sat down,

putting my head on the desk. Jeez, I was screwed and I meant that both literally and figuratively.

How could it be that Michael Hart, my one and only sexual encounter, was now front and center in X-Corp's first case? How would I explain to Finn and Ben my only connection to Michael Hart was my virginity? I sure as heck didn't want us all to sit around and explore the ramifications of my one-night stand and the embarrassing fact I hadn't even remembered his name.

I wanted to throw up.

When Finn strode into my office, I lifted my head and valiantly plastered a smile on my face.

"Dr. Gu agreed to see us tomorrow." Thankfully he didn't seem to notice my I'm-sick-at-heart look. "I'm having Glinda book us on a flight up to Boston tomorrow morning bright and early. Hopefully, we'll be back in time for that dinner at my place in the evening."

I swallowed hard. "Yeah. That would be great."

"Any luck remembering more about Hart?"

"I'm working on it."

He stood. "Good. I'm off in an hour to meet with those potential investors. I suggest you turn in early and get some sleep. I'll pick you up about six in the morning, so we can make our seven-forty flight."

"Okay," I agreed. Guess I wouldn't tell him about my plans for the strip club tonight.

At four-thirty I left the office and reluctantly headed for Shay's Hair Salon. I wasn't happy about it, but right now my life was in the crapper anyway. Following Ursula's advice, I sat down, shut up and let Karen work her so-called magic. I kept my eyes closed the entire time, not wanting to know what she was doing to me. When she was finished, I took a deep breath and opened my eyes.

It wasn't as bad as I had thought it would be. She'd cut my hair just a little bit, sort of angling it in the front so it framed my cheeks. It seemed kind of puffy and girly, but it wasn't awful. The highlights, on the other hand, were another story.

"It looks kind of streaky." I examined the chunks of blond.

"It's the rage. You look amazing."

"I look like a cross between a girl surfer and a skunk."

She laughed. "Ursula said you'd be a tough customer. You look fine, sweetie. Now it's time for the bikini wax. I'll make this as quick and painless as possible. Trust me."

What else could I do? Reminding myself change was good and I was strong enough to handle it, I followed her.

She led me to a small room with a long, cushioned table covered by several plush yellow towels. Several scented candles had been lit about the room, casting warm shadows on the walls.

"Take off your clothes from the waist down and lie down on the table," she instructed, pressing a button on a stereo. The soothing sounds of waves lapping against a shore filled the room.

I hesitated. "Um, why do I have to undress from the waist down? I mean, it's November and I'm not planning on wearing a bikini any time soon. I think we can safely skip this part."

"You want to impress this man of yours, right?"

"Yes. But not if it involves a bikini. We're just having dinner."

Karen pointed a finger at the table. "Ursula warned me I might have to get tough. Look, I've got my orders so park it, sister. Now."

"Fine. No need to go all commando." I unsnapped my jeans and pulled everything off. I gingerly hopped up onto the towels, feeling weird with my naked nether regions on full display. "Is now a good time to ask what exactly a bikini wax entails?"

She pressed me back onto the table and laid a warm washcloth against my privates. "No."

"Is there ever going to be a good time?"

"No."

"That's what I thought," I moaned, staring at the ceiling. "This doesn't involve pain, does it?"

She was ominously silent, doing something behind my head so I couldn't see what it was.

My stomach started doing weird, nervous flips. "Will it take long?"

"I sure hope not. Now I need you to hold as still as possible."

I gasped as she dropped a warm goopy substance in the crevice where my thigh connected to my pubic bone.

"What's that?" My heart started beating fast. I wasn't going to like this.

"Wax." She showed me a white strip of cloth. "I'm going to press this against your pubic area and pull out the hair."

"What?" I screeched. "What do you mean by *pull?*"

Before I could draw a breath, she'd pressed down the cloth and *rrrriiiip,* up came the hair. And up came me.

I screamed at the top of my lungs. "Mary, Mother of God!"

Karen had apparently anticipated my reaction because she was ready for me. Although she wasn't more than five foot three, she moved like a linebacker. She wrestled me back onto the table and pinned me in place until my breathing returned to a semi-normal state.

"Let me up." Tears filled my eyes. "I'll give you a hundred-dollar tip."

She reached over with one hand and turned up the music. Loud. "Sorry. It's a matter of professional honor. I gave my word I'd do you right."

I wasn't too proud to beg. "Two hundred. Please."

About ten strips and lots of screaming later, she was finished and I was a trembling, shaking mess. She rubbed some special ointment on me and permitted me to sit up. I nearly rolled off the table, but managed to get my feet under me.

"Don't use any perfumed soaps." She took a clean strip and wiped it across her forehead where I noticed she was sweating profusely. I gingerly pulled on my undies and jeans.

Leading me out the door, she pointed to another room nearby. "That's the recovery room," she said. "Aromatic therapy, spiced chai and relaxation music if you need some down time before driving home."

I'd already been in the salon three hours and there was no way I was spending a moment more in the torture salon. I paid up, giving Karen just over a fifteen-percent tip against my better judgment, and got out of there as quickly as I could.

I headed home, cranky because my hair smelled like flowers, my private area felt like a hundred bees had stung me, and I was starving. The minute I got home, I took four ibuprofen, swallowing them at the same time. Opening a can of chicken noodle, I heated it on the stove while slathering some saltine crackers with peanut butter and eating them standing up at the counter. After I finished my wretched dinner, I went online and spent the next several hours reacquainting myself with Michael Hart.

It turned out over my four years at Georgetown, we'd had seven classes together, but I'd never noticed him in any of them. Not that I was big on noticing people in the first place, but there you have it. I racked my brains and I'm certain we had exactly one conversation during the post-lecture party on nanophotonics followed by an utterly forgettable sexual encounter. Now I wondered if everyone had been wrong about the possible sexual relationship between Darren and Michael. Maybe Michael had been experimenting or maybe he'd never been gay. More ominous, perhaps our sexual experience had somehow turned Michael off women from that point on. That was a seriously depressing thought, although I suppose in all actuality, it didn't matter much at this point except to my now at-an-all-time-low sexual confidence.

But it did connect me in a peripheral way to Darren Greening. If Michael had talked about me, this might have been Darren's way of searching for a kindred soul with a person we both had in common. He trusted me because he had no one else to trust.

By ten o'clock, the pain in my private area had almost completely subsided. Grateful, I stuffed some cash, my driver's license and keys into my jeans pockets, logged off my laptop and checked the address for the club where Ursula worked. I more or less knew the area, so I got there a bit earlier than I expected. The club was located in an interesting part of Jessup. There were several gentlemen's clubs and X-rated bookstores along the street, but just one block away stood the imposing silhouette of St. John's Catholic Church, Jessup's oldest structure.

I know there had been many protests and complaints over the years of the proximity of the X-rated area to a house of God, but so far, nothing had changed, and life continued.

I double-checked the address and pulled into the parking lot in front of a red-and-black building. The lot was completely full and I had to circle twice before someone vacated. When I walked to the front of the club, I noticed the neon sign for the club: Boobie and Bush Bar. I hunched my shoulders and pulled the collar of my coat up against my cheeks. Jeez, I hoped I wouldn't run into anyone I knew.

The bar was crammed with men and stank to high heaven of sweat, alcohol and smoke. Waitresses dressed in super short shorts and bras carried trays above their heads through the teeming mass. A dark-lit stage held two women gyrating against an iron pole to the grinding beat of a song. While I watched in surprise, a young guy, clearly drunk, half crawled on the stage and shoved some bills into one of the women's panties before being dragged away by what looked like a four-hundred-pound bouncer.

I seriously considered backing out of there when the bouncer made his way directly for me. His bald head gleamed unnaturally in the light and his arms were the size of small tree trunks. I had decided to scream and make a run for it when he grabbed my arm.

"Are you Lexi Carmichael?"

My breath hitched in my throat. "How'd you know?"

He smiled and I noticed he was missing two of his bottom teeth. "We don't get many female customers here. Ursula said you'd be coming. She wants to see you backstage."

"Okay." As if I had a choice. He dragged me through the crowd, once or twice actually lifting me off my feet until we reached a door at the side of the stage. He knocked three short times then two more in rapid succession before it opened.

"I've got Ursula's friend here." He shoved me into the opening. Someone reached out, pulled me in and slammed the door shut.

"Sorry," a woman dressed in a black bra with red tassels said to me. Her blond hair was piled high on her head. "Sometimes the men out there can be such jerks. I'm Susan." She held out a hand. "Glad you're here, Lexi. You're just in time."

I was just about to ask what I was in time for when Ursula rushed toward me. Tonight, she was dressed in a bright yellow bra and undies with black stockings.

"Thank goodness, you came," she said. "We need you to fill in for Michelle tonight."

"What?" I screeched as she thrust something purple and silky at me.

"We're desperate, Lexi. Michelle's baby is really sick. We've got another girl coming in to help, but she can't get here for a half hour. Look, Michelle desperately needs this job. She already missed yesterday. Hank will can her if she misses tonight. We need you to cover for her. Please, I beg you."

I stepped back in horror. "You're joking, right? Me? No, no, no. Absolutely not."

"This is not a yes or no situation. There is a young girl's job at stake here. You can do this. It's dark and you're about Michelle's height. We'll add this mask to your costume to hide your face." She held up a purple velvet eye mask. "Hank won't even know she's missing.

Just walk around on the stage like you did in your living room. You'll go on third and stay out for about seven minutes. Seven minutes. I swear, that's all. Susan will be out there, too, so you won't be alone."

I held my hand out like a stop sign. "I hope you're not offended when I say there is absolutely no way I'm going on that stage."

"For heaven's sake, Lexi, it's for a baby. Seven minutes of your life to help out a young girl and her baby."

I started to hyperventilate. How could I say no to a baby? "This is the worst idea in the history of worst ideas."

The other girls pressed around, urging me to help.

"Wait." I covered my mouth. "I think I might be sick. That happens when I get really nervous."

The girls backed off. Right at that moment the door slammed open and a fat guy with a cigar clamped between his teeth strode in.

"What's going on back here?" he shouted. "Tawny and Tickle are dancing three minutes over their set. Ursula and Tina, get on stage. *Now!*"

Ursula and Tina scrambled out onto the stage while the other girls slid in front of me protectively. But the guy noticed me anyway and squinted suspiciously. He shoved the girls out of the way. "Who are you?"

Susan stepped forward. "My sister. She's visiting."

"Well, I don't pay you to visit. And why is she half-dressed? Get back to work and get her out of here." With that he stomped out, slamming the door behind him.

"Great." Susan pulled my shirt off. "Hank's in a foul mood tonight. Do your best, girlfriend. We appreciate it."

I clutched my shirt to my chest like it was my last anchor to the world. "Look, Susan, I'm really sorry, but

I don't think I can do this. Besides, Hank just said he wanted me out of here."

"Don't worry. He says that about everyone."

She yanked the shirt from my hand and slid the purple bra on me, fastening it in the back, ignoring my protests.

"You should know I'm *totally* not cut out for this kind of thing," I protested weakly.

"Honey, you're a woman and that's all we need for tonight. You'll do fine. It's a really good deed you're doing." She handed me a tiny pair of purple undies. "What size shoe are you?"

"Shoe?" I stared at the panties.

Susan was examining my feet. "Wow, you've got big feet. Macy is the only one of us that might have something to fit you."

I kept staring at the panties until another one of the girls came by. She was dressed in a schoolgirl uniform with fishnet stockings. I would have eaten the panties if she were a day over eighteen.

She gave me a shy smile. "Thanks for doing this. Michelle is my best friend and she loves her baby so much. If she didn't have this job, she'd have to turn tricks. It's really nice of you to fill in until Jody gets here."

"Jeez," I moaned.

Susan rushed back with a pair of mile-high black shoes. "Hurry, Lexi. Please. You're up next."

I exhaled a deep breath. Telling myself it was for the baby, I slipped out of my plain white underwear, tennis shoes and socks. I slid on the panties, careful not to brush the area where I'd gotten the bikini wax. The panties covered exactly diddley in the back and barely diddley in the front. I wasn't even sure it was legal. My breath was coming so fast I thought I might pass out.

Before I could stop her, Susan helped me into the shoes. Then she swiped some blood-red lipstick across my lips, fluffed my hair and slipped the mask on my face.

We reached the side of the stage. I saw Ursula look over at us and smile in relief. Just then a waitress walked by the stage below us with a tray held high. Bending over, I snatched a glass of amber liquid and downed most of it in one gulp.

Susan looked at me in surprise. "Do you drink?"

"Not much." The alcohol burnt a trail down my esophagus.

"I was afraid of that," Susan said, pulling me out on stage. Ursula gave me a hug as we passed, whispering, "Be the perfect Bond girl. Be strong. Go conquer those Bonds."

"Agghhh," I muttered, thankful at least Susan was out there with me.

It might have been my imagination, but I swear the sound in the club lowered about six decimals and it seemed like every eye in the room was on me. That's when I realized Susan had started dancing and I was just standing there like a frozen idiot.

I quickly started moving my hips like I'd seen Ursula do. It didn't feel at all natural and it seemed to me that the bar had become even quieter. My heart was racing so fast, I was having trouble breathing. Susan sashayed up to me and hissed, "Relax."

I strutted forward a couple of steps and grabbed the pole. Closing my eyes, I visualized Ursula in my living room, whipping her head around and sliding up and down the pole. I shook my head, my streaked hair flying all over the place, and in the process banged my ear on the pole. Thankfully, the sound was muffled, on account of the overly loud music, but for a moment I saw stars. I'd started to feel light-headed, maybe from acute anxiety, the bang to my head, the alcohol or all three in combination. I tried to hold it together and leaned backward provocatively (I hoped) still holding on to the pole. I lifted my leg to the ceiling and gyrated. I had no clue if this was appropriate and since it was dark, I couldn't tell if the patrons were frowning or smiling. Couldn't hear any booing.

Yet.

Unfortunately, my hands were slick and before I could bring my leg back to the ground, I lost my grip on the pole. I half fell, half slid to the stage, bashing my butt on the floor with a loud unladylike thump. For a second I froze in horror. Then, in a moment of inspired desperation, I laid flat on the stage, lifting both my legs up in the air and crossing them back and forth like scissors. I hadn't seen Ursula do this, but I think I'd witnessed something like this once in a yoga demonstration.

I did this frantically until the room erupted in loud cheering. Surprised, I sat up and positioned one high heel beneath me to stand up. That's when I realized someone had spilled something on the stage. Before I could get my other foot under me, I started to slide like a greased pig right toward the edge of the stage.

I had time to give one horrified yelp before I slid off the stage and onto the nearest table. My butt hit something wet and gooey and my elbow overturned a glass directly onto the lap of a chubby guy wearing a Hawaiian shirt. Still in motion, my body slammed into him, my knee wedging somewhere in the vicinity of his throat.

The breath knocked out of me with a sickening

whoosh and the ceiling whirled. After I blinked a couple of times, I saw the bald bouncer come into focus as his face loomed over mine. With amazingly little effort, he extracted my knee from the chubby guy's neck and lifted my butt back on stage, dumping me there like a sack of potatoes.

Mortified I managed to stand up and saw the entire club had gone wild. Guys were pumping their fists in the air and chanting something at me. My head spun.

Task her?

Fast girl?

What the heck were they saying?

Mask Girl. They were calling me Mask Girl.

Scared, I started to back up toward the side of the stage. Surely my seven minutes were up. I'd done my duty and saved Michelle's job. I'd helped a baby in need. I deserved a freaking medal.

That's when I heard Hank shouting at me, "Michelle! You stay on stag*e!*"

He had climbed onto the stage and now blocked the exit at side stage. Crossing his arms against his chest, he practically dared me to try to get past him. I shot a frantic glance at Ursula, who stood next to Hank looking as if she were in shock and staring at me like I was an alien from Mars. Maybe I was.

I started to hyperventilate again. I had to go home right now or else I would pass out. Once I fell unconscious, an ambulance would come to remove my body, the police would raid the club and arrest the young schoolgirl for underage dancing, Michelle would lose her job and become a prostitute, and my mother would disown me after having to be hospitalized for massive heart failure.

I started to see black around the edge of my vision when Ursula and another girl came to my rescue. They pushed past a surprised Hank and onto center stage, starting a very sexy dance together. The guys began to cheer and yell at the girls, taking the spotlight, at least temporarily, off me. I frantically tried to figure a way to get the heck out of there when I saw a dark-haired man moving methodically through the crowd to the front of the stage. As he got closer to the stage light, I saw it was Slash. I had no idea what he was doing here, but I had never been happier in my life to see him.

I almost started crying when he smiled and held out his arms. He mouthed one word.

Jump.

Without wasting another second, I ran to the edge of the stage and jumped into his arms. I almost knocked both of us to the floor, but, somehow, he held steady. At first I felt a hundred hands grabbing at me. Then Slash said something I couldn't quite make out, wrapped an arm around me tightly and pulled me through the crowd. Whatever he said apparently did the trick or he gave off a dangerous vibe because, to my everlasting relief, everyone left us alone. We exited the club and stood on the sidewalk where he promptly gave me his leather jacket. His holstered gun was now on obvious display but I was freezing to death. I shivered as I slipped it on and he pulled me close, rubbing my back. The jacket only covered my upper body and my butt was literally hanging in the wind, but I appreciated the gesture.

"You constantly surprise me," he said after a minute. "And you smell like nachos."

My teeth started to chatter as I looked down at my

high-heeled feet which had cheese sauce on them. "I think I slid into a plate of them."

"I'm not sure what I should say to that."

"Aren't you wondering why I'm in a strip club?"

"Actually, I'm beyond intrigued. But I warn you, I have quite an active imagination—one that you seem to enrich on a regular basis."

I hiccupped a sob. "Oh, no. I don't even know what that means. Could this night get any worse?"

"Lexi?"

I glanced up and saw a dark shape hurrying down the sidewalk toward me. I squinted, wondering if I now needed glasses for everyday life, when the shape came sharply into focus. I inhaled a sharp gasp.

"Father Mulrooney?"

"Lexi?" he repeated, staring at me in surprise and disbelief.

"Aaaahh." I clutched the jacket tighter to my chest, wanting to run shrieking back into the club, but I was frozen in mortified shock and indecision.

"What are you doing here?" He glanced up at the flashing neon sign that read Boobie and Bush Bar.

I discreetly tried to tug the jacket lower to cover my purple panties, but it wasn't helping much. Why couldn't Slash have worn a trench coat?

"What am I doing here?" I repeated in an unnaturally loud voice. "As in *right* here? I...ah...um..."

Father Mulrooney looked between Slash and me, and everywhere else except below my waist. I wanted to die. Really. Just pack it up and end it all. What was the point of going on?

After a minute of the most awkward silence in the history of the universe, Father Mulrooney cleared his throat. "Well, I'm here because I was visiting an old friend's mum who lives out here near St. John's. The bus stop is down this way."

"It's…ah, nice to see you. Done any crossword puzzles lately?"

He didn't reply.

"Okay, I know this looks bad. Not even nominally bad, but horribly, awfully, disgustingly bad. But it's not what you think at all. There is a perfectly innocent explanation."

"Alright." I could tell he didn't believe me.

"See, there's this girl named Michelle. She has a baby and would lose her job. She didn't want to be a prostitute, so I thought I could help her and the baby. It was all for the baby. Technically, I was only here to watch. I mean, I didn't really *want* to watch, but it was my homework and then I…"

Slash sighed and took the father's arm, pulling him to one side and out of my earshot. They spoke quietly for several minutes with the father occasionally glancing my way. I shifted back and forth on my high heels, my legs and butt literally freezing, but I didn't dare interrupt. After a while, Father Mulrooney waved at me and detoured into the parking lot toward a black SUV.

I clutched Slash's arm when he came back to me. "What did you say to him?"

"It doesn't matter."

"It matters to me."

Slash slid an arm around me, pulling me close. His breath was hot on my cheek. "I told him you were working undercover."

I stopped and considered for a moment. "Oh, good.

That's really good. Except I'm a computer geek for Finn's company. Why would I be dressed like a stripper?"

"Sorry, that's classified information."

"That's good, too. I'd buy it, but Father Mulrooney is no fool."

"No, he's not. That's why deep down he figures there really is a good explanation for your appearance. *Cara,* don't worry. He doesn't make you for a stripper, a lady of the evening, or even sexually loose."

"Really? You convinced him of that?"

"I didn't convince him of anything. He's a man of the cloth. I assure you, he can see more deeply to the truth than you and me. However, I also promised to take him home, so let me walk you to your car now."

"Okay, but my keys are in my jeans in the club."

He reached into his pants pocket and pulled out two keys. As he dangled them in front of me, I looked at him suspiciously. "You have a key to my car?"

"*Cara,* I have the key to your car *and* your apartment. I have the key to many things."

Deciding I really didn't want to try to figure out that cryptic statement, I sighed and took the keys. We started moving toward my car when it occurred to me I had no idea how he'd even known I'd been at the bar. "What are you doing here, Slash? Were you following me?"

"I needed to talk with you. We think you know where Darren Greening is."

I shook my head. "Sorry. I'd help you if I could. But proprietary information and all."

"I know, *cara.* I just wanted to remind you that we're on the same side, *si?*"

"Okay." We reached my car. "And, Slash, thank you. I mean it."

To my surprise, he abruptly reached over, unzipped his jacket and pulled it open. I started to shrug out of it, but he stopped me with a hand on my shoulder. Instead, he gave me such a long and thorough perusal I thought I would die of embarrassment.

"Did you get a bikini wax?"

I had thought I couldn't be any more embarrassed this night, but I was wrong. Did the entire world have to know all my freaking secrets?

Before I could say anything, he zipped the jacket back up.

"Keep it. I'll collect it later."

Without another word, I climbed into my car, removed the offensive heels and drove home. I staggered into my apartment, so beyond exhausted that I didn't even bother to brush my teeth. Instead, I fell fast asleep, face-first, on top of the covers still wearing the lipstick, my purple bra and a pair of barely-there panties.

Chapter Twelve

I woke in a panic when I heard the incessant knocking on my door. Letting out a shocked gasp, I glanced at the clock and saw it was six-thirty in the morning.

Crap.

I'd forgotten to set the alarm and now I was later than late. "Oh, crap."

Racing to the door, I threw it open. "Oh, Finn, I'm so sorry." I reached out and yanked him into the apartment. "I overslept. It will just take me five minutes to get dressed. I'm an idiot."

I started to run back to the bedroom before turning around and dashing back. "Oh, I almost forgot, happy birthday."

That's when I realized Finn stood staring open-mouthed at me, his eyes about popping out of his head. "Do you always sleep like that?"

I looked down, realizing I was still dressed in my stripper outfit. "Agggh. No. Never. Holy cow, let me go change."

I raced back to the bedroom and stripped off the bra and panties. As I headed into the bathroom, I stopped in surprise. Folded neatly on a chair near the bed was my sweater, T-shirt, jeans and underclothes from last night. My tennis shoes with socks tucked inside were beneath the chair and my keys and driver's license sat atop my underwear.

Slash.

Far more disturbing was the fact that his leather jacket had been picked off the couch in the living room where I'd tossed it and now hung perfectly on the back of the chair where my clothes were folded. That didn't make any sense to me. If Slash had been here, why didn't he just take his jacket home?

Realizing I didn't have time to ponder the implications of this, I quickly brushed my teeth, washed my face and pulled my hair back in a long straight ponytail. I took a moment to wash my butt and feet of the nacho remnants that had dried on them before dragging on a pair of jeans and a baby-blue blouse. On the way out, I shoved my feet into a pair of shoes and grabbed my keys, a navy-blue blazer and my purse.

"I really am sorry, Finn," I said as we exited the apartment. "I know this is important and I'm not normally so scatterbrained."

"Did you do something different to your hair?"

My cheeks flamed. "Um, sort of. I'd rather not talk about it, if you don't mind."

Finn looked like he was going to say something, but instead, closed his mouth and put his hand in the small of my back, guiding me toward his Jag.

During our ride to the airport, Finn asked me again about my connection to Michael Hart. I told him I hadn't *exactly* figured it all out yet. Technically, that was true. We then rehashed some of the finer points of the case, but didn't really come up with anything new. I waited until we got to the airport and through security to buy a bottle of water and take two ibuprofen for my pounding headache. Whatever alcohol I'd consumed had definitely not agreed with me.

Once on the airplane, Finn amused me by telling me about his evening escapades with Colin. They mostly involved Colin trying to attract the attention of a woman he wanted to meet at a bar, including purposely spilling a drink on her. Their antics were *totally* tame compared to mine of the previous evening, but there was no way I was about to enlighten him on that. I only prayed Father Mulrooney wouldn't either.

Thankfully, the flight was smooth and on time. Finn had rented a car in advance, so once we landed in Boston we were able to quickly pick up the rental car and head out to Dr. Gu's place, using the handy-dandy GPS system.

I put on my sunglasses. "You rented a convertible?"

"Cars are my weakness. No point in spending time in a car if you aren't going to be comfortable."

"But it's November and we're in Boston. So, what's the point of a convertible?"

"It's a bloody lot of fun to drive."

"And, you look good in it, too."

He laughed. "I may deserve that, but I won't apologize for it."

"No apology necessary." I sighed, easing back into the plush leather seat. "I think I'm getting spoiled."

We listened to the jazz station on the way to Dr. Gu's house and before long we arrived at a neatly kept two-story brownstone. A car was parked in the driveway, which I assumed meant Gu was home.

Finn rang the bell and after a minute, a distinguished-looking Asian man opened the door. He wore tan slacks and a white shirt with a dark brown cardigan sweater. His trimmed beard held more than a hint of gray, but I noticed his eyes sparkled with interest.

"You must be Mr. Shaughnessy and Ms. Carmichael." He ushered us inside.

"Yes," Finn answered. "Thanks for seeing us on such short notice."

We followed him into a study completely lined with bookshelves. A gorgeous oak desk stood as the room centerpiece. Dr. Gu had lit a fire in the hearth and motioned for Finn and me to sit on a comfortable brown leather couch with burgundy pillows.

He pointed to a tray that held a blue-and-white teapot and three cups and saucers. "Can I offer you some tea?"

"Thank you," I said and Finn also agreed to have some. Dr. Gu poured while I looked around.

Finn picked up his cup and took a sip. "We appreciate you having us. As I mentioned on the phone, we're looking for a young man by the name of Darren Greening. He went missing about two weeks ago. We're worried something may have happened to him."

Dr. Gu leaned forward and put a spoonful of sugar in his tea. "I see. Why, pray tell, do you think I might know anything about his disappearance? Was he one of my students?"

"He attended your class on nanomechanics when you were a guest lecturer at Georgetown University several years ago. He was friends with the son of one of your old classmates from Johns Hopkins—Gene Hart."

"Ah. Gene Hart. Yes, his son named Michael passed away in a car accident not too long ago if I remember correctly. Horrible tragedy."

"We're not so sure it was an accident," I said. "That's

why we're worried about Darren. He and Michael were working on some pretty radical energy-replacement nanotechnology."

"Hmm…is that so? Still, I'm afraid my connection to Darren Greening seems pretty tenuous."

I opted for the element of surprise. "Do you belong to STRUT?"

I saw the shock in his eyes, but he hid it quickly. "I assume you are referring to the Society for the Responsible Use of Technology?"

"Yes."

"I am a member."

"Do you ever use the chat room?"

"Occasionally."

"Do you have a call name?"

"I actually have more than one."

Finn fell silent, letting me take charge of the conversation and for once, I was glad. I realized it had come down to whether or not Dr. Gu would trust me. I hoped he would.

"Would RawMode be one of those call names?"

"And if I said yes?"

"Then I'd tell you I'm CryptHead."

He laughed. "So, I thought. You are clever, Ms. Carmichael. How did you find me?"

"I hacked in to your profile in the STRUT chat room."

"I assure you, there is no useful information there."

"True. But I managed to trace your internet provider."

"Ah, good thinking."

I shrugged. "It was more interesting to me that I traced Grok to this ID as well."

"Fascinating. I take it you assume I know Grok as more than someone in a chat room."

"He used your provider at this exact location. I'd say it's a reasonable assumption."

He paused for a moment, setting down his teacup with great care onto his saucer. "He knew you'd find him."

I held my breath, feeling Finn tense beside me. "Darren?"

"Yes."

"Do you know where he is?"

"Yes."

When he didn't extrapolate, I asked, "Here? In your house?"

Dr. Gu shook his head. "No. Darren is not that careless. He wants to see you, Ms. Carmichael. That's why he left a trail. I personally thought it too obscure, but now I see I was wrong. He was right about you."

"I hope you mean that in a good way."

He smiled. "Indeed, I do."

I leaned back on the sofa and lifted my hands. "Okay, so what now?"

"Now you meet Darren."

"How?"

Dr. Gu held up a small black cell phone and I looked at it in surprise. "Go outside to your car. In approximately three minutes, Darren will call you with instructions."

I exchanged a long glance with Finn and then reached over and took the phone. Finn and I stood up.

Dr. Gu shook his head at Finn. "I'm sorry, but Ms. Carmichael must go alone."

"No," said Finn.

"But Mr. Shaughnessy is my partner. He's the owner of X-Corp. He's been in on this case from the beginning. If Darren can trust me, he can trust Finn."

"I'm sorry. You must go alone. That's the deal."

I glanced at Finn who had the darkest scowl on his face I'd ever seen. After a moment, he pulled the car key out of his pocket and handed it to me, frowning. "I don't like this."

"I'll be fine. I know how to drive a stick shift."

"Lexi, it's not the car I'm worried about."

"Right." My insides warmed. "Well, don't worry. It's just Darren. I can handle him."

"I still don't like it."

"Unfortunately, it can't be helped." I reached over and shook Dr. Gu's hand. "I hope I can help Darren."

"I do, too." He motioned Finn back to the couch. "I'm sorry it has to be like this, Mr. Shaughnessy, but it really is the safest way."

Finn muttered something in what I think was Gaelic, but I decided not to ask for a translation because I was sure it wasn't polite.

Instead, I walked out to the BMW, started the engine and waited. Three minutes later, the phone rang.

"Darren?" I said, flipping the phone open.

"Lexi?"

"What's going on? Where are you?"

"I need you to get me to safety without being followed."

I turned in the seat of the car and looked out the window. I saw nothing out of place. "Do you think I'm being followed?"

"It's a likely possibility."

"You do realize you're paranoid."

"Absolutely," he said with conviction. "It's kept me alive this long. Hope it keeps me breathing a little bit longer."

"Okay. What's the plan?"

He rattled off instructions and for the next forty minutes, I traveled around Cambridge, sat in parking lots and made so many right turns my head was spinning. Finally, Darren had me park the car and go into a bookstore. Once inside, I quickly exited out the back and made an immediate left that led into an unmarked building. I was mathematically certain there was no way in God's green earth anyone could have followed me.

It turned out the building was an apartment complex and I was told to climb six flights of stairs to room 603. When I got there, I lifted my hand to knock when the door opened and someone pulled me inside, slamming the door shut and bolting it.

"Darren," I said. "Don't worry. No one followed me."

He turned from the door. In his photo, he'd been geeky thin, but now he was pale, gaunt and haunted.

"I knew you'd find me."

I don't know what possessed me, but I walked over to him and gave him a hug. He collapsed in an emotional heap, sobbing on my shoulder. I patted him awkwardly on the back for a few minutes until he could compose himself. After that, we went to sit down together on an old sofa. The scarred coffee table was covered with books, papers and a fancy laptop, most likely the missing one from his apartment.

After a moment, I said, "Well, it's nice to finally meet you."

He fumbled for something in his pocket and pulled out a tissue. "Yeah, it's nice." He wiped his eyes. "Michael used to talk about you."

"Really?" I said, surprised.

"He did. Said you were a prime hacker."

"Well, I used to be, but I'm reformed. Except I had to reengage to find you. You do realize that you caused me to fall off the wagon."

"I'm sorry about that. But I knew you'd find me."

"I'm glad I did. The treasure box helped. The postcard from Mars, the Martian code name Grok, it clicked for me."

He gave a watery smile. "You found the box and made the STRUT connection. I knew you would. I only hoped it wasn't too obvious."

"Obvious? You're lucky I figured it out."

"I'm certain luck had nothing to do with it."

I sighed. "Well, even the Mars to Mars connection might not have been enough. Thankfully, Rudy remembered you played GURPS Robots."

He looked up, surprised. "Rudy from the Lighthouse Cyber Café?"

"Yeah. He mentioned you were a king of the game or something. I checked it out and hypothesized you were the MasterNano, since you've played for so many years. On a hunch, I traced the ID. For the first trace, the originating ID for the account was to a location in the Dulles, Virginia area—your neck of the woods. But when I ran a second trace from the last time you played, two days ago, it led here to Cambridge. That corresponded coincidentally with Grok's location from the STRUT account. After that, Dr. Gu's address was just one more hack away."

"Smart girl."

"Incredibly lucky girl. It was unbelievably risky putting GU front and center. Everyone, myself included, assumed you meant Georgetown University."

"It's all been a big risk. But you're here, so it paid off."

I couldn't argue with that. "So, any chance you're finally going to clue me in on what's going on?"

Darren rubbed his pale cheeks with his hands and leaned back on the cushions. "I'm in a boatload of trouble."

"You don't have to understate the obvious with me."

"I'm alone."

"Not now, you're not."

He shook his head. "I mean, I'm alone in what I must do. You of all people understand what it's like to be different, to stand on the outside of the norm of society."

"Yeah, I do."

"Well, after my folks died, I'd never felt more isolated. Then I met Michael at Georgetown. He became my best friend, my only friend, a kindred spirit. His dad took me under his wing as well. I became happy again and that's when I made my biggest scientific advances. Michael had this amazing head for figures and business, but even better, he also understood the science of what I was doing. We were a perfect match to get Flow off the ground. We just needed some cash to get started."

"Michael's dad provided the start-up capital."

"It was an amazing time, Lexi. Until then, everything had been theoretical. At last we had the chance to put our ideas to the test. But as our research and experiments grew and became wildly successful, we had to expand. We needed more money and staff to continue."

"Enter Niles and company," I said.

"The match seemed good at first. Things were fine until several months ago when Michael and I informed the board that we were at the *earliest* seven to ten years away for a working prototype. To our surprise, Niles was furious."

Darren closed his eyes. "Neither one of us understood why he was so angry about our progress. After all, we were light years ahead of any other corporation on an operational prototype. It didn't compute. So, Michael decided to do some investigating of his own. He hacked into Flow's computer system and subsequently Niles's account and that's when he discovered the company was in serious debt. Niles had apparently led our investors to believe that my energy-replacement prototype was just three to five years out. He needed that prototype soon or we were sunk financially. Both of us were stunned he made such rash promises to investors without even consulting us."

I held up a hand. "Why couldn't Niles just tell the investors the truth? The work you're doing, Darren, well, it's breathtaking in scope. If it works, it will be a scientific breakthrough on a scale the world has never known. For heaven's sake, you could single-handedly save the planet from pollution or eradicate hunger. Why wouldn't the investors be willing to wait a few more years?"

"Money. It's all about money, Lexi. Even if the prototype works, nanotechnology is inherently unstable. It's more than likely the manufacturing process will encounter unforeseen issues that will make it another ten years or longer before anything can be produced on a mass scale. Twenty years or longer is a significant wait to see any cash flow."

"But the science is sound."

"Yes, the science is sound. I assure you, I know what I'm doing and what needs to be done. Perhaps it's a gift or a curse, but for some reason, I'm the one destined to present this technology to the world. It *will* be fruitful... if I live long enough to finish it."

"You're truly in fear for your life?"

Darren nodded. "Michael's death was not an accident. He was murdered."

"You're not the only one who suspects this. We did our own checking and the accident seems suspicious. The government agrees."

He looked up in surprise. "The government?"

"Yes. They are looking for you, too, Darren. They've caught wind of the progress of your research and are naturally interested."

"We have a spy at Flow. He's been reporting on my progress. I don't know if he's reporting on me to another company or to the government, but Flow itself is no longer secure."

I rolled my neck, trying to loosen the tension knot that had formed there. "Let me guess. You suspect Evan Chang is that spy."

Darren gasped. "How did you know?"

"A hunch. He was visibly nervous talking to me when I interviewed him about you. Besides, it makes sense. He replaced Michael and would have the best understanding, not to mention access, of where you were with the research and development."

"He seemed solid as a scientist, but I didn't trust him."

"You trusted no one," I pointed out.

"Except for you and Dr. Gu."

"Okay. But that still doesn't explain why you are in fear for your life. Industrial or even government espionage is one thing, murder is another. Why would someone murder Michael or you? You're the key to this entire technology—a walking gold mine—despite the fact it could take years. Besides, Flow's investors took out a twenty-five-million-dollar insurance policy to protect you as an intelligence asset. Okay, they may get the twenty-five million if you were to die in a so-called accident, but that's a drop in the bucket in terms of their initial investment not to mention the billions, maybe even trillions, they stand to make if they'd stay with you for the duration. I just don't get it."

Darren leaned forward, clasping his hands between his knees. "Lexi, the investors aren't protecting me and they weren't protecting Michael. They never were. It's all a front. Michael and I...we were sold to the highest bidder."

"Excuse me?"

"Think about it. How many oil-rich countries in the world would pay millions or even billions to stop this technology?"

"Every single one of them. Your work is a serious threat to their livelihood." I paused for a moment, thinking it over. "You mean to say Flow agreed to or is actually a partner in a plan to *assassinate* you?"

"In a way. My death would have to look like an accident, just like Michael's."

"Unthinkable."

"I assure you, it's my reality. As it stands, there have been numerous technical and industrial malfunctions at the lab these past few months. Seeing as how I am pretty much the only one who understands the science of the process in its entirety, I'm also the only one who notices the small imperfections and have managed to avoid any unfortunate accidents. But my work and the lab have been tampered with on numerous occasions, certainly in the hope that I will be killed or seriously harmed."

"Well, that points to Chang as more than just an industrial spy. He's the only one with the science to be able to create such an accident."

"Perhaps. Then again, I don't know who frequents the lab when I'm not there."

I rubbed my temples with my fingertips. "How can you be sure any of this is really true? Not that I don't believe it, it's just easy to get sucked into the paranoia of the moment when under severe stress."

He paused for a moment, turning his serious brown eyes on me. "When Michael hacked into Niles's account he discovered that an oil-rich company was setting up a company in the U.S. to launder and provide funds for Niles that would pay for the hits. That company turned out to be NanoLab."

"Flow's manufacturing company. Why didn't you take this to the authorities?"

"Michael hacked in to Niles's account. None of what we discovered would be admissible in court. Besides, we didn't know who to trust. We didn't know how deep Niles's tentacles ran.

"In fact, we were still trying to figure out what to do when Michael was killed. We hadn't realized the threat was so immediate. For the few months following Michael's death, I was a mess. I barely functioned. They could have easily murdered me then, but they probably needed to wait a decent time before offing me as well. I suppose it would have been highly suspicious if both of us were killed in a matter of weeks."

"Jeez."

"I didn't know what to do, who to turn to. The only person I had left in the world was Michael's dad and the last thing I wanted to do was to endanger him in any way. I had to find someone to help me, someone who could understand what I needed to do. I went first to Dr. Gu because I remembered him from his lectures at

Georgetown and because he was friends with Michael's dad. He gave me a place to stay temporarily, but I needed to find someone with contacts both in the private sector and the government to take me to the next step because I didn't know who to trust."

"You found me."

"Yes, because of Michael. He had a crush on you when we were at Georgetown. Then one night he got drunk enough to make a move. It was his experimental period."

"Experimental?"

"Yes." Darren ran his fingers through his hair and hung his head. "I loved him so much. You have no idea."

The anguish in his voice stabbed at my heart. I reached out and put a hand on his arm. "Darren. You okay?"

He nodded, but didn't lift his head. "Yeah." His hands trembled. "You see, I knew Michael loved me, too, but he needed time to figure things out. You were his first and only sexual experience with a woman. After that, he knew. Just knew. It was the two of us."

I stared at him. What should I say?

"Well, we only…um…met…um, once."

Darren lifted his head. "I know. But the emotional attachment stuck around. He kept tabs on you. He often talked about a spectacular hack you made in one of your classes together. He admired you, Lexi, thought you were ace. I suppose it didn't hurt that you aren't all that bad-looking either, for a geek."

"Thanks. I guess."

"I was a little jealous of the way he followed your career. He knew when you got a job at the NSA. After he died, I checked up on you. You had left the NSA and moved to X-Corp. Then it hit me that if Michael had trusted you, so could I."

"Okay, you've got my full attention. You can trust me. What do you want me to do now, Darren? How can I help?"

He hesitated, considering my words. "I have to continue my research, my work. But it must be supported in the right way by the right people. I'm too paranoid now to figure out how to get the help I need."

I considered for a moment. "Do you have to do your work within the private sector?"

"I can't limit myself anymore. It's too important now."

"Agreed. And lucky for you, I know just the guy."

Chapter Thirteen

It took Slash just under three hours to get to Cambridge. It probably involved a private jet and a car service, but I really didn't care. He was here and he could help Darren. In the meantime, I'd called Finn and assured him I was okay. Darren still refused to meet with anyone other than me and Slash, so Finn had to wait it out—albeit impatiently—at Dr. Gu's place. He sounded inordinately stressed and must have told me a half dozen times to be careful and not to take any chances on anything.

Darren permitted me to order pizza from some local joint he trusted and to my delight he also liked anchovies too. We gorged on pizza and beer while watching reruns of *Jeopardy.* Darren had a perfect record, answering every single question correctly, even those on sports, culture and entertainment.

"You do realize you have a future in game shows if this nanotechnology thing doesn't work out," I'd told him.

I'd almost forgotten the time when I heard the knock on the door. Darren must have leaped a good three feet off the ground.

I walked to the door. "Chill. Slash is a professional. I assure you, he wasn't followed."

Nonetheless, I looked carefully through the keyhole

before I opened the door. It was Slash all right, but I hardly recognized him.

He entered quickly and shut the door behind him. I stared at him in amazement. "Wow. What's with the suit?"

I had never, *ever* seen Slash in anything but jeans or cargo shorts. Now he wore a navy-blue suit with a light blue tie. His long black hair had been slicked back and secured at the neck and he carried a large black duffel bag. He looked amazingly handsome, but it was a more dangerous mafia-hit-man vibe than a nine-to-five-office-worker vibe.

"You like it?"

"It's different."

To my surprise, he pushed past me and lifted a hand in greeting to Darren. "Nice to meet you. Now both of you go to the bathroom."

"Huh?"

He slowly enunciated every word. "You and Darren go to the bathroom."

"Together?"

He rummaged around in his duffel bag. "Yes. And put these on."

He tossed something at each of us. I barely caught mine and Darren's fell at his feet.

"A bullet-proof vest? What's going on, Slash? I thought you said you'd take every precaution not to be followed."

"*Cara,* please just do as I ask. You too, Darren. We are going to protect you and keep you safe. Then we'll talk. But now you must follow my instructions exactly."

Darren looked over at me with wide eyes and I lifted my hands. "I trust him, Darren. I don't have a clue what he's doing, but I really do trust him."

Without a word, Darren picked up the vest and carried it into the bathroom. I followed him and together we managed to get the things on and properly secured. The vest fit me like a cross between a very large padded bra and a life preserver. Darren looked completely swallowed up by his, but to his credit, he didn't say a word. I guess the vests were sized for the average adult, not a couple of skinny geeks like us. I occasionally glanced out the bathroom door and saw Slash lifting the blinds and peeking out and then pacing back and forth across the room, pressing something to his ear.

Darren and I waddled out of the bathroom and Slash nodded approvingly. "Do you have anything essential that must go with you, Darren?"

"My laptop and some papers."

Slash pointed to his duffel. "Put what you need here."

"Thanks, but I've got my own bag."

"Are you going to tell us what's going on?" I watched Darren close his computer and slide it and some papers into a dark green gym bag.

"Not now. No time."

Slash hoisted his bag over his shoulder, Darren grabbed his, and we dutifully lined up at the door. Slash stepped into the hallway first, looked up and down and then motioned for us to follow him out of the room. I had Darren go next and I took up the rear. I didn't know what was going on, but my heart was racing like a jackhammer. On the other hand, Darren seemed eerily calm. Apparently, he'd been preparing for this day for a long time and now that it had arrived, he was able to deal. I hadn't had enough time to prepare and just felt sick to my stomach after all the beer and pizza.

We approached the stairwell and Slash motioned for us to wait in the hall. We pressed back against the wall as he opened the door and disappeared. After a few long moments, the door opened again and Slash indicated we should follow him. I'm sure the idea was to be quiet, but Darren and I lumbered along like whales in our vests. Darren's duffel bag kept banging against the stair rail and every time it thumped, my heart gave a startled jump. We had gone down a couple flights of stairs when I heard a popping noise and the plaster on the wall behind my head disintegrated.

"Go back," Slash yelled at us, crouching in the stairwell and pulling out a gun. "We're under fire."

Darren and I scrambled back up the stairway. The popping and pinging noise intensified.

"Fire as in gunfire?" Darren shouted.

"That would be the winning scenario, so move it."

Darren gasped like a fish out of breath as I dragged him up the stairway. He kept stopping to rummage around in his bag with one hand until I yelled at him to knock it off.

We finally reached Darren's floor and I flung open the door to the stairwell. I nearly collided with a guy dressed in black fatigues that said SWAT across the front of his chest. He held a gun and was apparently startled to see us because he took a step back and gave a shocked yelp.

"Ahhhhhh," I shouted in turn, leaping back into the stairwell and instinctively shielding Darren behind me. "You scared the freaking daylights out of me. Thank goodness, you're here. Someone is shooting at us down there."

He leveled the gun at my head. "*Da.* That would be my partner." He laughed and with one arm made the motion of snapping a neck while making a slicing noise.

I shrieked. "Oh, no! You're the neck-snapping guy from the garage."

"Yes, and looks like exercise won't help you now."

From that point on, everything seemed to move in slow motion. I noticed the way his nostrils flared, his finger tightened on the trigger and the jolt he gave when he was blown halfway down the hall.

I screamed again, glad I could be so helpful in this do-or-die situation. My ears were ringing as I turned and saw Darren kneeling, one hand beneath his elbow and the other holding the biggest freaking pistol I'd ever seen. He had a grim expression on his face, but otherwise he was utterly composed.

I yelped and jumped back. "Holy crap. Did you just shoot him?"

"Yeah. And you're welcome." Darren rose from his crouch just as Slash raced up the stairs and came to a sudden halt. Darren's pistol was still smoking.

He looked between Darren, me and the guy lying in the middle of the hall. "That's one big gun."

Hysteria bubbled in my throat as I pointed at the guy. "He tried to shoot us. He has SWAT on his shirt, but he's the guy who tried to snap my neck in the garage."

There was no further time for comment because at that moment, complete pandemonium broke out. The stairwell was swarmed with police and a boatload of black-clad SWAT guys with radios and guns. Slash gingerly relieved Darren of his gun and gave it to a uniformed cop. Still in shock, Darren and I leaned back against the wall, trying to stay out of everyone's way.

At one point, a guy identifying himself as a medic asked Darren and I if we'd been hit. We both shook our heads, numb from the events. Slash spoke furiously to a uniformed cop and a guy in SWAT fatigues, both of whom looked duly chagrined. Since Slash is Italian, or at least I *think* he is, there was a lot of hand waving and cursing going on. I don't think I'd ever seen Slash so livid. After a few minutes, he finally wound down and strode over to us, his face still thunderously dark.

"Che gran seccatura!" He stopped, pressing a hand to his forehead. "The local police will be the end of me. Let's get out of here."

We obediently followed Slash down the stairwell, over the body of another black-clad guy who was surrounded by police, and out the front door of the apartment complex. There were more police cars with flashing lights, a couple of dark vans surrounded by a bunch of guys in black carrying rifles, and a gaggle of spectators who were being pushed back as uniformed cops ran yellow police tape around the entrance to the building. To the left of the building a black SUV sat idling. A guy dressed in black fatigues and an earpiece with a dangling cord waved to Slash. We headed in his direction and piled into the SUV, Darren and I in the back and Slash in the passenger seat.

Without a word, the driver jumped in, gunned the SUV and off we went.

"Where are we going?" Darren asked Slash.

"The airport."

For a minute, no one spoke. My stomach still felt queasy, so I pressed a hand to it and willed myself to calm down.

Slash turned around in the seat, facing Darren. "So, when did you learn to shoot?"

"After Michael's death, I bought a gun. Practiced at the firing range."

I snorted. "That wasn't a gun. It was a freaking cannon."

"A GLOCK 34. No way was I buying a sissy gun."

Slash nodded. "Excellent for serious tactical duty or

Slash held up a hand. "We weren't spying or stealing, only monitoring you, Darren. I'll admit there is a fine line here. However, let's be frank. Both you and I know there isn't a soul alive today that could keep up with your thinking on this issue. You're in a league of your own in this field and that's an undisputed and unshakable fact. No one could steal what you have locked in that brilliant head of yours."

Darren sniffed, but Slash's comments seem to mollify him, probably because they were the unadulterated truth.

"I'm sorry to admit that Michael's death caught us completely by surprise. At first, we considered it an unfortunate accident. But after Evan reported on your state of mind and the fact that all progress on the program seemed to be halted, we began to wonder. We understood you would have to grieve, but it didn't explain your increasing isolation or paranoia."

"Michael was murdered. You'd have been paranoid, too."

"*Si.* After that we conducted our own quiet investigation into Michael's death. What we discovered was quite unsettling. We didn't believe it had been an accident either, although we had no hard proof. However, Michael's death led to our discovery that Flow was in more serious financial trouble than we had suspected."

"Did Evan tell you that, too?"

"No. But he was in Flow's system. You know full well it's easier to do a hack from the inside."

Darren pressed his lips together, looking increasingly unhappy.

Slash continued, "As soon as we heard that Flow had entered into a manufacturing partnership with NanoLab, red flags went up."

"Why?" I interjected.

"It wasn't sound financial sense that Flow would wholeheartedly enter into an agreement with a manufacturing partner when the prototype was still years away."

Darren's eyes blazed with sudden anger. "You knew about the delay of the prototype, too?"

"You were grieving after Michael's death. In fact, you still aren't thinking clearly, Darren. It wouldn't take a genius to realize the prototype was still years out. Evan figured that out almost immediately. He may not have understood the big picture in its entirety, but it was clear the prototype was not going to be anywhere ready in the near future. So, that left us with the troubling puzzle of why NanoLab would agree to come on board at this point."

"Because they had no intention of doing any manufacturing," Darren spat out.

Slash nodded. "*Si.* But what we didn't know is what they intended to do until just a few hours ago."

I looked at Slash in surprise. "How did you find out?"

"Ben Steinhouser contacted us about an hour before you did. He'd made a disturbing link between NanoLab and Boris Oleshinsky."

"Boris who?"

"Oleshinsky. A Russian billionaire."

A light bulb went off in my head. "Hmm…let me guess. He made his fortune in oil."

Slash smiled. "She doesn't have a high IQ for nothing."

I rolled my eyes. "You think this Boris guy is the one paying to eliminate Michael and Darren?"

"We just don't think it. We know it, *cara.*" He leaned forward, his elbows resting on the seat. "Think about it. Russia is the world's second-largest exporter of oil behind Saudi Arabia. A multimillion dollar hit on Michael and Darren is nothing compared to the billions in profit they stand to make if Darren's and Michael's work is interrupted."

"So, you're saying that Oleshinsky involved Niles and the others at Flow when it became clear the prototype would not be available for another seven to ten years," I mused. "He offered Niles a quick way out of his current financial crunch."

Darren looked thoughtfully out the window. "Niles could have the cash flow he needed and all he had to do was sell out Michael and me."

"*Si.* I believe that Oleshinsky thought you were a lot closer to manufacturing the prototype than Niles let on."

"Enter NanoLab to become the front to launder the hit money for Niles," I said. "In exchange Niles kept Oleshinsky apprised of Michael's and Darren's activities and whereabouts so that the hits could be done in a way that would make them look like accidents. That way the suspicions of the authorities wouldn't be raised and Niles could potentially claim his twenty-five-million-dollar insurance claim, as well."

"We'd actually traced some of the money for Nano-Lab's set-up back to Moscow, although, by no means is all the money coming from there. Some of this was done above board. After all, it's not against the law for Russia or other foreign countries to invest in America's private sector, but as you can well imagine, we do keep close watch on it. At first, we assumed Oleshinsky was making a potentially profitable investment. Naturally, once we dug deeper, our opinion changed. But we weren't certain of anything until Ben Steinhouser contacted us."

"His part of the job was focusing on NanoLab," I said. "I take it he found out about the hits."

"Yes, which is why he contacted us at once. Cybersecurity is one thing. Murder and assassination are something completely different."

Good for Ben. "So how does all this relate to what just happened back there in the stairwell? Who were those guys?"

Slash ran his fingers through his dark hair. "We had a problem, *cara*. Although technically we knew what Niles and his cohorts were up to, we had no way to bring them to justice. Ben employed, let's say, *unconventional* methods to find and tie the hits to Oleshinsky. We also used nontraditional methods of confirming his suspicions."

"Hacking."

Darren swore. "None of the evidence would be admissible in a court of law. Been there and had that same problem."

"Therein was the dilemma," Slash explained. "Once you found Darren, we knew we could protect him, but we knew we wouldn't be able to bring down Niles or Oleshinsky. We could shut down Flow, but there would be no justice for Michael or Darren." He paused for a moment. "Unless we could force Niles's hand."

"Jeez. Someone tipped off Niles that I'd found Darren."

Slash nodded. "Steinhouser. We instructed him to go see Niles personally to let him know you'd found Darren and that the boy wanted to leave Flow, change his identity and work for us. Ben assured Niles that no one believed any of his paranoid stories, but that we'd send a government worker to Cambridge to escort him back to Washington. Despite Darren's paranoia, Steinhouser told Niles that the U.S. government felt Darren would be a useful asset to our energy-replacement program. Therefore, at Darren's request, the government would provide Darren with a new identity and help him start anew."

"Bet Niles didn't like that one bit. Was Finn in the loop on any of this?"

"*Si.* Shaughnessy was kept abreast of the developments."

No wonder Finn had sounded worried out of his mind when I talked to him earlier. He knew what was coming and he couldn't warn me. There hadn't been a thing he could do about it.

"However, it was imperative for us to catch Niles in the process of contacting Oleshinsky to let him know Darren's whereabouts," Slash continued. "That would directly link him to the hits. But we couldn't risk Niles using something other than his own computer, cell or work phone. So, we had Steinhouser place bugs in Niles's office as well as directly on Niles himself."

I looked at Slash in surprise. "Physically on Niles?" It would have been a walk in the park to slip a bug beneath the chair or desk, but putting a device *on* a person requires actual touching. I couldn't imagine Niles permitting anyone to touch him.

Slash smiled. "We told Steinhouser to give Niles a hug in celebration that X-Corp had finally found Darren. Probably shocked the heck out of Niles, but somehow the bug was planted in his jacket pocket."

The thought that Ben had managed to hug a guy like Niles *and* slip the bug in his pocket was amazing in my book.

Go, Ben.

"Anyway, minutes after Steinhouser left, Niles contacted Oleshinsky's office just as we expected."

"You got him?" I asked.

"Indeed, we did."

Darren frowned. "Are you sure all of this will stand up in court?"

"The court order for the wiretap and the listening devices came in minutes before Ben entered Niles's office. Niles and company have already been taken into custody."

"Great," I said. "But why the drama in the stairwell? Was Neck-Snapping Man one of the Russian hit men?"

"*Si.* We had Niles, but we couldn't pin Oleshinsky unless he actually ordered the hits. By this point, Oleshinsky was very concerned that Darren would disappear for good and there would never be a chance to finish him off. The Russians have no idea where the U.S. government is in terms of nanotechnology energy replacement and they certainly didn't want Darren helping us along, so they figured they'd have this one and only chance to finish off Darren."

"So, you let the hit continue to pin Oleshinsky," I said. "I suppose that by now, Oleshinsky didn't care whether Darren's death looked like an accident or not. Eliminating Darren became a priority."

"We figured Oleshinsky would have the hit go immediately into motion. That meant I had to play the role of an office drone and couldn't let the hit man know I was on to him. I dressed as an ordinary government worker who came to escort you and Darren back to Washington. I let him pick up my trail from the airport and led him directly to you. Cambridge authorities had been notified and a SWAT team, as well as undercover police, were in place at the apartment complex before I even arrived. But the *idioti* authorities made a couple of important miscalculations."

"Which were?" I asked.

"There was more than one hit man and they both

recognized the undercover cops as soon as they saw the building."

"So, why'd they proceed?"

"Arrogance? Money? I presume they thought they could outwit the local police. I was informed that one of the SWAT guys had gone missing when we were already in the stairwell. The evacuation was to proceed as planned. The team leader suspected only that a sniper had taken the missing man's post and sent agents to the spot to secure him."

"But instead of taking over the sniper post, one of the hit men took his uniform," I speculated.

"And blended in with the operation. Then, while I was busy with the first one, the other one came from the rear for you and Darren. *Mai più!*"

"What does that mean?"

"Never again," Slash muttered. "Never again will I let anyone run an operation for me. My operation, my team only."

"Well, I kind of put you on the spot. I didn't give you a whole lot of time to prepare anything."

Slash's jaw tightened. "Never again."

After that, we sat quietly, watching the scenery pass. Finally, Darren spoke. "Okay. It's over and we're safe. What now? Where do I go from here?"

"Your life is still in danger. But the U.S. government can protect you. We can help you start a new life with a new name and a safe place to live."

"And continue my research?"

"Absolutely. We'll have to shut down Flow, but your legacy and work will continue. We're also willing to talk about ethics and the practical environmental concerns of the technology. We know that's important to you."

Darren perked up a bit. "An oversight committee of sorts?"

"Si," Slash assured him. "But consisting of scientists and ethicists, not politicians or businessmen."

They discussed that for a while and I was impressed by Slash's knowledge of STRUT and the ethical issues of energy-replacement nanotechnology. Like me, Slash had probably done his homework. The only major drawback I could see to this whole arrangement was that the lab was presently situated in some godforsaken town in Iowa.

After several minutes of discussion, Darren's brow furrowed. "I think it will work. It's not like I have much of a choice. It's what I was born to do."

I couldn't argue with that but it somehow seemed rather sad that he would have to move to a new place surrounded by unfamiliar people and be guarded round the clock as a top military secret. Hollywood is always playing up how amazing it is to be the Chosen One or the Gifted One, but I could see having a special destiny isn't always what it's cracked up to be.

We were all silent thinking over what Slash had said. Then I turned to Darren, putting my hand on his arm. "Well, the good news is that Michael gets his justice after all. His death will not be in vain thanks to you."

"Thanks to us." Darren took my hand and to my surprise, he lifted it to his lips. "I'll always be indebted to you for that, Lexi, *meus amicus.*"

I hadn't taken six years of Latin for nothing. I squeezed his hand in return. "Hey, you're my friend, too, Darren. *Totus est puteus ut ends puteus.*"

"All's well that ends well," he repeated and we both smiled. At that moment, I thought no phrase had ever been truer.

Chapter Fourteen

The airport loomed before us in what seemed like record time. We were whisked through a few airport security checkpoints and permitted to drive right up to a fancy silver-and-blue plane parked on the tarmac. The plane was already idling and a dozen or more suited guys with corded earphones surrounded the plane. Finn stood at the bottom of the stairs, pacing back and forth. As soon as he saw the SUV he made a beeline for us.

"Lexi." He pulled me into a hug. "Are you okay?"

"I've been better. But we're fine, so that's the upside."

Finn released me and held out a hand to Darren. "Nice to finally meet you." He shook Darren's hand. "You sure kept us busy these past several days."

"It's been a heck of a ride."

Slash hopped out of the SUV and hustled us all up the stairs and into the plane. Several of the suited guys with earphones got on the plane with us and before we could even decide where to sit, we were instructed to separate for a debriefing. For the next hour or so, we were swarmed over by different agents, required to sign papers and reminded the secrecy of the government's energy nanotechnology plans should be considered top secret.

At some point, the agents decided they had beat me to death with the reminders and left me alone. I leaned back against the seat and closed my eyes. When I opened them, Slash sat beside me.

"How are you feeling, *cara?*"

"Weird. I'm glad that we found Darren safely and got the justice that Michael deserved, but I'm really worried about a kid who has a lot riding on his shoulders."

"That kid is the same age as you."

"True, but I don't have the responsibilities that he does."

"It's the life of a prodigy. We are all gifted in certain ways for a higher purpose."

I remembered the gold cross Slash wore beneath his shirt and the fact that he had spent several years as a part of Vatican Intelligence.

"It's nice to believe that all things have a purpose."

He lifted a dark eyebrow. "And you do not?"

"I'm not sure. It just doesn't seem fair somehow. Darren has no one now. I mean Michael's dad is the only person in the world that is close to him. Will Gene Hart ever know the truth about what happened to his son and Darren?"

"*Si, cara.* We will tell him. And there are methods we can employ so that the two of them can see each other and communicate. We no longer operate as in the old days."

"That's good. Call me a mother hen, but I think Darren deserves some happiness. I'd hate to think he'd be holed up in a government lab with nothing more than the good of mankind on his shoulders. He needs a life. He needs some friends."

Slash leaned over and patted my leg. "I think he's already made a good one."

At some point later in the flight, Darren extracted himself from the agents. Right about the same time Finn begged off any more debriefing and the two of them joined me simultaneously.

Finn plopped down in the seat. "How did you stand it, Lexi? The government is driving me crazy with regulations, secrecy and paperwork."

"You worked for MI6. You should be used to this."

"Even the British version of the CIA doesn't have regulations like this."

"Still, you're a foreigner, Finn. They have to take extra precautions."

Finn rolled his eyes, but it got a laugh out of Darren.

"You know, I really don't know how to thank you, Lexi," Darren said. "I've made your life horrible and I'm sorry for it. I hope you'll forgive me."

"Hey, all is forgiven and I mean that. And don't thank me. Thank Finn. His company is what enabled us to find you."

Finn grinned. "Perhaps. But it looks like I've got the company's most important resource right next to me." He leaned over and kissed me on the cheek.

I blushed. "Well, I suppose it helped that we were also able to employ a little good old-fashioned cyber-sleuthing."

"Hacking," Darren corrected.

I glanced over at the agents. "Jeez, Darren. Keep your voice down. We're in mixed company after all."

Darren grinned and turned to me. "So, will I see you again, Lexi?"

I shrugged. "I don't see why not. Slash says there are ways around the whole secret-life thing. I think at the very least we should be able to stay in touch."

"I'd like that."

"Me, too."

We landed a few minutes later. After a final good-bye hug, Slash and some other suits quickly whisked Darren away in a black sedan. Finn and I were left standing on the tarmac.

One of the agents turned to us. "Can I drop you two somewhere?"

Finn shook his head and glanced at his watch. "Thanks, but I've got my car. Lexi, are you still up for something to eat? I'm not sure I've enough energy to prepare linguine tonight, but we can pick up something and bring it back to my place."

"Sure, it's your birthday. I'll do whatever you want. But I should warn you, I didn't have time to get you a present."

He grinned. "I think solving our first case is probably the best present anyone could give me."

"Lucky for me, I didn't even have to wrap it."

He laughed and while in the car we decided on Chinese food—Hunan Chicken with fried rice, won-ton soup and egg rolls. I held the food on my lap as Finn drove home, enjoying the warmth and the heavenly smell. As we got closer to Finn's place, it occurred to me that I'd never been there. And since it was an unknown, I began to obsess.

Where the heck did a guy as loaded as Finn live? What if it were some weird-ass mansion with fifty rooms or something like that? I'd feel completely out of place in a museum full of expensive furniture, tapestries and artwork. Where would I sit, what could I touch?

On the other hand, maybe he lived in a playboy-style penthouse condo with a vibrating bed and mirrors on the ceiling. Jeez, I knew for *sure* I wouldn't be able to do that.

I started breathing through my mouth as Finn told me we were getting close. Then, to my enormous relief, Finn drove into a nice residential area with pretty townhouses and parked in front of a row that backed up to some trees.

He pointed to an end unit with a brown brick facade. "I'm the end unit right here."

I exhaled a loud breath. "It's normal."

"You thought it would be abnormal?"

I smiled too brightly. "I mean, it's a quiet neighborhood."

"Well, there are lots of young professionals here. Although a young couple with twin toddlers recently moved in three houses down. The girls are cute as buttons."

The banter relaxed me as I juggled the bags of food and followed Finn up the sidewalk. He let me in, disarmed his alarm system and pointed me to the kitchen. "Let's eat in there." He shrugged out of his coat and tossed it on the banister.

I walked into the kitchen and flipped on the light, noticing the beautiful tile floor, dark green granite countertops and stainless steel appliances. Modern, but inviting.

"We can eat at the bar." He pointed to a counter with two stools and a silver light fixture that hung directly over it. "I'll get us some plates and pour some wine."

The wine would be excellent. Since Finn's family owned one of the most profitable wineries in Ireland, he was always plying me with different years and flavors. I'd become so accustomed to the expensive stuff, my palate would never be the same. If things didn't work out between me and Finn, I'd probably have to swear off wine forever.

Finn handed me two plates, forks and empty wineglasses. He then sat a bottle of wine in front of me and asked for my opinion.

"Pinot Gris 1979. It's a challenge finding just the right wine with Chinese food. What do you think?"

"Your family label?"

"Of course."

"Then you know I'm going to like it."

He twisted the corkscrew in. "You're so easy to please."

"You ruined me. I used to like the cheap stuff."

Grinning, he pulled out the cork. With a flourish, he filled our wineglasses while I served up the won-ton soup and egg rolls.

We ate while companionably discussing some of the finer points of the day's activities. Finn refilled my wineglass twice and it wasn't long before I felt a nice warm buzz coming on.

Finn cleared the dishes and dumped them in the sink while I packed up the leftovers and put them in the refrigerator.

When we were done, Finn leaned back against the kitchen counter. "Want to see the rest of the house?"

I was curious about how a guy like Finn lived. "Sure."

Handing me my wineglass, he said, "Follow me."

We walked through a simple dining room with a dark wood table and chairs and into the living room. A worn brown leather couch and two reclining chairs were positioned in front of a gas fireplace, above which hung a large flat-screen television. The room wasn't pretentious as I had feared, just warm and inviting. Kind of like Finn himself.

I followed him up the hardwood stairs, past a hall bathroom and into a comfortable guest room. Next to that room was a home office with a bed, presumably to accommodate more guests and a simple home gym with a treadmill, weights and a bench.

"Hey, Finn, this is really nice."

"Glad you approve."

"Well, not that it means much as I don't know anything about interior design."

"Then we're on the same page."

He led me to the last room on the floor to what was obviously the master suite.

I stopped in the doorway and whistled. "Sweeeet."

Finn had a simple platform bed in mahogany wood, behind which was a matching headboard with floor-to-ceiling bookshelves on either side. The bedding was light brown with a scatter of silk brown pillows. Track lighting inside the bookshelf and over the bed gave the room a soft glow. A brown leather chair with an off-white pillow sat to the right of the bed and a dark rug had been positioned directly under the bed.

"I can't claim credit," he said, taking my hand and pulling me into the room. "I hired a designer just for this room. I wanted a place where I could get away, lock the door and completely be myself."

I sighed. "It's perfect."

He set my wineglass on a matching mahogany dresser and pulled me into his arms. "You're perfect. What would you say if I tried to steal another kiss?"

"Didn't we already have this discussion?"

"Okay. I admit I'm hoping for a repeat performance where I'm desperate to get a certain woman off my mind and a pretty lass takes pity on me by giving me a kiss."

"Am I the certain woman or the pretty lass?"

"Both, of course."

"And what does the pretty lass do, exactly?"

"Hmm…she kisses me."

"Like this?" I lifted my mouth to his.

"Like that. Only open your lips slightly, perhaps."

I parted my lips. "Better?"

"Infinitely. I like when the pretty lass is a quick study."

"I like it when you call me pretty."

I stood on tiptoe, wound my arms around his neck and pressed my lips to his. This time he didn't let me pull away. He kissed me back, his mouth slanting over mine. He tasted spicy and sweet.

After a moment, he threaded his fingers in my hair and started nibbling his way down to my throat. "You smell like smoke," he murmured against my skin.

"You would, too, if you were anywhere in the near vicinity of a GLOCK 34."

His chuckle vibrated on the sensitive area near my collarbone, causing me to shiver. Jeez, where *was* he going with that mouth of his?

"I wouldn't mind taking a shower," he said. "How about you?"

I froze. Was he suggesting a shower? Together?

A million thoughts raced through my head. I'd practiced being a Bond girl. I'd danced nearly naked in front of a room full of guys I didn't even know. I could handle a shower with Finn. Right? Then why couldn't I breathe?

Apparently sensing either my fear, indecision or both, he nipped at my earlobe. "You get undressed. I'll get the towels."

He was giving me time to figure this out. "Ah, okay. A shower is probably a good idea."

Taking my glass of wine from the dresser and swallowing a big gulp, I walked into the master bath. It had a huge jetted tub and a pretty glass-enclosed stand-up shower. I reached into the shower and turned the hot water on, letting it run over my hand.

"Jeez, that feels good," I murmured. I slipped out of my jeans and unbuttoned my blouse, laying them on the sink. Feeling a bit light-headed from the wine and the possibility that I might be completely naked in a minute with Finn, I sat atop the toilet seat in my boring white panties and cotton bra. I wished I'd worn something sexier, but then again, I'd thought I'd have plenty of time to return to my apartment for a change of clothes before coming over to Finn's place. Well, the best-laid plans...

I jumped when he spoke.

"Here you go." He stood in the doorway to the bathroom with some towels in his hands.

My cheeks heated although I pretended like it was no big deal to be half-naked in front of a guy. "Ah, thanks."

"You're lovely." He set the towels down and walked over to me. Pulling me to my feet, he slid his arms around me and nuzzled my neck. I melted into him. His warm hands slid up my bare back until they reached my bra hooks. In seconds, without any visual aid, he'd unfastened my bra. The guy was a freaking genius. It always took me at least two or three attempts. Apparently, Finn was a master bra unhooker because, *boom,* just like that, he stepped back from me, my bra dangling from his fingertips.

I resisted the urge to cover myself. He didn't stare at me, just held the bra and sort of lingered.

Suddenly I realized he was waiting for either an invitation or a rejection. I opened my mouth, but no words came out. I cleared my throat and tried again, but whatever I wanted to say was locked up good and tight.

I felt like crying. Oh, great. It was official. I was a big, honking, clucking chicken.

Finn knew at once and was gracious, as always. "You go first. I'll wait out here."

I liked him more than ever.

I still couldn't say anything, so I just nodded. He left and I sat back down on the toilet, putting my head in my hands.

Idiot, idiot, idiot.

After a minute, I stood, shed my panties and started to step into the shower.

There was a soft knock at the door. "Lexi?"

I snatched a towel and wrapped it around my naked body. "What?"

"You'd better come out here."

I opened the door a crack. "What's wrong?"

"I think there's someone in the house."

"What?"

He grabbed my hand, pulling me out into the dark bedroom. At some point, he must have turned off the lights. Leading me to the bedroom doorway, he stopped, placing a finger on my lips.

We stood quietly listening.

Thump.

I squeezed his hand in fright, leaning over and pressing my mouth against his ear. "What was it?"

Finn shook his head. We waited some more and then we both heard it again.

Thump. Creak. Bump.

"Stay here. I think I forgot to set the alarm. I'm going to go check it out."

I gripped his hand harder, whispering back with high intensity. "I don't think so. I've had enough of being stalked by assassins for one day. I'm not staying up here alone. We'll do this together."

Finn made a sound of protest in his throat, but didn't

argue when I followed close behind him. I bumped into his back as he stopped at his dresser and pulled out a gun from the top drawer.

"You keep a gun in your underwear drawer?"

"Would you have me keep it in the bathroom?"

"Good point."

Taking my hand, he led me out of the bedroom and down the hallway. Finn paused at the top, listened and then mouthed against my ear, "Follow exactly in my footsteps."

Figuring he knew exactly where the creaks were, I did as he said. To my enormous relief, we climbed noiselessly down the stairs. At the bottom, we paused and listened.

Still nothing.

Gripping my hand and holding the gun, Finn tugged me toward the kitchen. We crept past the living room when someone flipped on the lights.

"Surprise! Happy Birthday!"

I jumped backward and lost my towel. Finn cursed beside me. A very pretty woman with blond hair stood with her arm around a young woman. To their side stood a very tall man with brown hair, dressed in black slacks and a white shirt. The young woman held a dozen colorful balloons and there was what looked like a chocolate cake on the coffee table.

"Finn." The older woman gasped.

"What are you doing?" Finn shouted at them. "I could have fekin' shot you."

The younger woman began to laugh. "I told Mum this wasn't a good idea."

We all stood staring at each other in complete shock until I yelped in horror and reached down to snatch the towel off the floor and cover myself. Then to my dismay the young woman walked straight up to me and offered me a hand.

"Hello. I'm Maureen, Finn's sister. I bet you're Lexi."

"Oh, hello." I tried not to bawl.

The older man discreetly turned away from us, but not before I saw him stifling a laugh.

Finn laid the gun down on a side table and ran his fingers through his hair. "Lexi, this is my family. My mum, da and my younger sister Maureen."

Finn's mom hadn't stopped staring at me. At that moment, I wanted nothing more than for Scotty to beam me up and get me out of here.

"Okay, awkward." Maureen laughed again. "Let her get dressed, Finn, then introduce us proper, for God's sake."

With those words, I fled up the stairs. I heard Finn talking for a moment more and then he followed me. I had already dressed by the time he entered the bedroom. Without a word, he went into the bathroom and turned off the shower.

"They wanted to do something special for my birthday. So, they flew in from Ireland to surprise me."

"It was definitely a surprise."

He put a hand on my shoulder. "Will you stay? I can set them up in the guest rooms and we can pick up where we left off."

I gulped. "I just met your parents for the first time, Finn. The *very* first time. I was completely, utterly and bone-chillingly naked. How does that factor into a first impression? As it is, I suck at social skills and now I've been handicapped beyond even the ability of Pussy Galore."

"Huh?"

"Never mind. The point is I need time to regroup and

restore my pride. Truthfully, I'm not sure I can ever face them again."

"I'm certain they'll love you."

"Jeez. I'm sure your family is wonderful. I just don't think I can ever look at them again."

"Give it a bit of time. Soon we'll all be joking about it."

"Maybe in ten years."

"I feel awful."

"Probably. But you also think it's funny. Go ahead, laugh. You know you want to."

He chuckled and then started laughing. After a minute, tears ran down his face. "Jesus, Joseph and Mary. It was a truly brilliant moment, a once-in-a-lifetime kind of thing. I almost shot my family and you were standing there completely starkers."

"I'm glad you find it all so amusing."

He swiped at the tears with the back of his hand. "I'm going to find a way to make it up to you, Lexi. I swear on my grandda's grave, I do."

"That might be hard since now I *really* have to move to China."

He pulled me into his arms and kissed the top of my head. "Come down and meet my family proper, won't you?"

"I'm crazy about you, Finn, but there is no way I'm ready to face your family just yet."

He kissed me and then exhaled a breath against my cheek. "I'm sorry. Really."

I sighed. "I know, but I'm going to look on the bright side. It will give me time to find you a proper present."

He grinned. "You were doing just fine."

We both laughed and I felt a lot better. We climbed back down the stairs, hand-in-hand and my heart began to race. To my enormous relief, the group had moved into the kitchen. Finn walked back alone and told them he was taking me home. I could hear his family arguing, urging him to permit me to stay, but he told them we would all be more comfortable this way. I really appreciated him for respecting my wishes.

Finn drove me home, walked me to the door and gave me a very, very nice good-night kiss.

"Now I feel like it's *my* birthday."

"Hold that thought, lass," he murmured.

We kissed once more and I went inside my apartment. Leaning back against the door, I sighed. It had been a heck of a day in a lot more ways than one. I felt ready to drop dead from the roller coaster of emotions.

Walking back to the bathroom, I stripped again and took a hot, hot shower. After combing out my hair and pulling on an oversized T-shirt and a pair of sweats, I rummaged around for the blow dryer. That's when I heard the knock. I went to the door and looked through the peephole.

Slash.

I disarmed my alarm and opened the door.

"Hey. I think this is the first time you've ever knocked. You come for your jacket?"

Slash slipped inside. He'd changed from that amazing three-piece suit and was now dressed in black jeans, boots and a dark sweater. Sexy, mysterious and smelling really, *really* good.

"No." He closed the door behind him. "Set the alarm."

"What? No more hit men. I seriously can't take any more today."

"There are no more hit men, *cara*."

I breathed a sigh of relief and dutifully set the alarm. "Thank goodness. Is Darren okay?"

"He's fine and resting. We'll start processing him tomorrow."

"Well, that's great, I guess." My brow scrunched into a frown. "Then everything is okay."

"*Si,* everything is fine."

We stood there for a minute in silence. I shifted uneasily on my feet. "So, if there are no hit men out to get me and you don't want your jacket, why are you here?"

He smiled.

"Another matter of national security?"

He shook his head, reaching out to twirl a strand of my wet hair around his finger.

"Slash?" I studied his face, but it was impassive.

Then, reaching into his jeans pocket, he pulled something out. I leaned in closer to get a better look.

"Tickets?"

"To the opera. Tomorrow night."

I knew exactly nothing about the opera. My childhood had not involved the opera or ballet despite my mother's best attempts to educate me. On the other hand, I was intrigued that an uberhacker like Slash had the time or an interest in something so…nontechnical.

"I'm not much of an opera connoisseur," I admitted.

"Ah, but are you game?"

The old Lexi was afraid of change. The new Lexi had a sparkling fresh mantra welcoming change. If I laid it out in mathematical terms, the opera equaled change. A harmless nonthreatening way to expand my horizons. Of course, I wasn't sure if he was asking me for a date or just suggesting an evening between friends. But Slash didn't seem the dating type, more like the one-night-of-passion type. Besides, he knew I was sort of seeing Finn and he wouldn't just cut in.

Would he?

I decided to err on the side of caution. "Um, we're friends, right?"

"Absolutely."

Well, that settled that. We were friends. It wouldn't matter to Finn one way or the other if I went out with friends. He would be busy for the next couple of days with his family and I still wasn't even sure we had a relationship. Besides, it wasn't as if Slash had invited me to an intimate and secluded dinner somewhere. He asked a friend to the opera. The opera was a popular and public place. Everything would be fine.

"Okay, I'm game."

"*Eccellente*. I think you're going to like it."

"Statistically, that's probably true. Opera has been around for hundreds of years and appeals to a wide audience of people. Maybe I'll be one of them. I don't see the harm in checking it out…as long as I don't have to sing."

He laughed. "*Cara,* I can promise you one thing. That's absolutely not going to happen."

I smiled back. "That's good to know, Slash. I'll hold you to it."

"I'm sure you will. See you at seven o'clock, then."

"Yep. See you then."

After he left, I leaned back against the door. In a matter of months, my entire existence had been turned upside down. I had more people coming and going in my life than I had ever had for all my twenty-five years combined. I still wasn't sure I liked it, but it had changed me. Change meant growth. For now, I'd decided to embrace it…if only to see what tomorrow would bring.

* * * * *

Read on for an excerpt from No Money Down,
*the next book in the Lexi Carmichael Mystery series
from Julie Moffett.*

My name is Lexi Carmichael and I hate the beach.

Okay, maybe *hate* is too strong a word. I don't really hate the beach. It's just the sun is too bright, sand is everywhere and seaweed gets stuck in my toes. Don't even get me started on how much I dislike bathing suits. It's not pretty.

I don't like people being crammed together in a mathematically disproportionate way in a very small area. Especially when they're half-dressed and strutting around like peacocks. It's too hot, too loud and smells too much of coconut suntan lotion. Beam me out of here, Scotty. Please.

Yet here I am, spending my precious vacation days at Ocean City, Maryland, on a beach without my beloved laptop, forced into this so-called "time away from technology" with my best friend and former roommate, Basia Kowalski. Somehow, I let myself get talked into it. Usually I can resist her crazy ideas. After all, I have a pretty high IQ and recently graduated from Georgetown University with a double major in mathematics and computer science. But sometimes she talks so fast and runs me in circles that I often will acquiesce just to quit trying to figure out what she's saying. Unfortunately, at that point it's already too late. I'm stuck, having agreed to God-knows-what just to end the conversation.

Don't get me wrong, I adore Basia. She's everything I'm not—pretty, social, fashionable and outgoing. She's also witty and has a remarkable flair for languages. She speaks about twenty of them fluently and has her own business as a freelance translator while working part-time for Berlitz, those folks who put out the small phrase books in dozens of different languages. She's brought me out of my shell more than any other person I've ever known, even if it does make me nervous and cranky most of the time.

She's always telling me, "Lexi Carmichael, it's time to log off and get a life."

She's usually right.

I'll be the first to admit I'm not the easiest person to be around. I'm neither a girly-girl nor a tomboy. I'm skinny in an awkward way, have no fashion sense and I don't date much (or at all), which is not surprising since my social skills suck.

I'm a geek.

That means my happy place is online. Computers, code, gaming. I'm also an ace hacker. Or at least I used to be. Then I sort of got busted. It wasn't a malicious hack, that's not my style, but it was still illegal. Lucky for me, my dad is a high-priced lawyer for a swanky firm in Georgetown so no one could prove anything. However, it scared the beejeebies out of me. It scared Dad too. Although I'm technically an adult, he threatened to take away all my computer equipment if I ever hacked like that again.

Now that I'm working for the National Security Agency, better known as the NSA, I've completely sworn off hacking, although what I do in my imagination is between me, myself and I. Secretly, I have a desire to fit in to the real world, at least sometimes, which is why I suspect I let Basia talk me into most of the things she does.

"Do you think this is a good spot?" Basia paused, setting the cooler down in the sand. She pointed at a very small spot sandwiched between an older couple sitting in a couple of lawn chairs beneath an umbrella and a greasy muscled guy asleep on his stomach on a black towel.

I shrugged. "Whatever."

"Great." She rolled out the colorful yellow Mexican blanket and I dropped the other bags at my feet.

"You can set up the umbrella here." She pointed at a spot near the head of the blanket. "We can adjust as the sun rises."

Sighing, I shoved the umbrella deep into the sand, angling it for maximum protection. No way would I spend more than a few minutes in the sun, if any at all. Roasting in the rays was not my cup of tea.

After a few minutes of unpacking, Basia shimmied out of a cute white beach dress, unveiling a teeny-tiny green bikini. She handed me the suntan lotion.

"Can you do my back?"

I smeared a considerable amount on her back and shoulders. She did the rest of her body and then faced me. "Your turn."

My cheeks heated. "Ah, I'm thinking of just staying here under the umbrella."

She gave me a look that meant I'd just said something really wrong. My mom had that exact look.

Basia planted her hands on her hips. "Take off your clothes. Now."

"But—"

"No buts. Undress."

Resigned, I took off my shirt.

"Good. Now drop the pants."

I slid the pants down my legs and handed them over.

She stared at me. "Where did you get that bathing suit?"

"Can you believe it? It was ninety percent off at Macy's."

"You mean you actually paid money for that?"

"Do you like it?"

"It looks like something my great-grandmother would wear."

I frowned. "It covers all the essentials."

"It covers a lot more than that. Okay, the first order of business after the beach is to buy you a new bathing suit."

"I like this one."

"It's beyond awful. Those panties reach your knees."

"I believe they're referred to as pantaloons."

"Please, don't start me laughing. I swear I'll never stop. For now, just get out from under the umbrella so I can slather you up."

I stepped out from beneath the umbrella and Basia shielded her eyes. "My God. You're white to the point of being clear. When was the last time you sat out in the sun?"

"In a bathing suit? I think I was twelve."

"Why is it my work is never done with you? Okay, I think an extra layer of lotion will be necessary." She wound my brown hair up into a ponytail, securing it with one of her scrunchies, and then smeared me with a ton of lotion. "You are skin and bones, girl. Do you ever eat?"

"If I don't have to cook it."

She swatted me on the arm and then rubbed the lotion residue on her leg. I thanked her and started to head back to the safety of the umbrella.

"Oh, no you don't." She grabbed my arm. "We're going into the ocean."

"Why? It's salty in there."

"That's the idea. Sun, fresh air, salty water. We're at the beach, remember?"

"I can get fresh air from here." The crankiness reared its ugly head and I felt oily and exposed.

"Lexi."

I figured she'd probably try and drag me, which technically I didn't think she could, seeing as how I had about five inches and fifteen pounds on her. But she'd try, which would attract more attention, which was even more loathsome to me than sticking my toes in salty water.

"All right." I supposed a little water couldn't hurt anything.

We had to make our way past the dozens of oiled people camped out on the beach until we made it to the water's edge. The sun felt hot on my shoulders and nose, but a nice wind softened the heat, and the water felt cool on my toes.

Basia took my hand. "Let's go in deeper."

I hesitated. "I can't swim."

"We won't go far."

The water lapped against my knees and then my thighs. As we went deeper, my nerves surfaced. "I think this is far enough."

"Just a couple of steps more." Basia laughed, let go of my hand and dived under the surface.

"Basia?" I yelped as the waves crashed into me, causing me to take a step back. "Where are you?"

She popped up behind me, nearly giving me a heart attack. With her dark hair slicked back and the green bikini, she looked like a mermaid.

"The water is great. You should try going under."

"Oh, no." The waves kept slamming me, keeping me off balance. "I think I've had enough."

Her pretty mouth turned into a pout. "But we just got here. Let's wave hop first." She took my hand again, pulling me deeper a few steps. "Like this."

A wave swelled in front of us and, as it reached its crescendo, she pulled me up and we rode the wave. It scared me at first, but after a few times, I realized I liked the exhilaration of riding the crest.

"Hey, this is pretty fun."

"The more you listen to me, the more you will say that."

After a few times, I started to get the hang of it. I didn't even get bothered too much when the water splashed my hair and face.

Basia giggled. "Look out, here comes a big one."

It didn't seem *that* big until it was pretty much upon us. By then it was too late. My hand ripped from Basia's as the momentum of the wave pushed me forward with alarming speed. I saw the blurry shape of a figure in front of me, and my brain instantly calculated that a crash with it was imminent. I opened my mouth to scream a warning, but water rushed inside. I slammed into the shape with the force of a speeding bullet, and we rolled over and over in a ball of tangled limbs, water and seaweed.

I pushed up to my knees on the beach, doggie-style,

sputtering and coughing. My hair dripped heavily on either side of me while I'm pretty sure I hacked up half the ocean with some seaweed to boot. I lifted my head up long enough to see the fuzzy shape next to me stagger sideways.

"Oh. My. God." I coughed up some more water. "I am so sorry."

"Are you okay?" He held out a hand to help me up.

I blinked, my vision hazy. Staggering to a half crouch, I reached out for his hand. Still unsteady, I missed and fell forward onto him, my hand still outstretched. My fingers got tangled in the waistband of his swimsuit. As I fell face-first into the sand, I took his swimsuit down around his ankles with me.

I looked up in horror. There he stood, a guy I'd never met, staring at me with an expression of shock and disbelief on his face while his privates were on display for me, and the entire beach, to see. Then he swore, reached down and yanked up his suit, while I let my face fall back to the wet sand in mortification.

"Hey."

Strong hands lifted me from behind. I stood, shaky on my feet, and rubbed my eyes. Two figures shimmied and swayed in front of me.

"Are you sure you're okay?"

I coughed, blinked a couple of times and tried to steady my shaking knees. "I'm not sure. I see two of you."

One of the figures put his arm around my shoulders. "Come on, let's go sit down on my blanket."

The figure led me to a blanket beneath an umbrella. He handed me a towel and I wiped my eyes with it. I set the towel on my lap as Basia came running up, kneeling on a corner of the blanket.

"Lexi, are you okay?"

"No, I think I'm going to have to move to another country. I nearly drowned, but not before exposing my rescuer."

"Ah, so *that's* what happened."

One of the figures nodded. "She confirmed my gender as male."

Basia snorted with laughter. "Well, leave it to Lexi to dispense with all social niceties and get right to the heart…or pants…of the matter. Most people go on dates first, you know."

"Jeez, Basia." I dared a look up and saw two skinny white guys with brown hair and piercing blue eyes wearing matching swimsuits. Both were staring at me.

I blinked three times. "Either I hit my head really hard or there are two of you."

"There are two of us."

I looked back and forth between them. "Twins. Identical twins."

One of them held out a hand. "I'm Elvis. The one you exposed."

Instead of taking his hand, I picked up the towel and hid my face in it. "I'm so sorry. I'm never coming to the beach again."

To my surprise, he laughed. "I'll admit it surprised me. Never figured that's how I'd meet a girl at the beach."

I lowered the towel. "Wait a minute. Did you say Elvis?" I glanced over at the other guy, who watched me with an amused expression on his face. "Your name wouldn't happen to be Xavier, would it?"

Both guys looked startled. Elvis leaned forward. "How did you know?"

"Mathematical deduction. If you take the current population of the U.S., which is about 300 million people, then make a reasonable assumption that a relatively small number of those people, say 1.6 percent, are both male and named Elvis, which is not a popular name, that puts us at about 2.4 million people. Only 0.4 percent of those are identical twins and half of that are male. Divide that by the 50 states and the District of Columbia, the number roughly equals 188 persons who are identical twins here in Maryland. Given this location, which happens to be a popular vacation destination for employees of the NSA, the odds that you are Elvis Zimmerman and he is Xavier are about 90 to 1 with an error percentage of 5 percent. By the way, I happen to work at the NSA too. I just joined the InfoSec division. My name is Lexi Carmichael."

"Optimum," Elvis breathed.

I blushed. "You guys are legendary, brilliant. Everyone in the know has heard of you."

Then realizing I sounded like a lame fan girl, I hid my face again. "Oh, jeez, this just keeps getting worse. I depantsed a legend."

"Hey, there could be more boring ways to meet, I guess." Elvis tugged at the towel, pulling it away from my face. "Don't worry about it. The ways of the universe are irregular."

Reluctantly, I let him take the towel. "I guess that's true. Perhaps this one act of randomness was just part of the predisposed nature of the universe."

He shrugged. "Stranger things could happen. Although, given this particular case, maybe not so much."

Xavier stared at Basia, his mouth agape. "And who are you?"

Jeez, I guess their social skills were about par with mine.

Basia shook her wet hair back, water droplets sliding down her body and making her look like a sexy girl from a Bond movie. "I'm Basia Kowalski, Lexi's best friend. Nice to meet you."

She held out a hand to Xavier and his eyes widened as he took it. "I'm...ah...ah..."

"Xavier. We know."

"Uh, yeah. Xavier." He shook Basia's hand vigorously for several seconds until she pulled it away.

Basia looked back and forth between the twins. "Well, if you two ever change places, I'm not going to know who is who. Identical twins down to the last detail."

I shook my head. "Not true. Xavier has a scar over his right eyebrow."

Basia leaned forward and peered at his face. "God, you're right."

Xavier blushed at her closeness but didn't seem to mind. "Good catch, Lexi. Elvis clocked me with a keyboard when we were arguing over the answer to a mono-alphabetic code."

Elvis shrugged. "I needed to get your attention. I was right and you weren't listening."

"I was too listening. You weren't right."

"I most certainly was."

Basia held up a hand. "Peace. How long ago was this?"

Elvis thought for a moment. "We were four at the time."

Basia's eyes widened and then she gave me a pointed look. "Well, if you're feeling okay, Lexi…"

Clearly it was time to make an exit while I still had a modicum of dignity left. "Right. Well, I've got to go."

I jumped up and smashed into the umbrella. The entire thing came down on us.

After we'd all extracted ourselves and crawled out, I stood, brushing the sand off my knees. I plastered a big, fake smile on my face to hide my embarrassment. Better to pretend that all was well and I wasn't the biggest idiot in the universe, the randomness of it be damned.

"Um, well, Elvis. Yes. It was cool to meet you guys. Ah, maybe I'll run into you at work."

I gave myself a mental head slap. What the heck was I thinking? I'd *never* run into them at work since they worked in the secret-most part of the NSA as lead architects of the president's network security. You had to provide like twenty-three palm prints, six retinal scans, and pass a colon examination to even get close to that section.

"Ah, sure, Lexi. If I'm ever in the InfoSec section, I'll look you up."

My cheeks heated. I was such a dork. "Okay, great."

It didn't escape my notice that Elvis kept one hand on his hip, his fingers holding the waistband of his pants. Just in case I fell again, I suppose. I think my face turned a darker shade of red.

Elvis shifted on his feet. "Well, maybe Xavier and I will see you around the beach again. We're here for the week, staying at the Hilton." He pointed to the looming hi-rise hotel behind us.

"Nice. We're over at the Crazy Parrot Hotel. Not nearly as nice, but it has a nifty beach bar."

"Cool. Well, see you around then."

"See you around." I turned to go when he spoke again.

"Ah, Lexi?"

"Yes?"

"Do you by any chance play Quake?"

"Quake? Absolutely. Expert level."

He smiled. "Ace. You, ah, want to play sometime? I'm also at the expert level."

"Here?"

"Well, not exactly in this spot on the beach, but while we're in Ocean City, yeah."

"I'd kill for it. But I don't have my laptop." I glanced over my shoulder where Xavier had pulled Basia aside and was speaking animatedly to her. "I'm on the wagon. Tech-free holiday per orders of said best friend."

"That's tough. But what she doesn't know won't hurt her. I've got a couple of extras with me."

My heart leaped at just the thought of touching a keyboard. "Really? You mean it?"

"Meet me at seven o'clock tonight in the bar at the Hilton. Quake is on the agenda."

"Deal." Giddy, I turned to see Basia saying goodbye to Xavier and waving me toward her. I caught up and she linked arms with me.

"Well, that was exciting."

"Way too much excitement for me."

"At least you met a man. Next time can you rip the pants off a guy who is a little less skinny?"

"Hey, he's a legend at the NSA. Do you have any idea who the Zimmerman twins are?"

"Geeks, first-class?"

"Hey, I resemble that statement." I rolled my eyes.

"No, Basia, they are not just geeks. They are the Kings of Geeks. Worthy of our admiration and respect."

"Is there some kind of geek magnet thingy I should know about? Because somehow you guys seem to gravitate toward each other."

"I'm telling you, they are amazing. Brilliant beyond words."

"Given my observation, they are as white as you. And that doesn't even count Elvis's backside, which is on a totally different level of whiteness."

I winced. "Do you have to keep reminding me of that? Besides, in the grand scheme of the universe, appearance is relative."

"Wrong. Appearance is important when you look like Casper the Ghost. Your body requires occasional fresh air and sunshine to survive. Remember, life is real, not virtual."

"Virtual is a lot safer and doesn't involve drowning, seaweed or guys with no pants."

"I think I've made my point."

We reached our blanket and Basia plopped down, opening the cooler and taking out a bottle of water. "They were kind of cute, though, in a nerdy, harmless kind of way."

I snatched my own bottle of water. "I'm not going to be offended by that."

"Of course you aren't. So when are you meeting with Elvis?"

I choked on my water. "What?"

She sighed. "He said something to you and your face lit up like a Christmas tree. There is only one thing that makes you go all gooey like that. My guess is he invited you to come over and look at his laptop. In the old days, it used to be etchings."

"Huh?"

"Never mind. The point is that I know you're planning to see him."

"I can hide nothing from you."

She smiled and took a sip of her water. "Remember that."

"So it's okay with you?"

"Only because at the bare minimum you are actually in the presence of a guy in sort of a social situation."

"You're a good friend."

She stretched back on the blanket and closed her eyes. "I'm your only friend. But someday I'm going to remind you that you said it."

Acknowledgments

Thanks go out first and foremost to my mom, Donna B. Moffett, and my sister, Sandy M. Parks, for their brainstorming, suggestions and beta reading of this manuscript. Thanks also to Carina Press for taking a chance on this series and to my amazing editor, Alissa Davis, who helped make this a significantly better novel. Lastly, a shout out to all my fans and friends, especially my Kubasaki High School classmates, who support, promote and cheer me on. There's no place like the Rock!